Isoline
and the Serpent-Flower

Isoline
and the Serpent-Flower

by
Judith Gautier

translated, annotated and introduced by
Brian Stableford

A Black Coat Press Book

ISBN 978-1-61227-152-1. First Printing. February 2013. Published by Black Coat Press, an imprint of Hollywood Comics.com, LLC, P.O. Box 17270, Encino, CA 91416.
Printed in the United States of America.

Table of Contents

Introduction

The first six stories translated in this collection were published in book form in *Isoline et La Fleur-Serpent* by
Charavay Frères in 1882, although *Isoline* had previously appeared separately in the same year. The remaining seven stories translated here are taken from *Le Paravent de soie et d'or*
[The Silk and Gold Screen], published by Charpentier et
Fasquelle in 1904. The title of the former collection is punctuated in such a way that it is more suggestive of a compound of
the two central motifs rather than merely a conjunction of the
titles of two stories, so I have done likewise in rendering the
title as *Isoline and the Serpent-Flower*. There is, in fact, a
sense in which all Judith Gautier's work, no matter how exotic
her stories eventually became in their form and substance,
remained overshadowed by those two motifs: the painful isolation of the individual, perhaps curable by love, but only with
great difficulty or extraordinarily good luck; and the destruc-
tive capacity of amorous obsession, ever likely to lead to trag-
ic extremes.

Judith Gautier (1845-1917) was the daughter of the great
flag-bearer of the French Romantic Movement, Théophile
Gautier, and Ernesta Grisi, the sister of the ballet dancer, Carlotta Grisi. Théophile Gautier was infatuated with Carlotta,
and it seems that it was because she was careful to keep him at
arm's length, perhaps out of concern for her career, that he
consoled himself with her sister, whom he never married, but
who bore him two children—children who thus found themselves in a strangely anomalous situation. Initially farmed out,
like most children of her class, to the care of a nurse, "Judith"
(whose actual forenames were Louise Charlotte Ernestine)
was then sent to boarding-school before eventually being ac-
commodated in her father's household, where she made the

acquaintance of all of his friends, including most of the leading lights of the Parisian literary community.

Reflecting much later on the peculiarity of her heritage and upbringing, Judith later remarked, sarcastically, that her father had only ever given her two pieces of advice, both of which she had ignored to her cost: always wear a corset, and don't marry Catulle Mendès. In fact, her marriage to the flamboyant but unreliable young writer Mendes, contracted in the teeth of fervent paternal opposition, in 1866—with Gustave Flaubert, Charles Leconte de Lisle and Villiers de l'Isle-Adam among the witnesses—not only worked out unhappily for her, but caused the break-up of her parents' relationship, when Ernesta was reckless enough to take her daughter's side. Judith eventually separated from Mendès in 1874, but did not divorce him until 1896, apparently having no desire ever to marry again, although she is rumored to have had a long series of affairs—including one with Victor Hugo, although she politely waited for her father to die before making that one public, Hugo having been the great hero of his adolescence.

Perhaps oddly, the friend of her father's who ultimately had the greatest influence on Judith's literary work was not one of the geniuses of French literature, nor even Richard Wagner—whose music made a deep impression on her, and of whom she wrote two significant memoirs—but a political exile from China to whom Théophile Gautier kindly offered temporary a refuge, and who taught her to read and speak Chinese. It was probably the sheer eccentricity and exoticism of that prospect that attracted her initially, but her interest in Chinese culture and legendry, and its reflection in her work, did provide her with a ready means of distinguishing her productions from those of everyone to whom she might otherwise have been compared to her detriment. If it did not make her entirely unique—Pierre Loti subsequently made a literary career out of studied Orientalism that inevitably led to comparisons, and to one drama written in collaboration—it did at least allow her to preserve the distinction that had, so to speak, been her birthright.

Judith had published a number of articles before her marriage—the first, a review of Charles Baudelaire's translation of Edgar Allan Poe's *Eureka*, is said to have delighted the poet, who was not easily pleased—but her first book did not appear until 1867. That was *Le Livre de jade* [The Book of Jade], a collection of poems translated from Chinese; it was followed by a historical novel set in the Orient, *Le Dragon impérial* (1869 as by Judith Mendès; tr. as *The Imperial Dragon*), but it was not until after her separation from Mendès that she began publishing books prolifically, on a regular basis. Her next novel, *L'Usurpateur* [The Usurper] (1876; reprinted as *La Soeur du soleil* [The Sister of the Sun]) also appeared initially with the signature Judith Mendès, but she reverted to the surname Gautier thereafter, for the novel *Lucienne* (1877) and her first short story collection, *Les Cruautés de l'amour* [The Cruelties of Love] (1879).

As the first three stories in the present collection illustrate, Judith Gautier experimented with various settings before settling into the Oriental groove, but even works that she set in contemporary Europe retained a calculated exoticism, which reacted, to some extent, to the peculiarities of her own life as well as to the literary models laid down by her father. There must have been a certain wry resentment inherent in being the daughter of a great writer whose lush romances stridently embodied the forceful conviction that ideal love is only possible outside the framework of real life, in safe havens of illusory or supernatural experience, and who provided the most striking but most outrageously impractical of all nineteenth-century female role-models in the classic *Mademoiselle de Maupin* (1835).[1] Whether she ever wanted to follow in Théophile Gautier's literary footsteps or not, the substance of such endeavors

---

[1] Judith Gautier wrote a dramatic adaptation of *Mademoiselle de Maupin*, but it remained unpublished, as did the other play she adapted from her father's work, *Une Fausse conversion*, and several of her original theatrical works.

were bound to cast a shadow over whatever Judith wrote or did, of whose oppression she was inevitably conscious.

While she was in love with Catulle Mendès, Judith Gautier presumably had some commitment to the ideas of the Parnassian Movement, whose guiding light he was, but when she fell out of love with him, she presumably felt little pressure to follow him, theoretically or practically, into the more cynical extremes of the Decadent Movement. Her work remained, however, solidly anchored within the precepts of Parnassian Romanticism, and she was well aware of its main exponents' increasing development of the techniques of symbolism and the sarcasm of the *conte cruel*. From the very outset, her work was consciously artificial and ironic, always inclined toward the bizarre. "Isoline" is one of the least exotic of all her works, but it nevertheless features an extraordinary heroine and recycles the plot formula of the Sleeping Beauty with a sharp ironic edge. Catulle Mendès was subsequently to prove more skilled as well as more cruelly ironic in such recycling exercises as *Luscignole* (1892), but Judith Gautier must have decided, long before she read any of her husband's endeavors in that vein, that she wanted to take her own work in a different direction.

"La Fleur-Serpent," a tale developing the Poesque themes of obsession, guilt and vengeance from beyond the grave, also remained unique within Judith Gautier's oeuvre, as did "Trop tard," here translated as "Too Late," which is as close as she ever came to a subversive pastiche of her father's tales of hallucinatory erotic obsession. Thereafter, she evidently found the ready-made exoticism of the Orient a more convenient costume for the deliberate artificiality of her accounts of the peculiarities of human relationships. Some of her stories in that vein are, or at least represent themselves as, straightforward renditions of pre-existent myths and legends, but her narrative method and style remained her own, and her best works in that vein are those in which she imposes her own mark upon her material the greatest verve, as in the flamboyantly melodramatic "Le Prince à la tête sanglante," here trans-

10

lated as "The Prince with the Bloody Head." She always felt that melodrama and the supernatural were far more appropriate to such distant settings than to contemporary European milieux.

The ten Oriental stories reproduced in this collection amount to considerably less than half of Judith Gautier's short fiction in that vein; there are two other collections entirely composed of such works, *Fleurs d'Orient* (1893) and the posthumous *Les Parfums de la pagode* (1919), although her collections do overlap slightly and she sometimes recycled her own works—thus, for instance, *Le Paravent de soie et d'or* contains both a reprint of "Le Fruit défendu" (here translated as "The Forbidden Fruit"), and a new version of "La Tunique merveilleuse," here translated in its original version as "The Marvelous Tunic," rewritten in a more elaborate supernaturalized version as a drama. The stories reproduced here are, however, a representative sample, and their spread reproduces the pattern of the evolution of her endeavors accurately enough.

Judith Gautier's works of that sort never won a wide audience, but they did command a considerable degree of critical respect and represented a considerable refinement of the primitive Orientalism pioneered by such early members of the French Romantic Movement as Joseph Méry. Her versions of China and Japan bear little resemblance to the actual countries, but that is hardly relevant to the kind of work she was doing, and she certainly made a highly significant contribution to the development of a literary Orient that was subsequently to be exploited by numerous later writers, of whom the best known exponents in the English language are "Frank Owen" (Roswell Williams) and "Ernest Bramah" (Ernest Smith).

These translations have been made from the versions of the first editions of the two relevant French volumes reproduced on the Bibliothèque Nationale's *gallica* website.

Brian Stableford

Judith Gautier

ISOLINE

I

A gray dusk is descending on the sea. The heavy clouds, driven by a harsh breeze and lowering over the horizon, threaten a further downpour. The rain that has just fallen slickens the slipway of Saint-Servan, whose slope declines into the turbulent water, and darkens the grey stones of the tall Solidor Tower, which seem to have taken root in the rocks that serve it as foundations and furnished the materials for its walls.

To either side of the slipway, fishing boats, their sails half-furled, are dancing with a kind of folly. Sailors and women carrying baskets are coming down the damp slope, calling in plaintive voices to the boats moored to the quay. A dyer, his arms blue to the elbows, is dipping various rags into the water flowing over the stone causeway, and momentarily tinting the first waves with improbable hues.

Close by, swaying in a disquieting fashion, an old boat with worm-eaten timbers, from which all trace of paint has disappeared, already filled with passengers, seems to be waiting for the moment to depart. The people crowding the vessel are mostly workers in their working clothes, stained with plaster and mud, and neat peasant-women with little colored headscarves knotted over the bosom: dainty Breton headgear, of which each town has a different form, quivering over their tresses. At the back are two Trinitarian sisters, their faces framed in bonnets folded beneath black veils, rattling the crosses and rosaries hidden in the folds of their coarse robes.

The boat is more than full , and yet new arrivals are hailing it and leaping on to the cluttered foredeck, without the passengers seeming surprised by the overloading. They merely exchange a few insignificant comments.

"So you're not going today, then?"

"Of course. There's still time."

"The tide won't wait."

"All the same, the wind is good and we'll make rapid progress."

And they close ranks again, some sitting down at the back of the boat, others remaining standing.

"Let's go!" cries the skipper, finally, whom nothing in his costume distinguishes from his companions.

The sail is hoisted above the heads, which duck down: a crude square sail that deploys slowly.

Just as a thrust with the gaffe is about the take the heavy boat away from the quay, however, hurried footsteps resound on the paving-stones and two people emerge from the town. One is a priest, who is making vehement signals to the boat that is ready to set sail, the other a young naval officer followed by a sailor carrying a trunk on his shoulder and a suitcase in his hand.

The latter couple head toward a pretty sloop that is making ready to sail at the end of the quay, while the ferry draws nearer again, responding to the appeals of the priest.

"Just in time, Monsieur l'Abbé."

"You'll hardly have room!"

"Come on, squeeze up!"

"How do you expect me to get aboard?" cries the priest, in a shrill voice. "You're already loaded to the point of collapse!"

"Oh, there's no problem," says the skipper.

"If I set foot on deck you'll sink, without a doubt. I'm too good a Christian to want to cause anyone's death." In an ill humor, he adds: "That's no joke!" And he darts a glance at the sloop into which the naval officer had just jumped.

"Are you going to Dinan, Captain?" he cries then, advancing to the edge of the quay, while the wind torments the black folds of his cape.

"Yes, Monsieur, I'm going to Dinan," the officer replies, with a sketchy bow.

"Will you make a little room for me, then, in your big boat, where you're all alone?"

"With pleasure, Monsieur," says the young mariner, scarcely dissimulating his lack of enthusiasm.

While maneuvering, the older of the matelots shakes his head, muttering in a low voice about the Churchman's presumption.

"They're mad!" says the priest, already installed in the sloop, pointing at the overloaded boat setting out to sea.

But the sloop has soon caught up with it and overtaken it. All its sails inflated, it leans over, catches the wind and flies like an arrow—not without rolling violently and taking on a few splashes of water.

The abbé holds on tightly to the banquette. "Shouldn't we take in a reef?" he says.

"Are you afraid?" sniggers the matelot. And with a touch of malice, when they quit the shelter of the rocks and the breeze redoubles in force, instead of spinning out the sheet and coming into the wind, he keeps the sail broadside and lets the boat heel over toward the surface of the water.

"I'm not a mariner!" cried the priest, hurling himself to the other side without the displacement of weight producing any effect.

"We'll get there sooner this way," says the officer, letting his gaze wander over the bay.

The admirable panorama unfolds, in fact, a trifle drenched in gray cloud: to the right, Saint-Malo, enclosed in its walls, dominated by the pointed spire of its bell-tower, seems like one of those cities one sees in the illuminations of a missal, carried in the hand by a king. Out to sea, the rocks and islets, edged by the whiteness of mobile foam, are brown patches. To the left, Dinard, with its elegant villas nestling in the verdure, hanging audaciously on to the rocky hillsides.

But the boat, which is bounding, prancing and falling back in a splash of flying water, comes about and takes its definitive course toward the Rance, whose flow in being reversed by the rising tide.

The scene changes then; now one thinks one is looking at a lake surrounded by verdant hills. The horizon is closed, but as one advances the hills seem to draw apart, like the scenery of a theater, opening a passage to other lakes, which seem momentarily to be devoid of any issue.

The waves calm down; they enter the river, and the individuals carried by the slender boat, which is now gliding without shocks, begin to examine one another.

The priest looks obliquely at the officer, and lowers his eyes when the other raises his.

Without knowing him personally, the abbé is well aware of who his host is; the sloop and the matelots manning it have allowed him to deduce, at the first glance, that the young man can only be Gilbert Hamon, a lieutenant aboard a State frigate, whom a convalescent leave has sent back to his family for three months. A bad fever, contracted in the Antilles, encouraged the belief that he would never be seen again; Abbé Jouan has heard mention of that from Madame Aubrée, Gilbert Hamon's sister. She even had a mass said for her brother's recovery; but this is the first time that the young mariner has returned to Dinan since Abbé Jouan has been the principal curate at the Église Saint-Sauveur—which is to say, for three years—so he knows of him without ever having see him.

Madame Aubrée being his penitent, the priest even knows something about the officer's family, his fortune, and his character; he is, for instance, perfectly well aware of the mariner's indifference in matters of religion—that is why he gives nothing away, giving no indication that he knows who the other is. The mere fact that he maintains in his service that matelot, Eugène Damont, the worst Christian on the coast, would be sufficient, in any case, to render the master of the boat suspect. Abbé Jouan even wonders whether he might not have been a trifle hasty in soliciting hospitality from this enemy vessel.

Gilbert Hamon's physiognomy, which he studies covertly, scarcely gives anything away. The young man is still very pale after his recent illness, as if listless and vaguely melancholy. His mouth, neatly shaped, is a vivid red, still excited by the burning of his fever. Short side-whiskers and eyebrows very clearly traced on a smooth forehead, the ivory tint of his temples, and the elegant correctness of his uniform, all add something Britannic to that physiognomy.

A veritable face of papier-mâché, concludes the abbé, privately.

What displeases him the most is the haughty gaze that occasionally springs forth suddenly, communicating a singular power to an almost feminine face. Its direct flame does not succeed in catching the priest's sly glances, but the young officer seems incurious about the face of his guest, darkened by a three-day beard: those gray eyes, anxious, as if ashamed; the features that frown and grimace continually—an ensemble that seems hardly worthy of interest—and he persists in staring pensively at the landscape. The feeble echo, immediately extinct, that the remarks uttered by the Abbé awaken, cause the latter to take refuge in the attentive reading of his breviary.

Already they have crossed the broad bay that curves around before Saint-Suliac, a curious village the color of ash, whose damp cottages are grouped on the very edge of the water, around the Gothic tower of its old church. Port Saint-Jean and Port Saint-Hubert go past to the right and the left; the hollow of a valley briefly reveals the large town of Plouer and white hamlets appear in the verdure, some near and others more distant, on the heights.

After the Châtelier lock, the wind, previously so keen, abruptly drops. The threat of rain is dissipated; the sky is now a soft gray and the water calm and silvery, as reflective as a mirror. Damont, muttering curses, slackens all the canvas; the other matelot, Pirouette, takes hold of the scull in order to assist the sails.

"Here's the calm," says the abbé.

The landscape is changing by the minute. The river is much narrower, describing large meanders through woods of tall fir-trees, whose dark perspectives deepen.

Gilbert continues his reverie, which grows gradually sadder. While gazing at the long reflection of the trees in the water, he interrogates his heart, which makes no reply to him—and that sensation of emptiness causes him an almost physical dolor. He searches within himself for the vibration of any sentiment whatsoever at the approach of his hearth, and experiences absolutely nothing. Powerful affections are no longer there; his mother, for whom each of his departures was an agony, has concluded her suffering; the ocean has devoured his father. He no longer has any family except for the sister, who sees him go away without any great sadness and sees him return without any great joy.

For him, therefore, after those incessantly-traveled seas, there is no port that he desires to see again; the native soil where he spends so little time is indifferent to him, and the distant lands of which he only knows the shores only seduce him fugitively. What remains to him even of those rapid amours, bound and unbound, condemned at birth? Nothing but a memory as slight as that of a slightly sweet perfume. He has not penetrated any further into the intimacy of his exotic lovers' souls than into the depths of the virgin forests whose florid edges smiled at him—only a few paces through the tangled lianas, a few fissures in the veil woven by uncomprehended language, and the frigate, floating toward the high seas, has already opened its large sails again and recaptured its prey.

The sea and its heavy solitude; that was all he found in his heart; the land was like a stranger to him; he had never had the sensation of being either far away or close at hand; nothing loved him and he did not love anything—so the death that had just brushed him had not drawn a single sigh of regret from him.

All mariners are like that, he said to himself—but his resignation was only external, and often, on the calm sea, without his cold visage allowing any glimpse of them, tempests were unleashed within him. At present, as he sought to experience a little of the joyous impatience of the return, he discerned more clearly than ever the destitution of his soul.

"Spleen!" The word came to his lips, and he felt enveloped, like the sky, in gray clouds.

Dinan appeared now, its gross towers still majestic, its ramparts powerful, the belfries of its old churches outlined at the summit of the high hill.

The abbé closed his book and got up to stretch his legs. "We're coming into port," he said.

Then the officer, ashamed of his long silence, strove to say something. He too stood up, in order to get a better view of Dinan.

"How somber the town is!" he said. "Those old walls, that dark greenery, those black houses, that river the color of ink! Everything is in mourning."

"It's the fault of the weather and the time," said the abbé. "Look at it again when the sky is blue."

"It's not a city like Paris," observed Pirouette.

"No, damn it," said Damont, leaping from one bench to another to haul in the sail.

"Ah! Here's Madame Aubrée and her children," said the abbé.

"My sister!"

They quickly moored at the quay and Gilbert found himself in the arms of a young woman clad in a gray dress, a black coat and a slightly disheveled hat.

"There you are! My God, how pale you are! It's obvious that you've been ill."

Two little girls, one six years old and the other four, looked on open-mouthed.

"Aren't you going to say anything to your uncle?"

"I'm scaring them."

The priest moved away, bowing deeply.

"Ah! Bonsoir, Monsieur l'Abbé," Madame Aubrée exclaimed, with an amiable smile. To her brother, she said: "Come on, then. Damont will bring your luggage."

They went along the old Rue du Jerzuale, unkempt and picturesque, as steep as the bed of a torrent, in order to reach the Rue de l'Horloge, where the Aubrée family lived.

II

On the bank of the Rance, outside the town, a modest cottage shelters beneath two large trees somewhat denuded by the wind. The roof, which projects to one side slightly beyond the wall, forms a sort of awning supported by two poles. It is beneath that shelter that the door of the hovel opens. It only contains two rooms, one very small and the other large; its floor is flattened earth. Its furniture includes a walnut cupboard decorated with a few brass plates, a Breton bed—which is to say, a second cupboard pierced by an oval hole, carefully closed by small floral-patterned curtains—and, in front of the bed, an oak bench that time and friction have rendered shiny, and as brown as a chestnut. From that bench, with the aid of an enormous stride, one can slip inside the bed. A table, a few high-backed wicker chairs, a stool under the mantelpiece of the huge rural fireplace, and earthenware or faience utensils hanging on the walls, complete the set.

The white hair of Marie Damont, who is knitting and watching the cooking-pot, is the only bright point in the somber interior, which only receives daylight through the door, glazed in its upper section.

Marie is the sister of the matelot Damont, who, after thirty years at sea, now lives with her, on his meager retirement pension and the small sums earned for him by the boat whose custody he has.

The life of the sixty-year-old spinster can be summarized in three words: devotion, poverty and resignation. She has seen nothing, owned nothing, hoped for nothing. Her blue eyes have and extraordinary clarity beneath their profound brows, and a seraphic calm. She is not married because it was necessary to look after her little brothers, and then her widowed and invalid father, and when he died at eighty she was past the age of amours. She knows that she is afflicted with the heart disease that killed her mother, and is expecting, without any terror, to die suddenly one night.

A few days after his arrival, Gilbert Hamon went down to the edge of the Rance through the miserable streets and the sodden fields, and opened the door of the cottage.

"Oh, Monsieur Gilbert!" cried Marie, getting up swiftly. "How kind of you to remember me, and to come to see me in such terrible rain!"

"How are you, my good Marie?"

"My old carcass still persists, in spite of the illness—but that's of no interest; let's talk about you. You've had a bad time, from what Eugène has told me—you, who ought to be so happy."

"Why is that, Marie?"

"Well, you're young, handsome, well-off—and a lieutenant, at your age."

"All that doesn't mean that I'm happy."

"Is it possible? We're all on this earth to suffer, then? They must be very happy at home though, to see you come back cured."

"Yes, I suppose so—but what can you expect? I'm stifling in that narrow environment."

"Mariners need air," Marie said, not understanding the true meaning of the remark, perhaps out of discretion. "Come on, I'll put an armful of wood on the fire to dry you off. You're soaked—but it's necessary to leave the door open so that the smoke doesn't choke us."

Gilbert sat on the stool and stoked up the brushwood fire, which was crackling and blazing brightly. "There, you're fuming like the meadows at sunrise."

And they remained face to face on either side of the fireplace, Gilbert plunged into a kind of torpor, Marie respecting that reverie and knitting rapidly.

The silence was broken by a joyful barking that resounded outside; almost immediately, a large dog bounded into the cottage. It was soon followed by a young woman, who came in impetuously and deposited a milk-jug on the table.

"Here's the milkmaid!" she cried. "She wants to be paid cash." And she threw her arms around the peasant with such vivacity that she nearly knocked her over.

"You're strangling me, my dear!" said Marie, in a soft voice.

Gilbert had risen to his feet and was looking attentively at the young person who had come in like a gust of wind. He found her so charming that he thought he had been deceived by the half-light of the cottage. She was dressed as a peasant-girl, but very carefully; her headscarf was embroidered and trimmed with lace, and she had button-less suede gloves on her hands.

The dog, a large black Newfoundland, growled at Gilbert.

"Who's that by your fireplace?" said the girl, turning round with a start. And she darted a glance at Gilbert full of a kind of scornful insolence. She had those strange bright blue eyes bordered by long black lashes that are common among Bretons, and which have a magical effect when they open in a lovely face.

"Are you afraid of a mariner?" said Marie. "It's Lieutenant Hamon, with whom my brother sailed for a long time."

"Oh, I know—you've often mentioned him to me." She took a step toward the young man and held out her hand. "Bonjour, Monsieur," she said, very gravely.

Gilbert felt a bizarre discomfort as he shook the gloved hand, which responded with a frank and firm pressure.

Then they said nothing more. She had lowered her eyes—but, irritated by the awkward silence, she frowned, uttered an abrupt *adieu*, and fled.

"Marie, I believe I'm dreaming," said the officer, going to the door in order to try to catch another glimpse of the fugitive. "Who is that extraordinary child?"

"Oh, there certainly aren't two like her," said the peasant woman, shaking her head. "She's wicked and good, wise and foolish, a beautiful wild plant full of thorns."

"Who is she?" Gilbert asked, coming to sit down again, his eyes shining with curiosity. "She's no peasant girl."

"That's Mademoiselle de Kerdréol. You don't know her?"

"The name seems to ring a bell."

"The Château de la Conninais—you know, a little way from here—belongs to her family."

"Yes, I remember. Didn't you raise the child?"

"Indeed, with the aid of a lovely white she-goat. She cost me a great deal of trouble—a demon that one adored! See, she brings me milk every day; she says that it's good for what ails me. I drink it to please her; if it were bile I'd still drink it; I've never done anything but what she wanted."

"How old is she?"

"As you said, she's a child—but she's twenty years old."

"How is it that she's not married yet?"

"Oh, she's much too disdainful; all the young men here make her shrug her shoulders; they're less than dogs to her. Then again, her life isn't commonplace."

"Tell me what you know about her, please," said Gilbert, with an urgency so marked that Marie looked at him anxiously.

"Lord! Don't go falling in love with her—that would be throwing yourself into an inferno."

"It would be strange," said Gilbert, trying to laugh, "to catch fire like a powder-barrel. I wouldn't be bored any longer, though."

"You've scarcely seen her," said Marie. "Don't see her again."

"Bah!" said the young man, gaily. "Mariners never retreat. I've seen enough of her never to forget her. She has dazzling eyes. Come on, I beg you—continue your fairy tale."

"There must have been a lot of bad fairies at her cradle," said Marie Damont, sighing. She sat down opposite Gilbert, picked up her knitting again, and remained silent momentarily. "I don't like talking about that, you see—it isn't my business. I've always kept my mouth sown shut about it. All that I can say is that Isoline isn't happy. Since she left my arms, she's been living alone in that great deserted château."

"What about her parents?"

"She only has her father; he only comes for one week every year, and never says a word to his daughter."

"Is he mad?"

Marie shook her head. "No, but it's something like that. Poor child! You saw her almost cheerful just now, but that's rare; she has fits of frightful despair, and fits of anger in which she's a Fury. She wants to know the reasons that condemn her to live thus, outside of humankind—she doesn't consider the people here as being part of it. She's never spoken to anyone of her own class; outside of us and her farmers, no one knows the sound of her voice—so I was dumbstruck when she held out her hand to you. She's got extraordinary ideas from books, you see, which one can no longer get out of her head. Oh yes, it's a fairy tale—a sad tale. But let's not talk about it anymore, for fear of making things worse."

The peasant woman got up and went to the door in order to swallow the tears that were reddening her eyes. She talked about her brother, who did not come back, and about the rain, which continued to fall, but she avoided the questions with which Gilbert wanted to interrogate her further.

"All, right, I'll be on my way," he said, eventually. "*Au revoir*, my worthy Marie. Tell Damont that I'll come back."

He went out into the rain, which was falling gently, but instead of going along the river bank, he went into a tree-lined path that rose up the hill almost exactly opposite the cottage. He climbed the slope of the wet ground without looking where he was treading.

His mind, so empty a little while before, but stimulated by a residue of fever, now had an aliment, which he devoured as a famished wild beast would have devoured a prey. Marie had missed her mark by identifying a danger in the possibility of becoming smitten by that young woman; she had precipitated the birth of an idea of love that would otherwise have taken longer to emerge. Gilbert wondered why it was so terrible to confront the charm of those splendid eyes. What did she know about it, that poor peasant woman ignorant of life? Had Isoline been loved before? Was it some romantic drama that rendered her life so somber?

He was curious to have another look at the Château de la Conninais, which he had only ever seen with an indifferent eye. If his memories did not deceive him, the path he had taken led to it.

He hastened his step beneath the thick foliage, on which the rain was falling rhythmically. Large rocks rose up on one side, velvet with moss and grass; to the right, beyond the trees, the terrain hollowed out in a narrow valley whose opposite slope was covered in fir-trees.

A mist rose up, hiding the ground. Everything was streaming, rows of droplets lined up under the boughs, which combined abruptly and fell, rills running between the stones, which were becoming sparser. The terrain, gradually becoming softer, lost all consistency; it was a marsh: a true Breton path in its wintry horror.

Soon, the descending path, framed between two banks, became a navigable stream. Gilbert climbed up, clinging on to wet branches; the earth, giving way beneath his feet, slid down, making the water spring up. Clumps of brambles, amassed in inaccessible places by the inhospitable humor of the peasants, tore his hands and snagged his clothing. He persisted stubbornly, walking through grass in which each of his footfalls left a hole that filled with water; he took large strides, leaping, aiming for a stone or a patch of ground that he thought to be solid, and which betrayed him.

Finally, sweating and out of breath, he set foot again on the main road to Dinan.

The Val de la Conninais descends sheerly on the other side of that road, which forms a rather steep ramp at that spot. Directly opposite the path from which the young man has emerged, on the far side of the valley, at the top of the slope hidden by the tall trees scaling it, the château is half-hidden by dark foliage. Fir-trees, green oaks and other species that winter does not strip bare seem to be mounting an assault on it, burying it in their impenetrable mass. Nothing can be seen but an old wall pierced by an arched gate, having on one side a square tower, topped by a modern slate roof, and on the other, a little Gothic chapel. The residential building, beyond the chapel, only presents is narrowest face to the valley.

The horizon is closed in every direction by high vegetation; the inundated meadows, covered with thick grass in which pools of water shine here and there, make beautiful ample folds between the clumps of woodland.

Gilbert went forward, to try to discover something more. He went down the road, traversed a crossroads where several paths intersected, and emerged from the bridge that overhangs and crosses the valley. Then he saw, beyond a pond, behind a thicket of bare branches, the long gray façade, pierced with window with narrow panes, of the château proper. He stopped, and his heart was constricted by the implacable melancholy that emanated from the landscape. The overflowing pond drowned its banks and seemed ready to pour down into the valley. A thick mist was fuming, slow and blue-tinted, and the bleak château, which it enveloped, seemed to be perched on a cloud. The heavy clouds in the sky hung down, as if to combine with that terrestrial vapor.

What! She had lived there for twenty years, alone, mute, in that damp prison, besieged by that swell of verdure that made the very gaze captive. It was even worse than a ship, a prisoner of the waves of the boundless sea.

The window were closed; nothing was moving; not a creature, not a sound.

Gilbert starred for some time, and was then gripped by vertigo. He thought that the mysterious dwelling, as if steeped in tears, was dissolving, evaporating like a vision. He no longer saw it as anything but the conception of a dream—and then it was effaced, and vanished.

Am I mad? he asked himself.

Abruptly, he turned round. In every direction, there was an opaque whiteness; he was a prisoner in a fog. While he was dreaming, the fusion had taken place between the dangling clouds and the mist; the countryside was no longer fuming. It seemed to him that the savage Isoline was opposing an impenetrable veil to the indiscretion of his gaze.

Blindly, he sought his path—painfully, for he dreaded getting stuck in some bog. He succeeded, however, after a thousand zigzags, in reaching the outskirts of Dinan and going back into the town through the Saint-Malo gate.

III

Gilbert had caught a slight fever from that walk in the rain. He came back shivering, and the state of his clothing brought loud protests from Jeanne-Yvonne, the little white-caped housemaid who came to open the door to him.

"Oh, Madame!" she cried, running upstairs. "Monsieur Gilbert must have fallen in the mortar." That is what Bretons call the liquid mud of their paths.

"What a state you're in!" said Madame Aubrée, coming out on to the landing. "Go get changed, quickly—you'll catch your death. Hurry up! Dinner's ready."

The dining room, which was rather gloomy, was on the ground floor. Old pearl-gray woodwork, brightened by a pink thread, hid the walls all the way to the ceiling. That woodwork, a witness to the previous century, had been conserved there purely for reasons of economy; Madame Aubrée would have preferred brown wallpaper with golden flowers, supported by imitation oak-wood, but had had be content, for good reason, when she first moved in, to wash down the walls and make repairs where the paint was missing. The mistress of the house offered excuses for her dining room, saying: "It's Gothic."

The rest of the house, however, was in perfect conformity with modern bad taste. The drawing room on the first floor—the narrow dwelling had only one room on the façade—was hung with a white and gold paper, on which there were a few engravings, a pearl-embroidered religious picture and a portrait of a man in oils. The furniture was upholstered in coarse blue rep, the curtains were embroidered muslin, with curtain-loops attaching them to brass rods. In front of the mantelpiece, garnished with an Empire pendulum-clock and two lamps, a brightly-hued felt carpet extended. A stereoscope with views of Switzerland and a photograph album never left the round table, covered in gray marble, whose prodigious weight rendered it immovable.

The Aubrées bedroom opened on the other sided of the landing and overlooked a little garden. Gilbert had taken the children's room, above the dining-room; they had gone down to their mother's room.

The Rue de l'Horloge, in which the house was situated, had nothing remarkable about it except that fifteenth-century tower with a double dial, whose large bell, donated by Anne de Bretagne, sounded the hours in a grave and resonant tone, and a few old houses whose first floors projected as far as the edge of the sidewalk, sustained by pillars. The young mariner, who, in accordance with a habit of his profession, often went out on to his balcony to interrogate the horizon, found the narrowness of the street oppressive; the house opposite seemed to hit him in the eyes. In order not to annoy his sister, he concealed his impressions, but he had no sooner entered that calm grey interior than an irresistible desire for air and space took hold of him; he fidgeted, and opened the windows, followed by the gaze of his sister, busy with some embroidery, who said to herself: *It's the fever!*

His mind was as uneasy in that environment as his body. Solitude, dangers and his perpetual voyages had caused him to grow. Abundant reading imposed on him by the interminable duration of crossings had amplified his intelligence and developed the pensive aspect of his character. Mingling little with other people, he formed an idea of them quite different from the reality; he only credited them with generous, noble, even heroic thoughts. It appeared to him that the Bretons, most of all, the sons of those corsairs who stupefied their epoch with improbable feats, ought to be devoured by the desire to raise themselves by some glorious deed above the ordinary level; the perfect quietude in the nullity that revealed itself around him reinforced his depression and his sullenness. In the midst of his own family, he seemed to himself to be a seagull captive in a chicken-run.

His sister, Sylvie Aubrée, had a flat face with quite pretty eyes; she did her hair badly and dressed in somber fabrics brightened by a few bright ribbons. She scolded her daughters and her maid, occupied herself with household matters and worried about the good opinion sand petty gossip of the town; beyond that she had no other imagination or ambition. Her husband was an inspector of indirect taxes—what is known in the provinces as a cellar-rat; he delved into the turnover of taverns, cafés and hotels, counting full barrels and bottles. He talked a great deal about the tricks that everyone attempted to play on him, the grievances of retailers and his skill in countering their ruses. He was a tall, stiff man with a deep baritone voice, who read *La Patrie* after dinner and fell asleep over it, when he did not go to his club in the Place Du Guesclin.

That evening, which was the day before Palm Sunday, a few ladies came to the Aubrées' home: Sylvie's sister-in-law, Madame Paul Aubrée, whose husband was a doctor and lived a few doors away; Madame Rochereuil, the Maire's wife, and her daughter Marguerite, a tall, slim blonde with a complexion veiled by red patches; and an aging spinster, Mademoiselle Taffatz, who had once run a boarding school for girls. Liqueurs were brought up from the cellar, served with finger-biscuits; one of the lamps on the mantelpiece was lit.

The little girls came to embrace everyone in turn and went to bed, each carrying a biscuit, and the chatter began, in the drawling accent of the region.

Gilbert, sitting in a corner with his gaze riveted to the floor, only heard a buzz that isolated him. He plunged into his new dream, seeing those large bright blue irises again momentarily, which were immediately extinguished, like stars, in the fog. He thought about the muscular hand that had shaken his, and that favor, which he could not explain, gave him a sort of confidence in the future of the sentiment that was growing within him.

An egotistical thought extracted him from his meditation. *All these gossips*, he said to himself, *undoubtedly talk about her, and can inform me in her regard.*

He lent an ear in order to discover what the topic of conversation was, and by means of what maneuver he might be able to seize its tiller and steer it into his own waters.

"He certainly has a great deal of unction," said Madame Rochereuil, "but he doesn't have the fervor of the reverend father who preached last Lent."

"You think so?" said Sylvia. "I like him a lot—he has a touching voice."

"He weeps; he doesn't thunder."

"He has pretty white hands," said Marguerite Rochereuil. "He lets them dangle on the red velvet like this."

"Père Saint-Ange struck it, with a furious fist."

"And dust came out of it," said Mademoiselle Taffatz, "which stayed there for Père Étienne."

"I think he's too fond of hearing himself talk," insinuated Madame Paul Aubrée, who was not very devoted. "His sermons never end."

"Oh, they're always too long for you," said Sylvie.

"What do you expect? They put me to sleep."

"They excite me," said the Mairesse. "I listen with all ears; I drink in the preacher's words, and when I get home, I write down everything I can remember."

"Really? You've never told us that. It's a very edifying idea."

"I retain the whole well enough," said Sylvie, "but as for the words, they don't stick!"

"You ought to show us that!"

"And allow us to copy them."

"Gladly," said Madame Rochereuil. "One day."

"Move on!" muttered Gilbert.

However, they went on to talked about the Grandmanoirs, who had offered the church an altar-cloth for Easter, which was said to be very beautiful."

"Are there many noble families in the châteaux nearby?" asked the mariner then.

They cited the Argentiers, at the Château de Mottay at Pontcadeux, the Rogers de Line, and others who lived constantly in their domains or only came during the summer.

"Is the Château de la Conninais deserted?" And his heart beat faster when someone mentioned Mademoiselle de Kerdréol.

"It's exactly as if there were no one there."

There was a pause.

"You're touching one of the questions that intrigues the town most," said Virginie Taffatz, finally.

"Nothing similar has ever been seen," the mistress continued. "A young woman who has lived alone since infancy, like a leper."

"A mystery," sighed Sylvie.

"If there wasn't a young girl here, I'd tell you what I think," growled Monsieur Aubrée, in his deep voice, exchanging a glance with Mademoiselle Taffatz.

"Marguerite, go see whether the children are asleep."

The tall girl left the room.

"Well?"

"Well, Baron de Kerdréol doubtless has reasons for thinking that he's not his daughter's father. The Baronne must have committee some folly, and he's making the child expiate the sins of the mother, that's all!"

"That's not Christian."

"The fact is that he detests her. He's never spoken to her; when he comes, which is rare, he orders her to remain in her room in order avoid the risk of meeting her."

"What an existence!" cried the doctor's wife. "And what if he's mistaken, if the child is really his?"

"Is it finished, Maman?" said Marguerite, putting her head through the partly-open door.

"Go on, you can come back."

"Have you ever seen her?" asked Gilbert. "How is she?"

"In truth, she has a lunatic air about her," said Madame Rochereuil. "Do you think she's pretty, Mesdames? Not me—she looks at you with a brazen gaze, which she wouldn't lower even before the pope. She's more like a boy than a girl."

"She has an English air about her."

The conversation deviated on that word. They talked about the English who were invading the town, with their extravagant fashions, their insolent airs, the manners of their young women, who had a sluttish air about them. But Marguerite brought them back to the original subject by asking whether the Kerdréols were related to Bertrand du Guesclin.[2]

"What makes you think that?"

"It's just that, in church, she often places herself close to the monument that contains Du Guesclin's heart, and looks at it as if she wanted to see though the stones."

"She goes to church?" said Gilbert.

"From time to time, but she doesn't have a very edifying bearing there."

"She isn't devoted?"

"No, and so much the worse for her," replied Mademoiselle Taffatz, harshly. "Devotion would soothe her pains and give her the courage to bear them."

The next day, Gilbert astonished his family by announcing that he would accompany them to High Mass.

"Have you been touched by grace?" asked Sylvie.

"It will distract me," said Gilbert.

They set out in great ceremony, Monsieur Aubrée carrying the umbrellas, Sylvie finishing putting on her gloves, and Gilbert holding the younger of his nieces by the hand.

---

[2] Bertrand du Guesclin (c1320-1380) was a Breton knight and distinguished military leader who became Constable of France in 1370. He was born not far from Dinan, and his heart was said to have been returned there, to the Basilica of Saint-Sauveur, when he was buried at Saint-Denis in Paris.

The bells were ringing fervently, the citizens in their Sunday best all heading in the same direction. They went along the Rue des Morts, which opens into the Place Saint-Sauveur opposite the church. The uneven paving-stones of the *Carroi*, as the large square surrounded by houses is also called, clattered under the heavy tread of the arrivals. The square has retained its Medieval design; the three fully-vaulted arcades of the portal make three black holes into which the crowd disappeared in groups. On the steps, beggars were seated beside large heaps of verdure.

The organs were rumbling when the Aubrée family let the heavy door close behind them. Gilbert was immediately enveloped by the splendor of those powerful sounds; the mysterious penumbra created by the stained-glass windows and the vague perfume of incense made an impression on him; he experienced a frisson that moistened his eyes. It was, however, an entirely poetic impression, which was quickly erased by the nasal voice of the cantors, the distracted air of the deacons and the rubicund complexion of the officiant.

He walked in the aisles where the dazzling headgear of the women of the people was devotedly inclined over the careworn parishioners. He admired the expression of naïve faith that some of them—the oldest—had, and smiled at the whispering of the young ones who were looking at him, jogging one another's elbows, holding their missals over their lips.

Abbé Jouan went by in a white surplice, seemingly busy. The gold braid on the mariner's cap attracted his gaze, which he immediately lowered to conceal his surprise.

Gilbert felt embarrassed; he did not know what attitude to strike, in the midst of all these people, who were examining him while responding with certainty to the formulas of the mass. Sometimes, an ill-contained squeak, murdering a Latin phrase, caused laughter to rise to his throat that he had difficulty containing. His footsteps rang on the flagstones; he was the only one standing, which attracted attention, and he sought to compose himself in a neutral manner that would not injury the ceremony.

The hope that Isoline might perhaps come rendered that spot attractive to him, and he did not want to leave it; the desire that he had to see her again astonished him by its violence. Was it possible, then, that the void in his soul had been filled so suddenly? That a being that he had not known at the same hour the day before had taken sovereign possession of his thoughts, as daylight invades the night! He was glad to feel alive, though, the leaden ennui that weighed upon him no longer crushing him, so he encouraged the commencement of the blaze with all his might.

He sought the stone beneath which the heart of the worthy knight is hidden, and having found it, in a lateral chapel, he sat down beside it and mechanically set about reading the inscription engraved in Gothic letters:

Here lieth the heart of Messire
Bertrand du Guesclin
in life Constable of France

But he got no further; his gaze fled, still seeking the person who had not come. In the end he became impatient and, to the great scandal of the faithful, went out during the communion.

The square, now completely deserted, was inundated with sunlight. Opposite, beyond the houses, the picturesque silhouette of the Tour de l'Horloge, with its long pointed spire, stood out against the serene sky. Gilbert, not really sure which way he wanted to go, paused momentarily under the porch, where the finger of time is gradually effacing the four evangelists sculpted in bas-relief, with their symbolic beasts, and the bizarre fantasies inscribed in the stone by unknown artists. Turning his back on the Tour de l'Horloge, however he took the little Rue des Chauffe-Pieds, which goes along the right flank of the church, and, as if involuntarily, raised his head as he went, letting his gaze linger in the delightful irregularities of the apse, from the midst of which surged the slender bell-tower, like an inverted lily.

The Place de la Duchesse Anne, which extends behind the church, is the part of the town about which the Dinanais are most proud. It is an English garden, albeit a rather mediocre one, which replaces an old abandoned cemetery, but which ends with one of the most beautiful panoramas that one can see. The esplanade that terminates the garden is the summit of an ancient tower; punctuated with gross round towers and bordered by a stone parapet with integral loopholes, it is raised at least forty meters above the level of the Rance. From there the gaze plunges into the valley with a kind of intoxication.

Far below, the river, like a steel ribbon, and the disorderly slate roofs, glisten in the sunlight. Nearer, the high viaduct that one also overlooks, crosses in a few spans the space that separates the cliff from the hills: everywhere on the slopes, thick woods are beginning to turn them green; there are villages of various sizes, hollows full of blue-tinted shadows, and, as far as the eye can see, valleys, meadows and landslides of russet foliage.

Gilbert did not pause before that scene, which was familiar to him. He began rapidly going down the abrupt path, which, sometimes a steep ramp, sometimes a stairway carved into the rock, descends with many zigzags from the esplanade to the bank of the Rance.

"Fool that I am!" he said to himself, hurrying along. "While I was playing the hypocrite and drinking in sermons, the person I'm looking for is down there, in Marie Damont's cottage."

IV

In the large solitary halls of the Château de la Conninais, Isoline wanders slowly, head bowed and arms dangling, as if lost in a semi-slumber. She goes from room to room, silently, like a phantom, trailing the pleats of a long white dress.

Around her, a modern luxury, grave and already a trifle faded, completes the ancient elegance of the old manor; to the oaken cavities of the ceiling, decorated with floral ornaments, to the extinct tapestries, to the smoke-darkened portraits framed in the paneling of the walls or over the monumental fireplaces, are added Baccarat chandeliers, new fabrics with beautiful supple folds, comfortable chairs and, in places, thick carpets.

Everything is in strict order; the parquet is carefully waxed; the interior shutters of all the high windows are half-folded.

Animated by a happy family, that dwelling would have had nothing sad about it, especially in summer; but this abandonment without disorder, this correct desert, this void in a place seemingly ready to receive guests, was perhaps more desolate than the solitude of a dilapidated château.

That young woman, condemned to such a cruel isolation, did not know the secret of her existence; the power that weighed upon her and enchained her liberty had not been explained to her. Her fate was merely written on a placard set under glass and hung from a wall, and it had been until now the summary of her life. It read as follows:

The child will be raised by Marie Damont, who will come to live in the château.

In seven years, Marie Damont will leave the château and never enter it again.

The Jesuit father I have designated will then come to attend to the demoiselle's education; he will teach her to read and wrote, nothing more.

That education terminated, no one other than the servants shall enter the château.

The steward charged with collecting the farm rents will furnish the expenses.

He will never give money to the demoiselle, who will notify him in writing of anything she desires.

Meals will be served at fixed times and in silence; in case of sickness, a sister from the hospice will be admitted to the château.

The upkeep of the house will remain as it is, reduced to the necessary.

At the time of my annual sojourn, and throughout its duration, Mademoiselle will not emerge from her room.

This being understood, let no one ever speak of it to me again.

And below, a large seal with a coat-of-arms, imprinted on red wax.

Only Isoline's early infancy had been happy; Marie Damont had given herself entirely to the child confided to her—but she was a virgin mother without experience of everything that was not attentive care and devotion; the scoldings and the severities necessary to discipline the imperious character of a child and direct her instincts were completely unknown to her; she adored, and was a slave. Little Isoline's exquisite beauty, those large eyes that opened like flowers, the flesh parallel to that of the camellias in the garden, drowned her heart in tenderness; she thought that she was dedicated to the care of an angel—but that angel, without ceasing to be adorable, became a devil as she grew older.

Marie lived then in continual apprehension, thinking of nothing but saving the child from the dangers in which it seemed to her that she threw herself incessantly. There were mad races with the nanny-goat over the steep slopes of the park, formed like an amphitheater; trees were climbed, in which garment remained, were little limbs were grazed; there was paddling in muddy pools that made the cherub into a guttersnipe. Everything became a subject of terror for the poor mother-by-appointment: candle-flames; the fireplace; the pond; the height of the windows. The child, frenzied by games and movement, never gave her a moment's peace, tortured her, but loved her passionately. There were very tender moments when she came, with the most affectionate caresses, to dry the tears that she had drawn by her mad caprices from her adorable nurse.

Marie never went out of the château or the grounds, and without the few household servants those two beings might have believed themselves to be the only ones in the world. Isoline never lived as a child; she believed that everything finished with the garden walls, and humankind, for her, was Marie and the white she-goat.

At the age of six, the child calmed down slightly; she became more sedate, more inquisitive. Marie poured into that young soul the treasures of her resigned and naively poetic mind. She told her the legends she knew: of mermaids, clad in algae, hiding in profound grottoes to which they lured imprudent fishermen; of marvelous cities swallowed by the waves, whose silver bell-towers and palaces of precious stones can still be seen when the water is clear; of white deer changed into princesses and rewarding the knights who have spared them; of elves, goblins and enchanters in flowery forests. There were also kings' sons, who went forth on behalf of their fathers in search of some golden key or precious relic.

"What is a father?" asked the child.

Then Marie became sad; she tried to make her understand that a father was the master of a child, that it was necessary to submit to him, which was easy and pleasant when one was beloved, but very sad when one was not. She talked to her then about the cruel separation whose deadline was imminent, and had no idea how to respond to Isoline's sobs except with tears.

The seven years elapsed, however, and the horrible separation took place. It was necessary to tear away the child, who was clinging to her nurse, leaving a shred from her skirt in her hands; she suffered convulsions, and for a long time was in danger of death. Marie, for her part, put herself to bed in the hut uninhabited for seven years, which damp was devouring. Fortunately, her brother the sailor returned from service at that time; otherwise she would have died, devoid of all help.

Damont rebelled where his sister bowed her head in dolorous submission; he talked about going to the police. The half-mad Baron did not have the right to martyrize an innocent, whether she was his daughter or not. He got carried away, swore all his mariner's curses, and thumped the worm-eaten table with his fist—but his sister demonstrated to him that there was nothing legally answerable in the Baron's conduct; he was free to impose any system of education that suited him. The steward, a cold and ambitious man, whose own interests lay in punctilious obedience, had made her understand that the best thing to do was to conform to the regulation without protest, for fear of seeing it become even more severe.

What did that regulation say? Marie knew it by heart; she had read it a hundred times over. Damont wrote it down to her dictation, read it and reread it in his turn, and thought about it for a long time.

One evening, he slapped his forehead with a flash of joy.

"She isn't forbidden to go out!" he cried.

Indeed, either by virtue of omission or forgetfulness, that prohibition did not exist.

Damont ran to the château and prowled around it all day long. The walls and thick foliage did not allow the gaze to penetrate, but on the side of the pond, the château was partly visible. He posted himself as a sentinel and watched. At the approach of dusk he saw Isoline climbing the steps, followed by a black-clad man.

Ah! The crow! he said to himself.

They disappeared into the house.

What should he do? How could he attract the child's attention? Marie had often come to that spot in order to be able to see into the distance, but she hid herself, for fear of being seen. It was necessary to show himself, to make signals. They had no result; the little girl only passed in the distance and did not look in that direction.

To get past the walls or the hedges would have been nothing to Damont, but there were dogs that would have given him away or perhaps attacked him; moreover, Mathurin

Ferron, the steward would not have hesitated to fire a shotgun at him.

He searched for an expedient for a long time, thinking about nothing else, sustained and consoled by the hope.

"It's not forbidden to write, either," Damont said.

"Wait until the poor thing can read," replied Marguerite, with her angelic patience.

And they counted the days, calculating the pupil's probable progress.

The Jesuit, a man already old, of repulsive appearance and mediocre intelligence, who signaled his presence with an unbearable reek, had caused Isoline a terrible fear that seemed to presage a return of her crises.

During her convalescence, she had become completely savage, retreating into a stubborn silence. Père Coüée was not a bad man, and he conducted himself very mildly; he came every afternoon, sat down and talked for a long time, without demanding either attention or any response. Those unctuous words ended up reassuring her and, one day, abruptly, she turned toward him.

"Where's Marie?" she said.

"In Heaven," the priest replied.

"Go find her for me."

Then the Jesuit glimpsed a means of reckoning with his recalcitrant pupil. Without knowing who Marie was, he promised that she would see her when she could read perfectly.

Isoline flew into a terrible fit of temper, stamped her feet and howled—but the next day, she asked Père Coüée how long it would take to learn to read.

"That depends on you."

Marie had already taught her the letters of the alphabet, in secret; the memory of them came back to her very rapidly and Père Coüée was amazed by the facility that the solitary child demonstrated.

She devoted herself to study with an astonishing discipline, applied herself with all her might. Her master obtained what he wanted by repeating to her: "You'll see Marie."

When he had gone she picked up the book again and persisted; she still had occasional fits of impatience in which books and notebooks were torn apart, but she buckled down again, even neglecting her white nanny-goat, which was, after Marie, the only creature she loved.

Père Coüée was not without anxiety on seeing his pupil's progress. What would he say to her when she achieved her objective and her hopes crumbled? He thought about bringing her a pretty plaster virgin and affirming to her, without lying, that it was Marie, but he saw the statuette in a thousand pieces on the parquet, and wondered how he would teach her to write.

The day came when the child read an entire page faultlessly. She clapped her hands and he saw her laugh for the first time.

"Marie! Marie!" she cried,

He became severe, claiming that she was still stumbling, that it was far from a perfect reading. He gained time, but not without storms; he came to the lessons hiding his shame.

Once she got up abruptly and said, with a bizarre dignity: "You're a liar"—and threw the book in his face.

The Père offered that insult to Jesus. He believed himself truly rewarded for his humility when, in traversing the courtyard after Isoline, who ran away from him, he saw a farm boy give the little girl a letter, of which he took cognizance by means of looking over the child's head.

My dear little Isol,

I hope that you can read now and you will be able to understand me. Listen carefully, if you still love me as before. It is not forbidden for you to go out. I cannot come to you, but I am waiting on the other side of the gate that opens to the valley. Go bravely through that gate and you will be in my arms.

Marie

Isoline uttered a strident cry, launched herself toward the large green gate, which was not far away, and started hammering on it frenziedly with her closed fists.

"Open it! Open it!" she howled.

Mathurin Ferron came running.

"What does Mademoiselle desire?"

"Open the gate, I want to go out."

"Go out!"

"By what right do you prevent me?"

Mathurin bowed and went away in order to reread the famous placard. He soon returned and withdrew the iron bolts of the portal himself.

"I know my duty," he said. "In all that is not contrary to the regulation, I am at Mademoiselle's orders."

The gate opened; the valley appeared, with its fresh verdure bathed in sunlight. With a single bound Isoline launched herself outside, crossing the limits of the château for the first time.

Marie, hidden behind a tree, stepped out into the open and received her in her arms. There was a nervous hug, moistened by tears in which words were stifled; then they sat down on the grass, huddled together, looking at one another through the tears. The child had become paler, grown taller; the mother's eyes were hollow and her little curls, beneath her headscarf, were entirely white. They stayed there until dusk, talking in low voices, fearfully. Marie exhorted her to be prudent, and submissive.

"When you can write," she said, "we shall be freer."

When the dinner bell rang at the château, the steward appeared under the arch of the gate, sketching a bow.

"Go, go, my darling," said the nurse. "Be very good and you'll see me again."

"Take me away," whispered the child.

"They'd soon catch up with us. Obey, darling; I'll come back tomorrow."

The child ended up giving in, and drew away with a heavy heart. "Until tomorrow!" she shouted, as she went back through the gate.

When Père Coüée reappeared, Isoline went to him gravely and said, with a contrite expression: "Forgive me Monsieur. You're not a liar, and I thank you with all my heart for giving Marie back to me."

"I forgive you," said the priest, still a trifle embarrassed, "and I hope that you'll continue to be good and assiduous."

Her handwriting made rapid progress and, after a year, Père Coüée bade his pupil adieu.

She missed him, having ended up becoming accustomed to him, and because the work had almost provided a distraction from the emptiness of her existence.

She was a big girl now, having attained the age of ten. Marie taught her, still in secret, a little about dressmaking and the great art of knitting, but Isoline found such work tedious. A little gaiety had returned to her; she played on the bank of the Rance, on the slippery rocks, and went fishing with Damont in the rain and the blustery wind, but she remained as savage as a beast of the forest; there were hectic flights when she perceived a passer-by at a distance, and if anyone came into the cottage she hid in the cupboard.

One evening she let the hour for dinner go by, and when she came in, found the table cleared and everything reset. She complained to Mathurin.

"The meal will be served at the appointed time," he said, bowing and pointing at the placard.

She went to bed hungry, and the next day drank sour milk and half-raw buckwheat pancakes at the Damonts. That nourishment gave her nausea, and after that she strove to be punctual. When the southerly wind blew, she could hear the bell from Marie's cottage; then she started running, and arrived in time. Sometimes she missed the soup. The steward, in a black coat, served it automatically, if she were absent, as if she had been there. Sometimes she did not arrive until dessert, and then stuffed herself with cheese.

At the age of fifteen she suddenly saddened, became dreamy and unquiet, wanted to know the secret of her existence and tortured Marie in order to get it out of her.

She watched out for the annual visit of the Baron, the man who was her father, but whom she had never seen.

He arrived at nightfall; the two battens of the gate opened to let his carriage in. Isoline, without a light in her room, glued her face to the window-panes and saw the lantern shining; then Mathurin went forward, obsequiously. A tall man dressed in black got out and went into the house; he went to occupy a bedroom on the first floor, which remained locked during his absence. Then trunks, which seemed light, were taken from the carriage.

An hour later the windows of the little chapel, to which the Baron alone had a key, lit up, and the light did not go out again for as long as the young woman stayed awake.

One morning, at daybreak, the Baron left again.

Isoline, who had until then confined herself to the wing of the château where she lived, began curiously to open doors of which she had previously taken no notice, visiting her prison on expeditions of discovery.

She saw large drawing rooms in sequence, soberly furnished, obscured by closed shutters; she sometimes folded one up in order to see better, and the light, falling upon a man of war, caused her to utter an exclamation. On the first floor were long corridors, and variously elegant bedrooms, including the Baron's—which was locked, and into which she tried to peer through the keyhole.

Opposite the staircase, on the broad landing, there was a tall door in carved walnut, decorated with gilt, which seemed to her to be very imposing. One day, the young woman opened it, not without emotion; she entered into a square room with divans all around and a carpet on the floor, garnished from floor to ceiling with bound books.

From that day on, the Damonts' cottage saw less of her; Isoline was discovering the world. She threw herself into reading with all the impetuosity of her character.

What amazement! All those existences that emerged from those pages, all those individuals born in her mind, evoked by words! At first it was an insensate chaos, a medley of history, poems and philosophy that confused her; then light dawned; she developed preferences. History seduced her, but the old romances of chivalry impassioned her. She no longer slept, hardly ate and never went out.

As she knew nothing and was completely ignorant about the real world, she believed in the one that populated her dreams, and lived there exclusively.

All sorts of aspirations coming to her, she could no longer tolerate the simple clothes that she had always worn. She demanded silk, rich fabrics, perfumes and embroidered underwear. Mathurin procured all that for her. She took her models then from engravings of all times, spoiled many garments, but ended up becoming skillful.

One day, she asked for a horse.

"There are some in the stables," Mathurin said. "Would Mademoiselle like to choose?"

"Not counting the farm horses, Isoline saw three of them: two grey Percherons for the cart and a black stallion of a good enough breed, but dulled by inaction.

"That one," she said.

Mathurin went to fetch a lady's saddle and saddled the black horse; then he held the stirrup.

"But I don't know how to ride," the young woman said.

"If Mademoiselle orders it, I can give her a few lessons," said the steward, who had once been a very good horseman.

"I'd like that," she said.

The riding lessons had taken place in the park, and Isoline, as agile as a boy, was soon accustomed to that exercise.

The first time she went out on horseback, the stable-boy donned livery, mounted one of the Percherons and followed her at a distance. She weren't straight ahead without going far the first few times, then became bolder and went on longer excursions, plunging into superb countryside, and saw the sea.

But the disgraceful and thoughtless individual who followed her, always at an equal distance, made her impatient; she forbade him to accompany her, and wandered alone for entire days.

Nature intoxicated her, the wide horizons, the changing skies and the infinite variety of locations caused her first joys, but that happiness soon wore then; the bad weather arrived, rain barred the roads, the fog blotted out the landscape and the wind modulated its plaints in the flutes of locks.

All the books in the library had been read and reread. What should she do? What would become of her? A leaden despair overwhelmed poor Isoline. She understood now the horror of her life, and saw that it had no exit; she was already a woman; she would grow old there, die there; would all her youth and beauty be swallowed up, unknown, in that desert tomb?

And she sobbed and cried alone, facing her lamp, while the rainwater streamed in the gutters.

Why wait? she said to herself. *Why not hasten the end?*

The idea of killing herself took possession of her and rapidly grew. She caused Marie a thousand deaths be telling her about her mania. Several suicide attempts went awry; she wounded herself, and made herself ill, but came back to life.

"I'll succeed in the end, though," she said.

On the day when Gilbert had waited for her in vain at the church, she wandered through the château from room to room, gripped once again by all her miseries, firmly resolved this time to liberate herself from them. The idea of the pond attracted her; she was astonished not to have thought of it before. Was it not there at her feet, ready to envelop her, to close upon her, to erase every trace and memory of her? It was the remedy beside the disease; how had she failed, for such a long time, to understand that mute offer of consolation?

She opened the window, leaned on the sill, and gazed at the motionless water.

The bushes were leaning over, brushing the surface; clumps of irises widened their sheaves; tall straight reeds formed islets in places. All around it, the leaves of the tall trees were trebling gently in a warm breeze; a bright green, translucent foliage, contrasting with the dark hue of the wet branches, was beginning to spring forth everywhere; the sky projected a shred of azure into the middle of the pool.

Suddenly, a bird broke the silence; it launched a sonorous powerful whistle.

"What? Nightingales? Already!"

She raised her head.

At that moment, the sun was unveiled, its light falling like luminous rain through the bright leaves, lighting up the undergrowth. On the other side of the water, in the clearing formed by the road, a young man was wandering back and forth, pausing in front of the château, at which he gazed obstinately. A gilded gleam shone on his forehead, and Isoline recognized the naval officer.

She watched him curiously, but, seeing him as if transfixed by her presence, she gaily closed the window.

"Bah!" she exclaimed. "Spring again."

V

The next day, when he came to the Damonts' cottage, Gilbert experienced a choking sensation on seeing Isoline sitting under the mantle of the fireplace.

She was no longer the peasant-woman he had seen the first time, but a demoiselle—or, rather, a noble demoiselle, for, in the cut of her garments and her head-dress, there as a deliberate reflection of the Middle Ages.

She stood out clearly against the brown moss formed by the soot. Her bright gray dress in fine linen was decorated at the sides by a silken cord; her hair hung down in long tresses over her breast, and a little gray velvet bonnet, graciously indented, enclosed the top of her head; a light pale blue veil was attached to it.

The young man, after taking off his cap, dared not move forward, fearful of causing the wild bird to fly away, but

Isoline did not budge; she darted her haughty gaze at him, which gradually softened and became veiled.

"Come in," she said. "Marie will be back soon."

He sat down a short distance away from her, and while she lowered her gaze toward the cold ashes, he finally savored the joy of looking at her at his leisure. Her face was long, as pale as a communion wafer, there chin very delicate, her nose slightly curved; her eyebrows, often frowning, marked a slight pleat above the eyes; the corners of her mouth had a dolorous inflexion that rare and fugitive smiles did not erase; her hair, golden blonde, was wavy; from her entire person emanated something akin to a perfume of purity and nobility, a mystical, mysterious grace.

Nothing banal tarnished that solitary spirit, folded in upon itself, but never having been subject to the influence of narrow minds or any paltry prejudice.

Gilbert gazed at her with a religious admiration, paralyzed, unable to find anything to say.

She was the one who broke the silence; she seemed to be following a train of thought, and the question hovered, irresolutely, on her lips before resonating there.

"I'm told that you've been sad. Why?"

"I'm an orphan," he replied, "and until now, my heart was a desert."

"Yes," she said. "It's better never to love than to lose what one loves."

"Oh, don't say that!" Gilbert exclaimed, with an involuntary excitement. "Regret, poignant as it may be, still has its sweetness. One remembers those one has loved, and hopes to find them again in a possible eternity—but someone whose arid soul has dried up all tenderness can only have one hope, which is to die entirely."

She listened to him, surprised by the recklessness of that speech, struck by the singular gleam of those clear eyes; then she plunged back into the familiar silence, from which she soon emerged to hurl this remark at him, with a smile: "Would you like to love the spring with me?"

He looked at her for a moment without answering. "I want everything that you want," he said, finally, stammering with emotion and not understanding the meaning of the question.

Isoline started laughing at his confusion.

Marie came in; the young woman drew her to her by means of childlike caresses.

"Listen," she said. "Here's a mariner, very frightened; he thinks I'm mad!"

"What have you done to him, naughty girl? He's a noble soul who doesn't merit your scorn."

"I offered to let him be like a brother to me," Isoline said, becoming serious again, "and to celebrate with me the fête that's about to begin."

"What fête?"

"You don't know our Brittany, then, and the splendors of its spring? There are no carousels or tourneys worth as much as those fêtes. I've often traversed them all alone, searching enchanted gardens, forgetting my miseries in the midst of those riches." She lowered her voice. "I'd like to see them one last time, to bequeath them to someone, as if all those flowers were mine."

"At least wait until I'm under the ground, bad girl, to talk again about such vile things," Marie cried, understanding what Isoline meant. "It won't be long, moreover, for you're driving me toward the other world with your cruelties."

The young woman threw her arms around her. "Shut up," she said. "You can see that I'm quite cheerful. I can hear Damont mooring his boat; let's go join him and fly over the water." She turned to Gilbert, and added: "Are you coming?"

She held out her hand to him, and drew him outside.

From the doorway, Marie watched them draw away, with a tender smile.

"What if she could love him, though!" she murmured.

Damont, who was sitting in his boat untangling fishing lines, remained mute with astonishment when he raised his head and saw the young people standing in front of him, hand in hand, like old friends.

"Don't you recognize us?" she said.

"Slacken the mizzen, and forward ho!" proclaimed Gilbert, who thought he was in one of those dreams in which everything one desires is accomplished with the greatest ease. He was in haste to quit the land, to be beside her in that narrow boat, on the element that was his own, and where it seemed to him that she had just joined him.

"To Lehon!" Isoline had said, sitting down by the tiller.

And the sail was extended, and they had reached the middle of the stream.

Dinan immediately appeared at a bend in the river. The sun made the verdure rejuvenating its old walls shine. Everything was gilded; the sky, a very pale blue, drowned the contours. It was no longer the black and lugubrious town that had saddened Gilbert a few days earlier, but something joyful and resplendent, which put him in mind of a beautiful city in Italy.

"Look," said the young woman, pointing her finger at the ancient fortress, today a State prison, which seemed to be hoisting its formidable towers over the town. "Look, it's there that the hero Tristan was mortally wounded. It's there that he wept over Iseult's absence, while his page watched anxiously at the top of the tower for a ship at sea. It's incredible, isn't it, that one can see the sea from here; from the top of the tower, though, one discovers an endless horizon: meadows, hills, the jagged coast, and then the sea, and the islands almost distinct in the distance...but you're not looking."

"I'm listening," said Gilbert, drinking her in with his eyes.

"It's true," said Damont. "On a clear day, you can see Jersey and Mont Saint-Michel."

"I've often dreamed of finding their tomb," she continued, as if talking to herself, for they died here: 'He took her so forcefully in his arms, in bidding her a final adieu, that he burst her heart.'" She sighed. "I've loved them so much," she murmured, carried away by a dream.

"Do you think, then, that such a love can no longer be encountered?" Gilbert asked, in a tremulous voice.

"Who would inspire it," he replied. "Look at those superb châteaux whose majesty still moves us, and the blackened lacework of those high belfries. Compare them with miserable modern constructions; for me, there's the same difference between the men of long ago and those of today."

"Perhaps you're misjudging them—but its certain that Iseult was no more beautiful than you are."

She looked at him ironically, and stopped a cruel remark on the tip of her tongue.

He felt suddenly saddened by that cold gaze and the disdainful curl off her lip; why did he draw such forceful scorn from her? He was not wounded by that undeserved disdain, however; he dreamed of triumphing over it by making himself better known; something about him had pleased her, since she, so wild, had come to him; that was more than he had hoped. He caressed that fine proud profile with his gaze, those eyes whose irises resembled turquoises, as transparent as sapphires, and he pulled himself together.

Damont, whose keen intelligence had distinguished something akin to the rumble of a storm between the two young people, attempted a conciliatory remark, but the poor fellow stammered horribly at the slightest emotion. It was lost in an incomprehensible stutter at which Isoline laughed maliciously.

They passed under an old low bridge, the boat's mast brushing the arch, and then under the enormous viaduct, which resonated like a bell.

The fortress had disappeared, and the river became a stream between ravishing banks. They forgot Tristan and Iseult for the dragonflies, green or blue, quivering in a sunbeam above nenuphar lilies displaying their large leaves.

The narrowed banks are formed there by enormous rocks that loom up with a thousand cracks, presenting an exuberant climbing vegetation all the way to the rim. The leaves, brand new, cause the most tender shades of green to sing in all their freshness; it is an exquisite foliage, still light, full of birds, in which silvery willows interpose pale tufts. The river has a hundred caprices, describing curves and semicircles, seeming to slow down. It is as green as its banks; the sky finds no clearing in which to cast the slightest sheet of blue. Often, large trees protrude over the water, allowing creepers to hang down; they join up with the bushes on the other bank, to which they seem to be confiding some mystery.

Damont has furled his sail, for the wind is banished from that charming spot; the oars scrape the almost-pure mirror soundlessly, and a contemplative silence is allowed to fall, full of sweetness.

Suddenly, a song resounds over the water; mariners who are cheering up their journey; one might think it a slightly funereal canticle, so plaintive and sad are their voices. The shanty, however, has nothing sullen about it.

Let's sing to pass the time
The charming amours of a girl.
Leaving the port of Lorient
On her way to join her lover.

"Do you know that song?" said Isoline to Gilbert. "Damont has taught it to me, and I like the story very much; the lover is a captain, and in order not to be parted from him, the girl, disguised as a cabin-boy, signs on to the ship. He's struck by a resemblance, but the false mariner defends herself. Listen."

The boat passed close by
Monsieur you catch me unawares,
You're joking; you make me laugh;
I'm just a poor matelot,
Who has signed on with the ship.
I was born in Martinique,
I'm my mother's only son,
And it was a ship from Holland
That set me down in Calais.

"Yes, I remember," said Gilbert. "My matelots sometimes sing it."

The voices drew away:

They stayed for three long years
On the ship without recognition
They stayed for three long years
Unrecognized until they disembarked.

Why does that naïve song trouble me today? Gilbert asked himself. *I've heard it a hundred times without paying any heed to it.*

Isoline was looking at him more tenderly. Was he, too, not a captain who would soon depart on his ship, but alone and probably in despair? And since she did not want to live any longer than that spring, would not that departure be, for her, the last event in her futile life?

We'll both leave at the same time, she thought.

Then she thought about the places where he was going, and interrogated him about distant lands.

Gilbert talked about India and its giant forests, prodigious flowers with intoxicating perfumes, and butterflies, flying petals, and birds, living gems. She glimpsed brown-skinned women passing between the slender trunks of banana-tress, their blue-tinted hair finely plaited, with gold rings in their nostrils, and black slaves, and elephants beneath silken howdahs, brushing flowers and brushwood with their huge feet. Then he talked to her about Cochin-China and its superb ruins, the Antilles, Senegal and its perfidious climate.

A desire to escape, to flee, took shape in her. How many things there were of which the poor solitary creature knew nothing! Was the present truly worth the pain of living? Did those battling heroes by whom her mind was haunted have their equals in those singular lands? And she questioned him further about the mores about the people. The beauty of the costumes astonished her most of all.

"But why have you come back?" she asked.

"Duty."

That word threw her into a reverie. So one still devoted oneself, one still gave one's life to safeguard the glory of one's fatherland? Yes, but obscurely, without brilliant combats, without damascened armor, without helmet-plumes quivering in the wind; one could esteem modern heroes, but not love them.

Roland, beneath his bristling chimerical helmet, appeared to her as beautiful as an archangel, and she had wept a great deal over his sublime death in the gorges of Roncevaux, while the fat general who overlooked the square in Dinan made her split her sides laughing in spite of his alleged bravery.

They had arrived at the end of the journey.

"We're here," said Damont, sliding the boat into an inlet of the river.

More ruins, more past!

Gilbert sensed the enemy there. What could he do against phantoms, seen through the seduction of history and veils wove by time? He dreamed of single combats against that horde of specters, which defended the soul of the one he to whom was laying siege. It was necessary that the army in question be reduced to dust, dispersed, vanished, in order that he might enter as master. He admired, however, the power of the book, which had populated her solitude in that fashion, and understood her all the better because he loved the great heroes of the sea himself, and had acquired in their society a certain scorn for modern men.

In the ruined cloister, the young woman had sat down on a tomb only half-covered by brambles. The stone knight lying on his back joined his long hands together, verdant with moss, from the tops of cracked arched windows flowed a cascade of white flowers, while foliage stood in for panes and spread a green light.

With her gray dress, similar is hue to the tone, her pallor and her immobility, Isoline seemed to be a statue added to the sepulcher; the green daylight falling from above threw the same shroud over her and the knight.

Gilbert, as he looked at her, had a dolorous shock.

"Come on! Come on!" he cried. "You seem to me to be dead."

She stood up. "Jean de Beaumanoir lies here," she murmured.[3]

Outside the penumbra the illusion dissipated; the melancholy fell away with that wan veil. The young woman suddenly broke into a run, lightly, throwing back her hair, which the breeze scattered. She went through the black and sordid village, her dress held up on her arm, leaping over the greasy paving-stones; then she went down a stone stairway near a stream where women were washing clothes, and turned back to her companion, who had not allowed her to outdistance him, with a smiling expression.

"Now the charge!" she cried, pointing to a steep hill on which stood three stout broken towers.

Gilbert launched himself forward and, in a few moments, disappeared from sight. She was nimble, though, and climbed like her nurse the nanny-goat over the unsteady stones and the steep paths—but she could not catch him, and when she arrived at the summit, slightly put out, her cheeks pink and her heart bounding, she could not see him anywhere.

There were gaping abysses where the walls of the fortress had collapsed, bristling with stones without being complete filled. The grass, brambles and ferns formed a moving curtain in those hollows, capable of closing over a broken body.

Isoline was afraid. Surely he had slipped and fallen. Carried away by that insensate rush, he had not been able to stop on the edge of that gulf, which he had not anticipated. She felt that she was very pale, and was trembling all over. She had

---

[3] The earlier of the two knights with that name, who flourished in the mid-fourteenth century in the same era as Bertrand du Guesclin; there is a statue of him in Dinan.

not heard anything, however, no cry—but she had run so fast herself. Leaning over, her eyes wide, she interrogated the dark hollow, then made a circuit of the ruin.

A kind of pride stopped a shout of appeal on her lips. Nothing! Disappeared, mute, was he dead already, this companion she had chosen? She stood motionless, terrified.

A stone tumbling from the top of the highest tower caused her to raise her head; then the cry that she had suppressed escaped her lips—a cry of fright, and also of joy. Gilbert, astride a crenellation at the very top of the tower, attached there, like a flag, a piece of pale blue silky cloth. Shortly before, without her perceiving it, he had stolen her veil, and now it was floating in that inaccessible place.

"The fortress is captured," he shouted, gaily, "and my lady's colors are ablaze there alone.

"Oh, come down!" she said, in a distressed voice.

That descent was a torture for her. The stones, three-quarters dislodged, shifted underfoot; the tufts of grass to which he clung might suddenly give way and precipitate him along with them. She followed him with her eyes, her teeth gritted, and for a moment it seemed to her that the entire tower oscillated.

When he thought he was low enough, Gilbert jumped. Isoline thought that he was doomed, shut her eyes and fell backwards in a semi-swoon.

The young man ran to her.

"What's the matter? My God, how pale you are!"

"You're mad!" she said, furiously. "You've upset me!" And, incapable of mastering her nerves, she burst into sobs.

"Oh, you're good, you're a woman!" exclaimed Gilbert, kneeling down beside her. "You trembled momentarily for my life, but the childishness of that climb truly didn't deserve as much as that. Had you not cried: *Charge*? I was only obeying the order."

Ashamed of her weakness, she succeeded in calming herself.

"That's how you take a fortress that defied armies for centuries?"

"It's somewhat the worse for wear."

"But the tower is high and straight; I thought it quite impregnable."

"Mariners climb like monkeys," said Gilbert. "That's nothing—at sea, when a tempest is unleashed and it's necessary to go up to the top of a mast to attach a rope, it's harder. There, if you get dizzy, you're doomed. A mast is as tall as the tower, but less stable; sometimes its top brushes the waves and the man clinging to it is whipped by the water, the wind rages in order to tear him off and carry him away—but that still doesn't stop him attaching his rope."

"You've done that?"

"A hundred times. But can the reality trouble you thus, adorable child, you who only dream of the heroes of old whose principal merit was to shed their blood and that of others? Those butcheries would have been the death of you, since the slightest movement in which one risks a scratch draws tears from you."

"That's true," she said. "I'm foolish—let's not think about it anymore."

She raised her eyes, which she had kept lowered, with a hint of embarrassment.

"Look, look at all those crows. The sole lords of the castle today! Why are they croaking in those frightful voices? Perhaps they remember feasts of old, for there was, indeed, horrible carnage here, and the ground we're on has drunk a great deal of blood; it's said that it ran all the way to the Rance, whose waters were reddened. It was English blood."

"Or that of neighboring lords. Brothers readily cut one another's throats over a piece of land or a futile quarrel."

"You mustn't speak ill of heroes," she said. "Du Guesclin was once commander of this fortress."

"He was very ugly, the good knight."

"Which didn't prevent him from being loved by the most beautiful of demoiselles."

"Oh, let's leave the dead in peace," cried Gilbert. "We're alive and we're young, let's not part the flowers that veil tombs from us. Is this, then, the spring that you promised me—a vast cemetery of in regrets?"

"Well then, let's go," she said. "Tomorrow, we'll go out in the country."

When they were down below she turned round and saw her veil, palpitating on the old tower; then she squeezed Gilbert's hand with a sort of enthusiasm. That folly had served the young man better than years of tender submission.

They came back, followed by the last rays of the setting sun.

The boat, gliding beneath the branches and over the reflected foliage, seemed to them to be like a nest; they felt happy there, borne away by a somnolence; the gaze that weighed upon her numbed her gently, and he thought that the moment was one of the best of his life.

When he went back into his sister's house, without knowing how he had got back there, that return to vulgar life caused a painful shock. He was enveloped by a nimbus of happiness that isolated him; he was found to be sulky, the radiance in his eyes was not understood.

"What do you think of Marguerite Rochereuil?" Sylvie asked him, after dinner.

"I don't know her."

"What! You spent an entire evening with her here. The Maire's daughter."

"I didn't look at her."

"Really? Well, look next time—she has a dowry of two hundred thousand francs."

"So much the better for her," said Gilbert. "What does that have to do with me?"

VI

They set a course for Saint-Jacut on the coast, on horseback this time.

She wore a long dress the color of otter-skin and a musketeer's hat with a feather.

The sky was resplendent and fields of gorse turned the countryside golden; the perfumed warm breeze that was blowing made them intoxicated.

There were flowers everywhere, and nothing but flowers; the grass disappeared beneath a invasion of daisies, the smallest bushes hid under mantles of petals. Beside the road, paths opened and fled beneath vaults of sweet-briar and red or white hawthorn. In the moist grass patches of blue stood out, and swallows drank there as they passed by. There were perspectives in which the eyes became lost with delight, distances full of promises, veritably pathways to paradise, similarly impracticable.

At Ploubalay, when they arrived there, noon was chiming in the bell-tower of the new church.

"Shall we have lunch here?" asked Gilbert, thinking it a perfectly natural question.

Isoline reined in her mount and looked at him fearfully. "You want to stop? To talk to these people, to go into their houses?"

"What could be simpler? There's an inn. Aren't you hungry?"

"I'm very hungry," she said, "but it isn't the first time I've skipped a meal to run through fields. My pleasure is never complete; something always reminds me that I'm an impotent victim."

"Forget it today—give me that pleasure," Gilbert said, taking the horse's bridle and drawing the young woman after him with gentle violence.

She frowned, stiffened, and became very pale, but the surprise caused her by that determination, which did not give way to her own will at the first word, was not without charm.

The inn, which was a tavern and a farm at the same time, was dark and unappealing. In the first room, as dark as a cellar, men sitting with their elbows on the table, as if exhausted, seemed lost in the contemplation of their bowls of cider. The gracious hostess, with a pink and white smile, quickly showed them a door that led to the courtyard.

Large dilapidated buildings, which seemed very high, surrounded it in a square; it was considerable cluttered with dung-heaps in which chickens were pecking, and the ill-kept stables filled it with an acrid odor. At the back, an external staircase, which creaked underfoot, gave access to a room overlooking the countryside. The window on the side of the fields was garlanded by a precocious rose-bush, all in flower; that was, however, the only luxury in that vast whitewashed room, completely empty save for a long table and two wooden benches in one corner, and on the wall, as if lost, a colored picture of Jesus with a smoking heart in the middle of his stomach.

Gilbert had the table placed closer to the window. A white tablecloth was spread out; two wicker chairs replaced the benches; fresh cider in faience pots, salted butter, coarse rustic bread, heavy plates were laid out with rapid little shocks.

Isoline, leaning on the window-sill, stared out obstinately. She seemed to be suffering in that unfamiliar environment; her exaggerate sensitivity rendered dolorous the proximity of unknown beings who seemed to her to be a very inferior race and for whom she experienced a profound repugnance.

"Are you annoyed?" Gilbert asked her, drawing closer to her. "Are you so scornful of the friend you have chosen that you don't want to share his meal?"

The bad mood was not very serious. That solitary room where no sound arrived was nothing but reassuring. The young woman turned toward the laid table brought a thought to her mind that made her smile.

"Maître Mathurin Ferron, one of my jailers," she said, "is serving lunch at this moment to my phantom. He imagines that I'm going hungry; well, for once in his life, he'll be mistaken." And she sat down resolutely at the table

They obtained an exquisite omelet, but apart from that the menu was rather vague. They scarcely noticed it; Isolate was intoxicated by the pleasure, entirely new to her, of a shared meal, and the thousand attentions with which Gilbert surrounded her. The gaze that the habit of command rendered so dominating melted in tenderness when it rested upon her, giving her a beneficial impression. They chatted with increasing confidence, telling one another about their lives, comparing their harsh solitudes and finding that in many respects they resembled one another; that was what explained the sympathy between them, and why she had so spontaneously saluted him as her brother.

Brother! That title displeased the young man; he had never seen a sister in her. She was a dream, perfect happiness or mortal despair, but not tranquil and fraternal friendship.

He dared not speak of love, however; those pure eyes, that virginal gravity, froze the words of egotistical passion in his lips. He dreaded enlightening that reckless innocence, which confided itself so naively to an unknown and did not suspect any evil, where any other might have judged herself lost. He had to struggle, however, against an ardent youth; Isoline's hand in his caused him fits of dizziness; that tender palm disengaged a magnetism so powerful for him that it required all his will-power to take his hand away.

They left again, hastening toward their goal, for they had lingered chatting.

The sun poured down its warm light from one high over the increasingly beautiful. All the thorny hedges that jealously surround the smallest fields in Brittany were an admirable pretext for the spring to embroider its florescence. There was an abundance, an unparalleled prodigality; the splendid pink of apple-trees brought cries of surprise from the marveling couple, while the birds were chirping to proclaim their contentment.

The marshy bay of Saint-Jacut, in which tall gilded grass prospered, under which frogs were croaking, was dry when it was revealed to the riders' eyes; flocks were grazing there. Between the great brown rocks, which half-blocked the horizon, the sea appeared, the color of ultramarine, sending a breath of fresh wind.

They took a sunken path, and then launched themselves over the fields in order to reach the strand without passing through the village.

"I have an illusion of freedom today," said Isoline, "and I owe to you the pleasure of knowing that a joy shared is doubled."

Saint-Jacut is a bizarrely-indented peninsula offering variously-sized clefts to the sea, which comes to fill them at high tide. The deepest plunges between two chains of hills, luxuriant and fresh on the southern side, scorched on the surfaces that face north-west, the sea between them like a beautiful river.

They left their horses on the cliff and went down over the rocks on to the beach, which was still free.

The wind, which they had not felt in the country, was blowing briskly from the sea.

"You aren't cold?" he said.

"Oh, no!"

And she jumped up on a rock that protruded like a huge tortoise from the middle of the sands. He joined her there, enveloped by the whistling breeze, and they looked at one another.

A very gentle sky, of veiled azure. The sea, on the other hand, is the profound blue of sapphires. It is very choppy, but joyously so. Sequences of white waves dance around the islets; every rock is coiffed with a bright foam, which leaps, races, climbs, scatters in feathery spray, collapses in pearly cascades, flies away like smoke. It is cheerful, capering and gracious as if cadenced by ballet music.

"Do you love it, the sea, you mariners?" asked Isoline.

"It tortures us, and we can't get away from it," he replied. "Today, however, I'd renounce it for you—but she'll certainly be my tomb if you abandon me."

They looked at one another for a moment, he seeking to read the depths of her eyes, she with a kind of fear. They remembered abruptly that spring would come to an end.

There was a sort of solemnity in that minute, an anxiety and a kind of presentiment.

When they wanted to turn back, the water had surrounded the rock; it was now an island. What could they do? Take their shoes and stockings off and walk through the water? Modesty held Isoline back. Gilbert, who knew that he had nothing to fear from bold actions, seized her abruptly in his arms and jumped, with perfect surety, on to the sand from which the waves separated them.

The young woman was afraid; her hat flew off and she clung instinctively to Gilbert's neck.

Then a vertigo took hold of him; he pressed her against him madly, and lavished kisses upon the hair that was blinding him, and intoxicating him with its perfume. Immediately, however, he thrust her away, frightened by that violence; blushing in confusion, he turned his eyes away.

"Forgive me, forgive me," he murmured, his heart beating so fast that his voice almost failed.

"Forgive you for what?" she said, allowing the tranquil light of her irises to radiate.

"You don't understand?"

"No."

"It's just that I love you with all my being, and that you don't love me—that's al."

She pulled an enigmatic face and said, briskly: "You seemed to be suffering—I thought you'd hurt yourself jumping from the rock."

"The wound is of another kind," he said, with a bitter smile. "I beg you, though, let's go; this too delightful spring has made me lose my head; I'm afraid of myself. Come on, let's go."

They went back to their mounts and drew away slowly, returning through the shadows of the sunken road.

The marshy bay was now a beautiful lake that the wind did not reach; the water spread out gently and evenly, with the curvature of a camellia leaf, tinted with the most delicate hues of fading turquoise. Near a velvety brown cottage, a large apple-tree that leaned over crazily supported its black braches and pink flowers against the luminous background of the sea and the water.

On seeing the sun sinking rapidly they took to the gallop, afraid of being caught by nightfall. They took a short cut, devouring the distance, and finally saw Dinan on the far side of the plain, its hill still silhouetted against the clear sky.

They let the horses breathe for a moment.

A voice asking for charity made them shiver. It was an old man sitting under a little awning set on two poles.

"Oh! Give him something," said Isoline. "The unfortunate have often made me keenly aware of my poverty. Many a time I've stolen pieces of bread to give to them as I pass, so as not to be humiliated by a pauper!"

Gilbert threw a coin into the extended hat and they set off again.

A bell was ringing when they arrived within view of the château.

"My dinner!" she said, laughing. "I'll miss the soup."

They separated before the pool, and when he interrogated her with an anxious gaze she shouted to him, as she drew away: "Until tomorrow, no? At Marie's!"

VII

Isoline did not come to the rendezvous the following day, and they spent a day of anguish in the Damont's cottage. A hundred times, without putting down her knitting, Marie went along the little path and interrogated the mute château from afar. They lost themselves in conjectures. Was it a caprice? A cruelty? Was she ill?

Gilbert was convinced that he had displeased her and that she did not want to see him again. Marie had a more frightful thought, which she kept to herself, and covertly wiped away tears.

He went to prowl around by the pond, but he did not see anything; everything was closed, motionless.

Night fell—a clear and perfumed night illuminated by the moon. The young man drew away, then went back, unable to make up his mind to leave.

Suddenly, he heard running footsteps on the pathway; a form appeared, and before he knew what was happening, Isoline threw herself into his arms, half-fainting.

"My God! What's the matter?" he cried, drawing her into a moonbeam.

She was white, breathless, her hair disheveled, her dress in tatters, her hands bloody. "Take me away!" she sighed.

"Is someone chasing you? Has someone hurt you?"

"No, I've run away. I broke the lock and came through the hedge, where I left a great deal of my hair."

"Why? What's happened?"

"The Baron has come back," she said, in an agitated voice. "I'd forgotten that. In spring he stays for a time, because of the farmers. I was locked up, as usual, but a rage gripped me, a revolt; I wanted to get out, at all costs. I no longer want to submit to that slavery, since I have a friend who can protect me."

"He will save you, that friend," he said, emotionally, "but what strength he would have if you wanted him!"

"How?"

"By loving him not as a brother, but as one loves a spouse." He was speaking in a low voice, holding her in his arms, but she pulled away, perhaps sharing that disturbance which, the previous day, had not affected her."

"The horrible dread of finding myself separated from you has revealed to me how dear you are to me," she said, in an almost indistinct voice. "I found an incredible strength in order to escape and come to you. Look, I didn't even feel the brambles that grazed me." And she held out her pretty hands, all bloody—which, with a stifled cry, he cleaned with his lips.

"Yes," she said, "my cherished heroes have turned to dust since I have known you; you have slid treacherously beneath their beautiful armor."

"Isoline!"

"Well, now save me. Let's flee."

"No, my beloved. You're too pure and noble to want to use extreme means, without first letting me attempt to obtain you honestly. The Baron, in spite of his strange conduct, is your father, and he cannot hide from my request. If he refuses, then I will take you away from here, and you will be like an adored sister to me—but in year, you will be free, your own mistress, and the world will be ours."

"Is that true? Damont has already told me that at twenty-one, my chains would break of their own accord. I didn't want to believe it. It's necessary to obey you, then. See how submissive I am now—me, so unruly. I'll go back into my prison then."

"Tomorrow, I shall force its locks."

"All my strength is exhausted by having overcome the obstacles; now I'm going away from you."

He took her back and helped to get through the hedge again. The dogs did not bark.

She slipped through the dark pathways surreptitiously, in order to get back to her room without being seen, but the windows of the chapel, which were illuminated, attracted her gaze. She stopped.

If she could see what was happening behind those stained-glass windows, might she discover the secret of her destiny? The temptation was strong. Who knew whether what she saw might furnish her with a weapon to use in the battle in which she was about to engage?

She made a circuit of the chapel. One of the windows was ajar, and by pushing it a little one might look through it; it was just a matter of reaching it. There was no lack of ladders in the courtyard; she dragged one without making too much noise, and set it up. Her heart was beating rapidly as she set her feet on the rungs.

An infinity of lighted candles dazzled her at first; then she perceived an old man, correctly dressed, who was sweeping the floor.

She thought she was dreaming. The interior of the chapel was like a bedroom, very elegant but faded: blue satin wall-hangings, mirrors, candelabras, and, on a platform, a bed with raised curtains. A woman was lying on the bed, immobile and fully dressed.

The old man was tidying up, dusting with the greatest care. When he turned round, Isoline saw a face inundated by tears.

When everything was in good order, he went to the bed, fell to his knees and uttered frightful sobs.

"Armel! Armel!" he cried. "You can't hear me anymore."

Then he spoke softly, in a tender voice, murmuring indistinct phrases.

Isoline shivered at the tone of that dolor, which she did not understand. Who was that woman, who seemed to be simultaneously a corpse and a doll? And what was that man saying, so tender now, who hated his daughter?

"I've brought you the flowers that you love," he murmured, through his tears. "Roses, narcissi and lilacs."

He got up in order to look around and, doubtless having perceived that he had forgotten what he was looking for, he opened the door of the chapel to go out. Isoline climbed down rapidly, wanting to flee—but in her panic she took the wrong direction, and suddenly found herself, for the first time, face to face with the Baron de Kerdréol.

He saw her, and recoiled with a hoarse cry, his face distraught; the moon, which shone full upon it, rendered it pale and frightful."

"Back! Back, murderer!" he cried. "Get away, or I'll kill you!"

The terrified young woman fled, and barricaded herself in her room, trembling. Frightful nightmares followed her there.

When Gilbert had forced his way into the château, almost by violence, the following day he saw an old man of fifty, dazed by despair, who seemed mild, but who had the staring eyes of a madman.

As soon as Isoline's name was mentioned, he shivered, and his face took on a hard expression, but he listened with an apparent calm.

"The demoiselle does not want to marry," he said. "She wants to spend her life in retreat."

When Gilbert persisted, affirming that he would have none of it, a flash of fury appeared in the Baron's eyes. He restrained himself, however, and replied with great politeness. "Since you seem better informed than me, the person in question will be advised of the honor that you are doing her, and in a week's time you shall have an answer dictated by her."

The young man had no alternative but to withdraw after that very correct interview. He could not help being anxious, however, fearful of a trap. In spite of his apparent lucidity, the man gave the impression of being a madman; it was obvious that a great dolor, which had given birth to that inexplicable horror for the inheritor of his name, had ruined his life forever, and that time had not softened anything or caused anything to be forgotten. The obsession devouring him had become a mania. Gilbert sensed that there was everything to dread. He regretted the gesture of social convention that his respect for Isoline had suggested to him. He ought to have taken her away, as she wished, and only acted after having made her safe from all danger.

He ran to the Damonts' cottage; they shared his fears.

If the Baron had not lied, however, there was everything to hope for; it was necessary, in any case, to be patient for a week. That was a month in hell for the unhappy lover, who saw the return of his bouts of fever.

VIII

A few minutes after Gilbert Hamon's visit, a priest had been summoned by the Baron. It was Abbé Jouan who came. The two men conferred for a long time, and that evening, by means of a ruse, Isoline was taken away from the château.

The idea that the person he detested was about to escape him and might live happily had thrown the Baron into a fury. He had not foreseen the vulgar circumstance of a lover who might come to dispute her with him. Absorbed in his grief, he had forgotten prohibitions, bars and bolts; it was a miracle that she had not fled with that imbecile of an honest man.

"Happiness, for her, would be too much," he said to the attentive abbé. "She must expiate."

"What is her crime?"

"Her crime!" aid the old man, going pale. "Armel is dead; she killed her mother in being born."

The priest had craned his neck, avid for the secret that, like many others, had always intrigued him. "The child is innocent," he said.

"Innocent!" But the Baron, whose face had reddened, suddenly calmed down. "That's not the point at issue. Mademoiselle de Kerdréol is a minor, and I desire that she enters a convent. Her mother's fortune is considerable; I'm not poor myself, and I can't disinherit her; she will therefore be very rich one day. You have an entire year to gain that wealth for the Church."

The abbé was dazzled. "But we now live in an era when constraint is dangerous," he said."

"There remains persuasion."

"If there is no vocation...."

"Give birth to it."

Abbé Jouan referred the matter to his superiors, who ordered him to be both prudent and clever.

In the convent, during the first days, Isoline had fits of fury that caused anxiety for her reason. She did not eat, and at night it was necessary to hide her from view. The gentle consolations of the good sisters ended up calming her down, and being unfamiliar with hypocrisy, she even conceived a hope. In great secrecy she wrote a letter to Gilbert, telling him that she was more ready than ever to go with him and that he should come to free her from her prison. She confided the letter to the gentlest of the sisters, whom she paid with a valuable item of jewelry.

A few hours later, the note was in Abbé Jouan's hands.

The Baron had warned the latter to beware of the naval officer. "She's undoubtedly in love with him," he had said. "Let her be separated from him, and she will then know one of the tortures that she has inflicted on me."

The priest went into Isoline's room, holding the opened letter.

"My child," he said, "any attempt at correspondence with the outside is futile. It is necessary for you to submit to paternal will and pray to God to give you resignation. I want, however, to point out the danger that the man you love would run if he responded to your appeal."

Then, with the code in his hand, he made her understand that the abduction of a minor was a crime punishable by law, which was aggravated, in the present case, by the captation of a large fortune. He took advantage of the young woman's ignorance of the world to exaggerate further; he terrified her, making her feel the impotence of her situation.

"But what crime have I committed, that my father should be so implacable?" he asked.

"You have unconsciously destroyed his happiness; your birth cost the life of your mother."

"How?"

"But...." The priest lowered his eyes before the gaze of dazzling purity that was interrogating him. "It's difficult to explain," he stammered, "To you most of all."

"A crime of which the criminal must be ignorant!" she said, ironically.

"You are as innocent as the stainless lamb, my dear child," he said. "Offer your suffering to the Lord, and He will console you."

The Abbé was not mistaken in counting on his revelation. He had speculated on a noble sentiment and had succeeded perfectly—but the most naïve of women can thwart a priest.

Isoline's love, during recent weeks, had been exalted to the point of heroism. Immediately, she had resolved to safeguard her friend and only to compromise herself. She meditated all night, surprised herself to see her futile fits of fury succeeded by the calm of an indomitable determination.

The treason of the lay sister informed her of dissimulation; her dolor was seen to dissolve in tears and, in the chapel, she plunged into ardent prayers.

A rumor, cleverly launched, began to circulate in the town, and reached Gilbert's ears. The unfortunate man, after having sought in vain for Isoline's retreat, distraught with rage and dolor, had found himself nailed to his bed by a dangerous return of his illness. Sylvie took responsibility for letting him know what was being said about him; people were saying that a penniless mariner had asked for the hand of the rich de Kerdréol heiress, but that the father had insisted on opposing a disproportionate union.

"You wanted to marry her," Madame Aubrée added. "That's not stupid—but very ambitious, all the same."

Gilbert, who had no fortune but his future in the navy, was deeply wounded by this perfidious interpretation of his conduct. Although the avaricious motive that was being attributed to him had never occurred to him, he felt that he was immobilized once that idea was expressed—and that was exactly what his unknown adversaries wanted.

He was, however, firmly decided to do the impossible to recover the young woman, to reject all false shame. She loved him; do not all human prejudices fall before that certainty?

By a few words from Sylvie, still on the lookout for the slightest rumor in the town, he understood that Isoline was in

Dinan, in a convent, probably with the Ursulines in the Rue des Halles. As soon as he could walk without overmuch dizziness, he resolved to attempt something, to see the recluse at any cost. Walls and bars were nothing to him; if he could see Isoline, exchange a sign with her, nothing would be easier than to reach her.

His leave was approaching its end. His departure orders had already reached him, and his ship had been ordered to come to Saint-Malo—but he had decided to hand in his resignation, to give up his career rather than go away without having seen the person he considered, in spite of everything, to be his fiancée, without at least having exchanged a promise and a hope with her.

One night, he went out into the deserted town and went to the Rue des Halles.

On that side, the convent is enclosed by the neighboring houses, from which nothing distinguishes it but a cross sculpted in the wall above the door and bars on the windows. He judged it impenetrable from that direction and attempted to discover the internal disposition, and the extent of the gardens that were doubtless attached to the convent. He went around the block of houses and took the Gothic Rue du Jerzual, which a recent storm had changed into a river; all that could be seen there were trees behind a high wall.

Let's take a look! he said to himself.

A few crevices, robust mosses and the slightest projection served as points of support. The moon, half-lit between the clouds, permitted him to avoid the broken glass spiking the crest of the wall.

When he had leapt down on the other side of the wall something rigid and chilly told him that he was indeed in the garden of a convent. He walked carefully through the sandy paths, bordered with box-hedges, around flower-beds in the shape of crosses and hearts. He reached the buildings and saw a few faint lights at different windows.

Which was Isoline's?

Suddenly, a large dog barked furiously, pulling at its chain. The sister on guard duty, awoken with a start, came out into the courtyard, saw the man and uttered piercing screams.

Gilbert was obliged to flee like a malefactor, while an alarm bell rang precipitately behind him.

The next day, Abbé Jouan came to Madame Aubrée's house and demanded to see Gilbert Hamon.

"You committed a dangerous action last night, Commandant," he said, with a sickly smile and a fugitive gaze. "Perhaps you did not realize the gravity of your unauthorized entry, but we do not want the death of the sinner and I bring you words of peace."

Full of anxiety, Gilbert remained silent.

"You would like to see Mademoiselle de Kerdréol?" the priest continued. "What point is there in climbing over the wall, at the risk of killing yourself? It would have been simpler to knock on the door; it would have been opened to you. The convent's rule is not so very ferocious. Mademoiselle Isoline knows that you are leaving soon. She also desires to see you, and such is our weakness that we are prepared to facilitate that meeting, hoping that you will be discreet, unknown to the Baron."

"You'll let me see her!?" Gilbert exclaimed, torn between joy and the apprehension of some further misfortune."

"She's waiting for you. You graciously granted me a place in your boat on a day of danger, and I am glad to be able to be agreeable to you in my turn."

"Let's go!"

The door of the convent opened to the Abbé, who introduced Gilbert into a bare parlor, well waxed, with white cotton curtains at the windows, and left him alone there momentarily.

The young man's heart was horribly constricted, and Isoline's attitude, when she came in, froze the passionate words that were pressing upon his lips.

She was clad entirely in white, with a novice's veil, as white and cold as a statue.

There was a silence during which a heartbeat might have been audible.

The young woman kept her eyes lowered. Finally, in a slow voice that Gilbert did not recognize, she said: "I wanted to see you again, my brother, in order to bid you a final adieu; I am renouncing a world for which I was not made; grace had touched me; within a month, I shall enter into religion."

"You're under constraint, Isoline; it's not you who are saying this!" cried the young man, frightened. "A first love is not extinguished so quickly in the heart, and you love me. You, so spontaneous and so honest, would not betray yourself so cruelly. No, I don't believe you, I don't recognize your thought; say one word, make one gesture, and I will unmask the falsehoods and terrors that are being woven around you; I will get you out of here."

She raised her eyes, and a spark that she could not suppress sprang forth, but she continued in the same calm voice: "I have spoken freely, and nothing constrains my will. Forgive me if I have troubled your life. Forget me. I have understood my duties now; my determination is unshakable. Go, my friend, go; I shall pray that the sea will be merciful to you."

A horrible thought occurred to Gilbert. Perhaps she, too, had been persuaded that he was in quest of her fortune. He felt ice descend upon his heart. Any persistence would become shameful; a wall of gold loomed up between the two of them.

As soon as he had gone, Isoline let herself fall helplessly into a chair and burst into sobs.

Abbé Jouan hastened to her aid. "You were admirable, my daughter," he said. "I heard everything; you are now free from his pursuit; he will leave. Forget the vain hopes of the world and think of God."

"The sacrifice is made now," she said. "I will ask nothing more of you but one favor before I go into retreat. I would like to see Marie Damont, the devoted nurse who raised me, one more time."

Marie came in all haste and as gripped by a convulsive tremor when she saw her beloved child in a nun's shroud.

"It's the final blow!" she murmured, while her hollow eyes filled with tears.

Isoline took her in her arms, soothed her with caresses, and whispered a few words in her ear, which suddenly dried up her tears. Sensing that she was observed, however, she said aloud: "Don't weep, therefore. I shall do very well here; it's not as sad as my vile château. Come and see the garden; it's very pretty, and one has a charming view of it from my cell."

She didn't love the captain after all, said Abbé Jouan to himself, watching her draw Marie away almost cheerfully and show her the flower-baskets.

The pleasure of having acquired a considerable fortune for the Church was combined, for the priest, with that of seeing such a perfect beauty escape from the world and amour; there are people who love to tip over a cup that is not full for them.

IX

Gilbert's agony was bleak and frightfully calm. He made his preparations to depart, like someone who knows that he will never return. He gave away all his precious possessions, all the bizarre trinkets brought back from his voyages.

"One would think that you were making your will," Sylvie said to him.

"Mariners often travel permanently," he said, laughing dryly.

"Why don't you prolong your leave? You're not fully recovered. What's the hurry?"

"An important message for the Governor of Martinique."

"It's silly to leave like this. You're whiter than a wax figurine."

"That color will be a pleasure for the negroes there to behold."

Sylvie shrugged her shoulders, while considering the plumes of feathers that would look good on her mantelpiece.

Damont came to the Rue de l'Horloge to see the commandant, who no longer came to the cottage. The brave mariner had a favor to ask him. He was stammering horribly. He had been gripped by a desire to go to sea again; he was becoming stupid remaining perpetually on land. If the commandant wished to include him in the list of his crew, in the capacity of assistant helmsman, it would satisfy all his desires.

"I understand, my brave Dumont; you want to go with me, to watch over me, to prevent me from some despairing action whether I like it or not. It's futile—go away. When I've made a resolution, nothing can deflect me from it."

"If you were satisfied with my services when I was under your orders—if you have any concern for me at all—don't refuse me!" cried Damont, with a vehemence that triumphed over his stammer.

"So be it," he said, "if that's what you want." And he opened his trunk again to take out a book bound in green cloth.

Damont watched his name emerged from the grating pen. His agitation redoubled. "If it's not too much to ask," he said, "inscribe my godson too—a scamp who has no family and wants to go to sea."

"Who's that?"

"Ange Brune, a good boy; his father was a sailor."

"Good for Ange Brune. He'll be entered as a junior cabin-boy. Departure from Saint-Malo, tomorrow night."

"Thank you, Commandant."

"Hold on," said Gilbert, as Damont was about to leave. "Give Marie this little calico box; she can keep her needles in it, to remind her of me. Say goodbye to her for me; to see her again would be too painful for me."

When he was on his ship, when he felt himself overtaken once again by the powerful palpitation of the waves, all false hope being well and truly lost, Gilbert suddenly found his apparent strength vanish. A convulsion of agony, an irresistible need to cry out, to wring his hands, to allow himself to be racked by sobs, chased him to his cabin, where he let himself go.

The sea's swell beat the flanks of the vessel with regular strokes.

He saw himself once again on the rock that the sea had surrounded, as if it were reminding the excessively happy lover that it would take possession of him again, that it alone was faithful, and that it would retain a tomb for him.

One by one, he took all the broken flowers of his dead passion, evoked all the aspects of the woman who had said that she loved him—but a white face, compounded of harsh sails, interposed itself and effaced them.

On the deck, the first mate took the roll call. His monotonous voice reached Gilbert over the hum of the machine that was arming him.

"Jean le Guenn? Pal Houarn? Loïc Daulaz? Ange Brune?"

There was a silence.

"Ange Brune?" he repeated, more loudly.

The impact of a boat coming alongside the vessel was heard, and almost immediately, a young clear voice shouted: "Present!"

A few moments later, there was the beginning of an altercation at Gilbert's door.

"I tell you he's waiting for us," Damont affirmed, in a joyful tone.

And two people came into the tiny room, lit by vacillating lamps.

Gilbert did not make any gesture of impatience on seeing his door forced in this way. He merely demanded, in a faint voice: "What do you want?"

"Commandant, I want to introduce you to the cabin-boy."

He came to his feet with a start. "Isoline!"

"No, Commandant, Ange Brune, junior cabin-boy aboard the frigate *Armide*." With a passionate leap, however, she threw herself into his arms, and wept over that bruised heart. "Do you remember the song?" she murmured.

"You, here! Beside me!"

"Forever, now."

"Well, what do you think of my cabin-boy?" Damont stammered, his eyes moist.

"Yes, it's me," said the young woman, laughing through her tears; I lied to save us; I became a monster of hypocrisy; I deceived my jailers with a false devotion, put their vigilance to sleep—but Damont and the good Marie were warned. Oh, the nun hid a coarse sailor—look, here he is!"

And Gilbert, dazed by joy, admired her in her masculine costume, which made her smaller and younger.

"You've cut your beautiful hair?"

"Marie's keeping it as a souvenir."

"If I'm dreaming at present, I'll only wake up to die."

"Let's go, Commandant, let's go, if everything's ready!" Damont exclaimed. "The proximity of land isn't safe."

"Yes, yes! The water and the sky for us!"

And Gilbert hurried on to the deck, where he shouted his orders in a loud voice: "Raise the anchor; take to sea. Full steam and full sail!"

Electrified by the officer's surprising voice, the mariners made haste. There were shouts, the sound of chains, grindings, the flapping of sails in the wind, then effortful groans in the tautened ropes, a strident whistle—and the frigate moved off, quitting the harbor.

Soon, nascent daylight was running over the crests of the waves, outlining the rocky coast in black. A shaft of sunlight illuminated Saint-Malo, which appeared, one last time, above its sandy beach, which made it a kind of golden pedestal.

Ange Brune, leaning back against a mast, waved his cap and sang in a childlike voice:

I'm just a poor matelot,
Who has signed on with the ship.

The ship fled, over a sea the color of absinthe, as if she were being pursued by an entire enemy fleet. She was scarcely rolling, lifted up by her sails, rose-tinted in the dawn light, as if by wings—but the whole of her hull was quivering under the effort of the engine.

On the shore, the cliffs reddened, unfurling their long capricious line, punctuated by sands. Bell-towers rose up above the meadows that made a green crest for the rocks. All the mariners gazed at the land that they would soon no longer be able to see.

Then the fugitives remembered poor Marie, still resigned, alone now in the cottage on the bank of the Rance, dreaming—she, who had not had the happiness of others—of living long enough to see the two fiancés return, and to be happy in their joy. She would count the days now, huddled over her needlework in the corner if the dark hearth.

And those who were leaving, as happy as birds set free, sent her from their fingertips, over the waves and the fields, a tender and momentarily saddened adieu.

THE SERPENT-FLOWER

In the short distance that separates Naples from Portici, while the boat that was carrying me cut soundlessly through the immobile azure of the gulf, my mind, leaping backwards some years, saw once again the day on which the woman I was going to visit had appeared to me for the last time.

Five years already? Or, rather, only five years—for that time, so full for me, seemed to have been much longer: empty days and months of idleness certainly slide more rapidly into the past, without leaving any memory, than times of toil, activity, and travel most of all. How many countries I had seen, in those years! Japan, Cambodia, all of India. What surprising mores! How much beauty, and how much ugliness! Beneath all those new visions, however, the image of Claudia Viotti had not been erased; rather, it had grown, looming over my memories from afar; she had become one of the attractive charms of the absent homeland—personifying it, so to speak.

I had been madly in love with her, in secret, without ever telling her so, without any hope, and although I had been cured of that love for a long time, it was not without some anxiety that I was going toward her again, about to confront once more the danger of her beauty.

Already I could perceive the Villa Viotti, whose grounds terminate, on the shore of the sea, in a long terrace from which once descends a long staircase of stone steps, between sculpted vases, bristling with misshapen cacti.

As I leapt from the boat on to the sand of the beach, I heard the sound of voices at the top of the stairway, and Claudia appeared on the edge of the terrace, accompanied by three people who were doubtless visiting her. I recognized her elegant silhouette without any hesitation, outlined against a dark green background.

I had left a young woman; I found a young wife. When I had left, Claudia was due to marry one of my best friends, Count Scala, but a few days before the date fixed for the marriage, my poor friend had perished during a crossing from Naples to Genoa, where he was going to settle some business matters and look for a few family papers. During a storm, it appeared, a wave had carried him away. Claudia waited in vain, and, on learning of his death, did not manifest any considerable grief. Six months later, she married a young Neapolitan, Leone Vitti, who had tried to compete with Scala for her, and who was, as they say, much dearer to her heart.

As soon as she saw me, Claudia rapidly came down a few steps, with a cry of joyful surprise.

"What! It's you, Doctor?" she cried, in that sonorous and slightly husky voice, which my ear remembered so well. "So you've finally come back. We would have sworn that you had become a Brahmin or that some jungle tiger had devoured you."

And she held out her ungloved hand to me, to which I applied my lips affectionately.

"You've become more beautiful," I told her, admiring her lovely face, so warmly pale, beneath the dark mass of her undulating tresses, brightened by a large red flower.

"Is that true?"

"One can see that the sun of love is shining over you," I added.

"Yes, I'm happy," she said, looking up at me with a gaze full of fire. "I know that Scala was your friend, but what do you expect? I didn't love him, and he behaved badly with me. I begged him to release me from the promise that my family and I had made him, to renounce the marriage; he didn't want to." With a truly terrible expression, she continued: "I believe, you know, that the anger he ignited in my soul brought misfortune to him; I cast the spell of the evil eye upon him, involuntarily. If he hadn't died, I don't know what would have happened." She changed tack, cheerfully: "But why are we talking about that? Come on, I'll introduce you."

The visitors, two ladies and a young man, of whom my memory retained no trace, had remained on the terrace; they both came toward us, and the introductions were made, followed by a moment of embarrassed silence, difficult to break between people who do not know one another.

"Look! Look! This is my son!" Claudia suddenly cried, showing me with passionate pride a delightful three-year-old child who had just hurled himself at her skirts.

The child looked at me, laughing, and then escaped, bounding along the pathways. He disappeared behind a large clump of flowers, crying: "Cuckoo!"

"Come on, Pepino, come back," said the young mother, drawing us toward the villa.

The residence soon appeared in the midst of lush vegetation, so darkly green as almost to be black. The sun, which was setting, projected its light upon the façade and turned it blood red from top to bottom. I don't know why, but I experienced a painful sensation, a sort of vague dead, as if some danger or dolor were threatening me.

Oh, I wish to God that I had fled at that moment, never to return, stuffing my fingers in my ears in order that no echo of that terrible house could reach me!

But I crossed the threshold with a tranquil tread, already forgetting the fugitive apprehension that had just assailed me.

We went into a large paved vestibule, and then into a small drawing room that opened into a conservatory where the mistress of the house preferred to sit. There were pretty birds there, rare plants and, attached to a perch by a silver chain, a little monkey that was frolicking in a sunbeam.

"You rarely come to Portici," I said to the young woman, after installing myself in a wicker armchair. "I'm very glad to find you here; I'm told that you're almost never in residence here."

That's true. Leone has a kind of aversion for this villa, and we rarely leave Rome. My husband is horribly sensitive, and the sea air irritates him. He decided to come because of Pepino, whose health prospers on this shore."

The visitors took their leave at that moment, and Claudia left momentarily to show them out.

During that minute of solitude I couldn't help thinking about poor Scala, who had died so conveniently, and was so little regretted by the woman who was to have been his life's companion. I remembered that he had been desperately in love with her, to whom he had been betrothed since childhood. Claudia had seemed to me to have an affection for him, but she had been very young then, and when her womanly heart had awakened it had, it appeared been given to another. To renounce the marriage would have been more that my poor friend could bear, and he had wanted to have the woman, doubtless hoping to win back her love. Who could tell, though? His death had been very strange—perhaps it had been voluntary; perhaps a devotion, all the more sublime because it had to be unknown, had driven the disdained and desperate lover beyond life. If that were the case, Claudia would doubtless shed a few tender tears for the man whom her rancor had not yet forgiven.

She came back and sat down with me, cheerfully.

"Well," she said, "tell me about India, giant forests elephants as tall as houses, fakirs with birds nesting in their eyebrows and apple-green gods with thirty-six arms. Speak, speak!"

I told her about my most outstanding adventures, my labors, my fatigues; then I interrogated her regarding her new life and her family. She was entirely orphaned now, her father having died shortly after the marriage; except for a few cousins, no one remained to her. Her husband and child were all she had to love henceforth, and that love filled her heart to overflowing.

She smiled as she spoke, sitting facing me on a low chair, her chin in her hand, in a pose full of grace and relaxation. I studied her with mute admiration, thinking that the man who had her love must be very happy.

Suddenly, she uttered a cry, and I saw her face change completely, her eyes widening in fear. I turned round swiftly.

A maidservant came running, holding Pepino in her arms, writhing in frightful convulsions. "Oh, Madame, Madame!" she cried. "What's wrong with him? His mouth is all black."

Claudia was breathless, as if petrified. "Doctor!" she cried, with a heart-rending expression.

I ran to the poor child, whose contracted features were no longer recognizable.

He was writhing in convulsive spasms, but he wasn't crying. The dark red tint that stained the corners of his lips immediately made me think that he had bitten into some poisonous fruit, and I thrust two fingers into his throat in order to make him vomit—but I obtained no result.

"My God," I murmured. "What can this poison be?"

"Poison!" cried the mother, in a shrill voice. "What are you saying? There's no poison here; children sometimes have these frightful convulsions—but you can cure him, can't you?"

I suppressed a shake of the head.

The poor child's condition was exceedingly strange; I rejected in vain an idea that imposed itself upon me. It seemed to me that I recognized the effects, almost overwhelming, of a poison known in other climes but unknown in Europe.

"It's impossible," I murmured, "Where could he have found that frightful plant?"

I undressed the child and tried to arm him up by friction, but I had very little hope. His tiny clenched fist dropped something, of which I took possession. It was the crushed pulp of a fruit or a flower, crimson in color. In spite of its shapelessness, I immediately recognized what I feared by its penetrating odor.

I could not suppress a exclamation. "The Serpent-Flower! It really is! Alas, the poor angel is doomed!"

Claudia uttered a howl that tore my heart, and I would certainly have given my life at that moment to be able to return the child to his mother; she had thrown herself upon him, covering him with mad caresses, calling to him, and launching ardent prayers to the heavens, mingled with imprecations.

The maidservant had fled, weeping, calling loudly for the master of the house, the father. He soon arrived, his eyes haggard, his lips tremulous and livid.

"Leone! Leone!" Claudia cried to him, through her tears. "He's going to die!"

I stood there, stunned by emotion, receiving the repercussion of that frightful despair full in the heart, distressed by my impotence. The soul revolts in the face of sudden catastrophes that surprise people in the midst of the most perfect happiness, which they destroy forever.

It was in vain that the distraught mother strove to reanimate her cherub and warm him up with her lips; the pretty laughter had fallen silent forever; that life, scarcely begun, ended there.

I drew away in silence, painfully embarrassed by being the banal witness of that grief.

It was still light; I went out into the garden and wandered along the paths at a rapid, mechanical pace. But while my body was, so to speak, abandoned, a singular memory imposed itself on my mind, reconstructing itself there like a vision of a strange clarity. At first, I could not make out any connection with the drama that had just upset me, and I tried to dispel it as an unhealthy suggestion of the fever.

I saw myself back in Calcutta, on the evening of a fiery day; I was sitting on the veranda of my Indian house, reanimated by the relative cool of the evening, in which I was delighting. All around, the tall trees and arbors were rustling faintly in the breeze, which was bringing me gusts of warm perfume. The blue light of the moon was competing with the red light of a lamp set on the table in front of me; I was finishing writing a letter, while lending an ear, intermittently, to the distant sound of a guitar accompanying a song.

No detail of that insignificant, long-forgotten scene was spared me; I gave way reluctantly to the obsession, and I saw once again the large moths and insects of every sort that my lamp attracted, and where even brushing my sheet of paper, the clouds of smoke that I was drawing from a long pipe in order to defend myself from mosquitoes, and the glass of iced lemonade from which I had sipped a few draughts by means of a straw. I was writing nonchalantly. The letter was finished, but, before closing the envelope, I carefully dropped a few seeds into it; then I sealed it and wrote the address:

To Count Antonio Scala.

Suddenly, the objective of that stubborn memory became clear; the seeds that I had enclosed in that envelope had been the seeds of the Serpent-Flower! Yes, that was it. I had forgotten the missive and its contents; memory brought them back to me cruelly. I had asked Scala to sow the seeds in a corner of his garden and to tell me whether the plant was able to grow in Italy.

I was then studying the properties of the poison, which I thought I might be able to use medically. It was shortly after receiving that letter that my friend had died; it had remained unanswered. Had he, then, given the seeds—of whose dangerous properties I had definitely informed him—to his fiancée, or sown them in her garden? Why had he not warned her to beware of the deadly poison? All that was obscure, but I sensed that it was true: the Serpent-Flower could not have arrived in a garden in Portici by any other means.

But if that were the case, I was the one who had furnished the weapon that had just killed that poor delightful child! On the mild and perfumed evening that had just passed before my eyes again, I had, without knowing it, prepared the despair of a family and the death of a child who had not yet been born! And I had returned from so far away just in time to witness the denouement of the tragedy whose first threads I had knotted.

If the poor mother knew that, would I not be a monster in her eyes? Her son's murderer! Ought I not to flee that house, in which I had given birth to desolation?

I continued walking nevertheless, in increasing agitation, wandering through the bushes and the thick-crowned trees in the grounds. The descending darkness made a painful impression upon me; the quivering of the leaves was extended in my nerves, and when the moon, enormous and red-tinted, emerged slowly from behind the branches, I thought I saw a phantom covered in blood.

I made vain efforts to react against that feverish state; I don't know what dolorous assault squeezed my heart; something prevented me from leaving, and told me that the drama was not over yet. I hastened, however, to get out of the covert whose dense shadow weighed upon me.

Hushed voices, and a noise that I could not explain, attracted my attention. In the darkness, I perceived an agitated group of people, and, desirous of not being alone any longer, I moved toward it.

They were the gardeners and servants of the villa, who, on learning of the death of little Pepino, whom they all loved, had spontaneously thought of taking revenge upon the unconscious plant that had caused the evil, which they credited with a kind of venomous soul. They had, therefore, armed themselves with spades and pickaxes, and where mounting a frenzied assault on the roots of a large bush growing, as if by hazard, beside the stairway to the water. They were heaping insults, reproaches and curses upon it, with all the impetuosity of the Neapolitan character, and, needless to say, I was not far from thinking that they were correct to heap execration upon that homicidal plant.

The moon had risen above the trees, and was shining full upon the bush. I really had, in front of me, the Serpent-Flower, the terrible and fantastic plant familiar to the dwellers on the banks of the Ganges.

In those lands of prodigious exuberance, where the vegetation, unruly and as if crazed, seems to expend its overabundant force in extravagant creations, such surprising products are not rare. The Serpent-Flower is among the most exotic, and it is difficult to form any idea of it when one does not have it before the eyes. It is like a clump of slender snakes standing on their tails, leaning their flat heads toward a little orange-red fruit quite similar to a small pineapple or, rather, a large strawberry, but velvety and reminiscent of a flower. It is the leaves that resemble reptiles, broadening at the tip in the form of a head, and those heads being dotted with two eyes and a sharp thorn, projecting like a dart. The resemblance to a snake is striking: all those eyes, staring at you, and all those darts that seem to be defending the red pompoms, upright on their stems as if turgid with blood, have the most extraordinary and disquieting effect.

The roots were profoundly plunged into the soil; evidently, the plant had already been growing there for several years. The gardeners persisted stubbornly, the moon casting huge gesticulating black shadows behind them, with fantastic elongations.

I had stopped near the laborers, my head bowed, singularly oppressed. I stared at the hole that was enlarging beneath the thrusts of the spades.

Soon, my ideas became confused; I thought that I was in a cemetery; the nocturnal light gave an appearance of tombstones to the rum of the wall and the first step of the stairway. The marble vases were funerary urns, the men gravediggers.

Poor mite! It was the same place where I had seen him a few hours earlier, his laughter still vibrant in the air, and they were digging his grave already!

"Oh, accursed plants! Diabolical flowers! Nests of vipers!" growled the gardeners, straining their muscles to extirpate the roots.

Yes, it was necessary to destroy it, that horrible plant, to burn it, crush it, to let no seed fly away to give birth to the red poison elsewhere.

Abruptly, a part of the bush gave way, and, drawn by the momentum, the men took a few steps backward; but they came back immediately and leaned over he uncovered roots. Then I saw their faces fall and their eyes grow wide. A clamor of fear went up, and then they all fled, making the sign of the cross.

What, then, had they seen?

I was alone. The cry of terror uttered by the men had caused my heart to race, and a dread of which I was ashamed sent a frisson through my flesh. The mad flight of the fugitives was no longer stirring the gravel of the pathways, to which I was still listening, deceived by the sound of my arteries, motionless, as if rooted to the spot.

What, then, had they seen?

Were informal flames emerging from that accursed hole? Were they mad? And was I mad myself, not daring to look?

I rushed forward, and as soon as my gaze searched that shifted soil, the same cry that had just startled my ears emerged from my own throat. I had not been mistaken; there really was a grave there, with a corpse inside.

Oh, the horrible, hideous, abominable vision! The roots, like claws, held a skull in their talons, and limbs convulsed in an atrocious pose. It was a skeleton, not yet completely stripped of flesh, with the remains of hair and a beard mingled with the filaments of the plant and shreds of cloth. The hollow eyes seemed to be looking at me, fascinating me, and my hair prickled in horror. A plaint seemed to rise up, to become distinct, and I clearly heard the words: "Avenge me!"

Then a sudden clarity was born in my mind. I started running like a madman toward the house.

The unfortunates were still in the same room, now lit by large candles, funereal in appearance.

"Scala! It's Scala!" I cried, as I came in, finding nothing else to say in my mental confusion, strangled by indignation and frozen by horror.

I no longer had any pity for the dolor of that mother; I could only see murderers ripe for punishment. However, the little cadaver was there, as white as a wax Jesus, and Claudia, drunk on tears, could not even see me.

Her husband had straightened up at my voice; he looked at me wildly, his eyes bruised by black circles.

"You killed him," I said. "I know. He still had my letter on him, and it contained the punishment, the terrible poison, the seed of that accusing plant; his death is avenged now; he is the one who killed your child; but it won't stop there—the crime has been discovered, the alarm raised; the murderer cannot deny his sin."

My voice was staccato, menacing; anger took my breath away.

The guilty man shook her head slowly. "Deny it?" he said. "Why deny it? I can see full well that it's all over. It's true, I killed him. I bought love at the price of a crime; fate wanted it thus—and had it been necessary to strew cadavers along the road that led to my beloved, I would not have hesitated. Doubtless you have never been in love; it's your right to condemn me—but love itself will absolve me."

I had my back to the wall, my arms folded; I remained silent, slightly disconcerted by that frankness.

He raised his profoundly agonized wife to her feet. She had not heard anything. He drew her to him, looked at her for a long time with ineffable tenderness, and dried the tears that were blinding the beautiful Claudia's eyes with his lips.

"Listen," he said to her. "Listen, my darling; your poor heart with be swollen by a further grief; silence your despair for a moment. It is to you that I owe my confession, and when I leave, I want to take your forgiveness with me."

"Leave?" she said. And her eyes widened. With an abrupt movement, she placed her hands on Leone's shoulders and gazed at him with anxious fixity.

Then he began the following narration, to which I listened without saying a word.

"Do you remember, my dear Claudia, that dolorous evening when all hope was lost for us? I wandered around your abode, not daring to go in, mad with anxiety. I watched the windows of your lighted rooms, the bright bay of the open door. You were making one last appeal to your fiancé. You wanted to beg him, to soften his attitude, to confess your love for me to him. How hellish those hours of waiting were!

"Abruptly, you appeared to me in the lighted doorway. You came down the steps of the perron, and I received you in my arms, icy and livid, grinding your teeth. 'It's finished,' you said. 'He refuses to release me from the promise made; the day of our wedding is fixed. Adieu! I shall die of it!' And you plunged back into the red gulf.

"I tottered at first, as if I had received a sledgehammer blow on my skull; then a sudden calm succeeded the horrible agitation that had been consuming me a little while before. It was like an unleashed torrent suddenly frozen by a polar wind. A hard, implacable resolution had frozen my fury. Laughter contorted my mouth, and I shouted after your disappearing form: 'The one who will die will be neither you nor me.'

"The lucidity of my mind was frightful; so confused a few moments earlier, it now appeared to me to be stainless crystal, the purest water crystallized. I took a dagger from my pocket that I always carried and took it from its sheath. The blade shone, and, my gaze fixed upon that cold clarity, I calmly planned my vengeance.

"I knew that the boat that had brought my enemy was waiting on the strand to take him to the midnight ferry leaving Naples that night. The Count was going to Genoa, his birthplace, to take care of the final formalities necessary to his marriage. It was on that circumstance that I based the entire plot of the drama that, for me, was playing out for the second time, so carefully had I foreseen and meditated all its details in advance. It unfolded before my eyes, so to speak, of its own accord; my mind, in a state of clairvoyant acuity that I only experienced that once, was like a mirror, over which passed with great rapidity all the scenes that were about to take place. All the dangers to be avoided, all the precautions to take to ensure the mystery, presented themselves to me and were resolved effortlessly. I experienced no dread or hesitation; I felt as if I were inspired, surely guided by an external force.

"I don't know how much time elapsed between the moment that you went back into the house and the moment when the Count came out—minutes or hours—but I suddenly straightened up within the shadow in which I was lurking, as loud voices became audible outside the house.

91

"Your father was escorting his chosen son-in-law to the perron. I heard a few phrases. 'Don't be upset by her caprices; they'll pass.'

"'I hope so,' the Count replied, laughing conceitedly. 'In the meantime, I have love enough for two!'

"'Bon voyage!'

"'See you soon!'

"And my rival went lightly down the steps, his overcoat over his arm, and a cigar between his lips.

"I followed him, hiding in the shadows of the bushes, keeping low, as silent as a wild beast. When he set foot on the stairway to the water, I launched myself forward, gripped his throat with one hand to stop any cry for help before it emerged, and with the other hand, with a single thrust, plunged the dagger into his heart.

"Oh, no hatred can possibly equal that of a man in love, for I, who could not have cut the throat of a lamb without fainting, experienced no horror, no pity, but only a ferocious joy, a rage scarcely slaked.

"The stormy sky was very gloomy, the darkness thick. Even so, my enemy must have seen by whom he had been killed, for I leaned my face over his agony for a long time, without pronouncing a word, without my clenched hand letting a groan escape from the dying man's lips...."

"You merely anticipated me, Leone!" cried Claudia, who was drinking in her husband's words breathlessly. "I would have killed him on our wedding night."

Leone, whose narration had petrified me, darted a triumphant glance at me. His wife had not had an instant's hesitation in absolving him, and that forgiveness was sufficient for him. He clutched her to his heart, and continued, in a firmer voice:

"I stood up when the last quiver of life had ceased. Then I uttered a deep sigh, breathing with indescribable relief. The idea that had filled my nights with anguish, the thought beneath which I had writhed in rage and despair, was extinct forever. 'Claudia is his!' Those words could never be joined together now; I was finally free of him; they were rent asunder, scattered in all the winds of that tumultuous night. Punishment, separation, my beloved lost to me—those tortures were preferable to the one that had just shown me mercy. I was resolved, however, to do the best I could to conceal what people would call my crime, and in order to take full advantage of it, I neglected no precaution.

"I remembered—and it was a memory retained by my eyes rather than my memory—a wheelbarrow at the corner of a path, and in that wheelbarrow, thrown as if forgotten, a spade and a rake. I had noticed that while on my way to the furtive which we believed to be the last. If those tools had not chanced to be there, my situation would have been complicated. I ran to the path and, in my haste, collided with the wheelbarrow, whose implements fell out with a noise that frightened me.

"I drew nearer to the house. I looked at it as if in spite of myself. All the lights were out on the ground floor, but a few windows on the first floor were still illuminated; I looked for yours. Poor love! I divined the dejection in your tears, the wringing of your hands, as you cursed fate, and I had a desire to come and throw you a word of hope; but I resisted that desire; it was necessary that you be unaware of everything, in order that no fear could trouble your happiness.

"I went back to the dead man and dragged him into the corner of the balustrade, where the shadows were amassed with the greatest intensity. Then I readjusted my clothing, which the struggle with my rival had disarranged. I picked up his overcoat, which had fallen to the ground and I put it on. Then I went down the stairs rapidly.

"That overcoat was very distinctive and recognizable; it was an ample traveling cape with a loose belt that buttoned around the waist. It was a bright hazelnut-brown color, with large bone buttons. I was much the same height as the Count, and my beard was trimmed like his. The resemblance ended there, but on such a dark night, thanks to the recognizable coat, it might be sufficient.

93

"The boatman was asleep in the boat; he had not heard or seen anything—there was, in any case, nothing else to see but the dark night.

"I shook him as I leapt into the boat. He woke up immediately and stated rowing rapidly. The heavy atmosphere weighed upon the leaden, motionless water. On the other side of the bay the lights of Naples were reflected in long reddish trails. The rumors of the city were distinctly audible, but the sea was silent. We reach the quay and I headed for the ferry on foot, taking care to pull my hat down over my eyes and light a cigar.

"I knew that Scala's manservant was named Martino, but I had never noticed his physical appearance. I'd probably never even seen the fellow. That was something that made me anxious; Martino would surely be waiting for his master at the boat; he was bound to see me and mistake me for the other; what would happen then? The ship's lights spread a confused illumination; on the gangplank linking the boat to the quay there was the particular hubbub and bustle marking an imminent departure. I went forward bravely, enveloped by the smoke of my cigar.

"As I had hoped, Martino came straight toward the overcoat, raising his hat. 'I feared that the Signore might not get here in time,' he said.

"I replied with a kind of grunt, gripping my cigar in my teeth in order to mask my voice. 'I've reserved a god cabin,' he went on. 'The Signore's baggage is already there; here are the keys.'

"'Good,' I muttered. 'Let's see the cabin.'

"Martino went down ahead of me, and I followed him. It was a grave imprudence, for the entry-point as brightly lit and for a moment I thought I was doomed, but I had time to take out my handkerchief and plunge my face into it just as the lamp shone full upon it, and when the manservant stood aside to let me go into the cabin. I kept my back to him for the rest of the conversation, which I cut as short as possible but which seemed interminable to me. 'Perfect,' I said. 'You can go to bed. I don't need anything else.'

"He didn't go immediately, though. He made the bed, prepared a toddy and showed me the bag in which he had put provisions, listing everything he'd accumulated there; he also told me that the cigars were in the first compartment of the trunk. Those few minutes were full of anguish for me, but he finally went away without having conceived the slightest suspicion.

"Soon, I went up on deck, wanting to be seen by the captain. I went to greet him. 'Count Scala?' he said.

"I bowed. 'We're leaving in spite of the threatened storm?' I asked him.

"'We have to.'

"'How long will it be?'

"'Ten minutes.'

"I didn't have a moment to lose. I went back down to the cabin and opened the bags with a feverish haste. I took out the provisions and toilet items, which I set out in good order. I washed my hands in the basin, in case there was blood on them. I took off the overcoat that had provided me with such a good disguise and threw it on to the bed, which I crumpled; then I attacked the provisions, stuffing items of food into my pockets. I even drank an entire bottle of wine. Time was pressing. I cast one last glance at the cabin, which certainly seemed to have been occupied, and went out, carefully closing the door. I went back up and succeeded in leaving the boat unnoticed. A few moments later the engine's whistle blew, announcing the departure. The comedy was complete. Now it was necessary to get back to the more lugubrious scenes of the drama.

"I didn't want to take a boat to return to the villa; the boatman would have been a dangerous witness; I had to go the long way round the bay.

"The imminent storm rendered the roads deserted. I went part of the way at a run without encountering anyone.

"The first flash of lightning stung the horizon just as I set foot on the first step of the stairway, and a dull rumble rolled over the sea. I went up the steps slowly, vaguely frightened by the darkness, blacker after the flash of light.

"What if my enemy hadn't been completely dead? What if he were no longer there? What if it were necessary to re-commence the murder of a wounded man?

"I couldn't find the spot where I had left the victim right away. I groped and groped in the dark, in vain, dreading finding the cadaver beneath my hand, and dreading even more that I might not. I was inundated by cold sweat.

"Abruptly, I touched hi icy face, and an involuntary start of alarm made me step back with a stifled cry. At the same time, a further flash of lightning showed me his horrible face, his eyes wide open, his mouth agape.

"Although I had maintained an extraordinary self-composure until then, I almost succumbed to the superstitious terror than invaded me at that moment. The storm burst with a frightful fury; the suddenly swollen sea added its groaning to the racket of the thunder; the wind was blowing tempestuous-ly. I truly though that the heavens had been unleashed against me, and I had a desire to flee, to escape at any price that terri-ble face, which kept appearing and disappearing, and which seemed to be shifting in the intervals between the lightning-flashes.

"I had the strength to resist, however, and I set about digging in the ground.

"What point is there in telling you about the tortures in-flicted upon me by that labor? Beneath the torrents of rain that were overwhelming me, in the tumult of the elements, beneath that furious sky, which the reflections of Vesuvius reddened at times like the fires of Hell...that almost invincible lassitude that paralyzed me...the hole that filled with water...the dead man watching me, with his staring eyes, hollowing out his grave! Several times, I saw myself as the victim of a frightful nightmare, and I wished that floods of lava might come to bury, along with all memory, the victim and the murderer alike!

"When it was all done, dawn was breaking and the storm had died away. The wan morning light rendered me slightly calmer, and permitted me to erase all trace of the murder. The storm had helped me by softening and furrowing the ground; the rain had washed away the bloodstains. I put the tools back where I had found them, and fled to my house, where I slept for twenty-four hours solid, exhausted.

"The rest you know. The Count's presence on the ferry had been firmly established by my audacious appearance. The discovered overcoat, the cabin in disorder, the remarks exchanged with the captain and the manservant, left no doubt. It was nothing but the disappearance of a passenger, easily explained by one of those accidents so commonplace at sea; the crossing had been difficult, the night very dark; given the awkwardness of the maneuvering and the noise of the tempest, a man might have been carried away by a wave without anyone seeing the accident and raising the alarm.

"Liberated by that death, your father no longer had any reason to refuse me; you became my wife, and the heavenly happiness of that union filled my soul completely, drowning the memory of the sacrificed rival.

"I avoided living in the villa in Portici—but when you talked about selling it, since it displeased me, I came back here in order to deflect you from that dangerous idea. The first time I saw the habitation again I was alone, I had to announce and prepare for our installation.

"Something always attracts us toward that which we ought to avoid. I wanted to go back to that corner of the grounds that I ought to have fled, the terrace on the water's edge. So I went there, alone, my head bowed, unable to help passing once again through all the anguish of that criminal night, seeking for the location of that furtive grave, forever unknown.

"Suddenly I uttered a cry of fright; on the very spot that I knew so well, that bare place, deliberately chosen because it was free of all vegetation, any clump where the gardener's spade might dig, through the white pebbles with which the ground was strewn, I saw that terrible bush standing, that medusal cluster, those bloody flowers with menacing darts, like the whips of the Erinnyes!

"What was that frightful growth? All of it seemed to be howling at me, writhing, denouncing me! How had that plant grown over the dead man? I tried to tear it up, but it was immovable, and I bloodied my fingers on the thorns.

"I was about to return to the assault when I saw a gardener arrive. He came toward me rapidly. 'Just what I wanted to ask, Signore," he said. "I dared not dig out that strange plant without orders, which came here I know not how, and looks at you in such a diabolical fashion."

"'Dig it out?" I exclaimed. "Dig it out? What are you saying?' And I felt myself going pale; but I understood that I was losing my head, and I was able to control myself. 'On no account dig it out,' I said. 'The plant is very precious and I'm very fond of it.'

"'We could put it somewhere else?'

"'No, no, it would surely die. I forbid you to touch it, and you'll answer to me for that.'

"I thought I would be able to forget that hideous plant, which fear had obliged me to conserve, but it had wounded my mind with all those poisonous darts, and it was lodged there forever. It was a vengeful hydra that was devouring me, and my happiness was now lined with terror. I avoided the part of the grounds where the blooming remorse grew, but I sensed it growing, becoming a bush, a thicket, a forest; I could see its menacing gestures, I believed that I could hear its cries for vengeance. Oh, I knew full well that it would reach us!"

Leone, who had gradually lost his initial calmness, and had become excited to the point of fever, stopped speaking, and fixed upon his dead son a gaze charged with distress. Claudia was weeping on her husband's breast. They seemed to have forgotten my presence completely.

During the narration I had passed through various sentiments. The horror and anger that had turned me upside-down had given way, gradually, to an involuntary interest, a culpable weakness that almost drove me to regret that the crime had been discovered. I was the one who had furnished the dead man with the means to make his vengeance surge forth from his tomb; I was not far from regretting the fact. Love is a very powerful excuse; an individual possessed by it is certainly no longer in control of himself; if he is threatened in his passion, he defends it even more than his life, and is not a man defending his life always pardoned? Loved by Claudia, of what would I not have been capable myself?

All those ideas were agitating confusedly in my head, and were far from having the clarity with which I have just expressed them. Almost involuntarily, however, I said aloud: "How can you escape the law? The frightened gardeners will have raised the alarm. Is there still time to flee?"

My voice made the two spouses tremble. They turned abruptly to look at me.

"Yes, yes—let's flee!" cried Claudia. "Come, let's take our poor child and go to the far end of the world."

Leone shook his head, and held his wife in his arms. A kind of rumor was audible in the grounds. "Listen!" he said, pricking up his ears. "It's too late—but at least they won't take me alive."

Claudia uttered a scream, and clung to Leone passionately. "Kill me first," she moaned. "I don't want to see you die."

The young woman's beautiful tresses were in disorder beneath her husband's kisses; in that undulating fleece, the redness of a flower burst forth; he was looking around, doubtless seeking for a weapon with his gaze.

Suddenly, at the same time as his, my eyes paused on that flower. He shuddered, and recoiled involuntarily, but immediately leaned over his wife, first kissed her hair, and then threw his lips over the flower, which he devoured.

"Stop! Stop!" I cried, launching myself toward him. "The Serpent-Flower! Again! Ah, how it takes its revenge!"

Leone looked up at me, his eyes full of tenderness.

"Thank you!" he said to me. "Look after her."

Claudia had straightened up, as pale as a specter. She saw her husband's face, which convulsed, his bloodied lips; she opened her mouth as if to scream, but without making a sound, fell unconscious on the floor.

A year later, almost at the same time of year, toward the end of autumn, a caleche was waiting outside the door of a lovely house that I had rented in one of the most tranquil streets in Naples.

It was there that, for more than a year, I had disputed with death for the unfortunate Claudia, whom a sharp fever had struck down on the terrible day that had robbed her of her son and her lover. I had had her removed from the deadly villa, but her condition had not permitted me to do more by taking her away from Naples.

It was with a fraternal devotion, perhaps mingled with a keener sentiment, that I had cared for her during those long, dolorous months. Many times I had thought her doomed, but then her youth, and perhaps the fervor I put into saving her, brought hope back again.

This time I had definitely triumphed; several weeks ago, convalescence had set in—but it was only the body that was commencing a rebirth, omnipotent nature hastening its work of repair, while the excessively enfeebled mind was still slumbering. It was not without a certain terror that I waited for the reawakening of sentiment.

What would happen when the soul's wound reopened?— when the fever that it had been possible to overcome was succeeded by a despair impossible to cure? Would I not be reproached for having snatched the prey from the jaws of consoling death? And, in sum, why had I done it? Had I not been guided by an egotistical sentiment, an unconfessed hope? Did I really have the right to impose life in that fashion on someone who no longer wanted it?

Those ideas had only occurred to me after the cure; during the battle with the malady I had no such thought. This time too, nature would doubtless aid me to triumph over the danger. I would take Claudia away—far away—to another clime, and gradually, the egotism of life would take hold of her again; she would thank me for having saved her...and who could tell what might happen thereafter?

The excursion she was about to make was the first I had attempted; if she stood up to it well, we would embark in a few more days.

I arranged the cushions in the caleche, made sure that the horses were not too lively, made a thousand recommendations to the coachman, and then went in search of my poor invalid. She came down mechanically, seemingly unaware, questioning nothing. She was no longer a woman now, but she was a very beautiful statue.

I made her as comfortable as possible, and we set out. A chambermaid was with us, at the front of the carriage. We went through the tumultuous city by the shortest route; I was in haste to be in the open country. The air as very calm, the sky resplendent; it was a true day of convalescence.

I kept watch on my companion's immobile visage; it was tranquil, expressionless. The eyes, however, were gazing with a kind of avidity; consciousness had not returned, but I divined that it was very close, and menacing.

As long as nothing precipitated the crisis! I don't know why I wanted it only to declare itself once we were at sea. That immensity seemed to me to be capable of diminishing human dolors to some extent, and then, it would be easier there to talk about hope, a future life, to summon God to my aid.

Claudia appeared to be interested in the play of the sunset; its gleams seemed to fascinate her—but I was in haste to return, not wanting dusk to catch us unawares.

Alas! As we came back into the city, a traffic jam stopped us. I leaned out to see what had happened. Scarcely had I turned my head than a horrible scream from Claudia cut through my heart.

A little girl had leapt up on to the footplate of the carriage, her hands full of flowers, and, laughing, she was holding out toward us a large red bouquet made up of those accursed, murderous, terrible flowers: a bouquet of Serpent-Flowers!

I uttered a frightful imprecation, while an abrupt gesture from the chambermaid sent the wretched child who had doomed us back on to the roadway.

It was too late.

Claudia had seen; Claudia had understood; that scream was the first and last of her reawakened soul. She had stood up, bolt upright, but she soon fell back on to the cushions, laughing atrociously. Her reason had fled forever.

The Serpent-Flower had finished its work.

I am writing these dolorous memories on the steamer that is taking me away, I know not where, forever.

Was it truly hazard alone that directed the events of that fantastic adventure? Personally, I can't believe that; I can clearly see the vengeance of the dead man in all of it.

I even think that Claudia's madness is due to one last weakness on the part of the lover disdained by the woman he adored, for, if I can judge the matter by the frightful void in my own soul, the impossibility of ever attaching myself to anything again, Claudia's dolor would have been irremediable, and the Serpent-Flower was merciful in taking away her memory.

TOO LATE

Les Trembles, 22 November 1879
Dear Old Friend,

The weather is bitterly cold today; the sky is like black cotton-wool, a thin layer of snow is making the laws in the garden resemble large slices of gingerbread, and the north wind cuts one's face is one sticks one's nose outdoors. I shall never find a better opportunity to write you a long letter while roasting the soles of my feet in the fireplace.

You've often asked me to unveil for you what you call "the mystery of my life," but I've never found myself in a mood to satisfy that desire. Well, I'll do so today; I'll allow your curious and sympathetic gaze to plunge into the dark corners of my heart, and you'll finally know what you're so avid to find out: why I drag an irremediable melancholy around with me, why I've been completely disinterested in existence for thirty years.

I know that your dream-filled mind, somewhat inclined to mysticism, is capable of understanding me, and that you won't laugh at me. So, this is my story:

At the age when the first effervescences of the blood rise to our heads, that charming epoch in which we adore with all our soul all the female cousins that Heaven has bestowed upon us, I saw looming up in my mind, like a Sleeping Beauty emerging from a long slumber, the image of a delightfully beautiful woman, whom I did not know, and yet seemed nevertheless to recognize.

That vision imposed itself upon me and caused me all the disturbances and delights of a first love. It was because that singular creation of my brain was born fully-armed; the apparition had such an extraordinary clarity; no detail of her face, and even her costume, escaped me. She was blonde; her hair, piled up in a single mass and pinned by a comb, fell back in

103

light curls over the nape of her neck; her large irises, very pale blue in color, like a reflection of the sky on polar ice, gleamed beneath the penumbra of long and profoundly-arched eyelids; her mouth had an almost child-like smile. I always saw her clad in silk and lace, her hair streaming with gems, her shoulders bare and half-hidden in furs. By night, she leaned toward my bed, smiling at me, and I thought I felt her soft warm hand on my forehead. Sometimes she spoke to me, with a tone of voice that seemed foreign to me.

It must be admitted that it is conventional to denominate the ideal with less precise contours. I had no doubt that the woman in question, who gradually took possession of my entire being, existed and was destined for me. I even ended up persuading myself that she had had the mysterious power of revealing herself to me in order to prevent me from being unfaithful before meeting her. What oaths I swore, therefore, during my nights of insomnia, and how sincere I was!—for it would have been impossible for me to experience the slightest sentiment of love for anyone but her.

The phase of happy reverie of that bizarre passion came to an end, however, and gave way to a feverish impatience, an imperious desire to embrace my idol otherwise than in a dream. But how could I reach her? Where should I look for her?

I was in Paris, where I was supposedly studying medicine, but I soon needed a physician myself. That tension of all my faculties toward an ungraspable being, those mad desires struggling in a void, procured me a nervous fever whose delirious ardors only served to increase my folly.

My mother left Les Trembles in haste and came to install herself at my beside. Her presence did not calm me—but one morning, I threw into the middle of my room the powders, potions and pills that had been murdering me for months, and declared to my mother that they were not what I needed, that my illness was moral, and that the physicians knew nothing about it.

"My God!" she said, thinking that I was in the grip of a bout of delirium. "What's got into you? What do you want?"

"What do I want?" I cried, with a vehemence that frightened her. "I want to go to balls, to soirées, to fêtes, in order to search, until I find her, for the woman I love, and to conquer her amour."

"You're in love," said my mother, smiling. "I'm glad about that. Well, we'll go to balls; there's no need to look at me with such a terrible expression."

"Oh, how good you are!" I cried, embracing her. "Come on, let's go."

"Come now, Hothead," she said. "Let's give it some thought. For a start, it's nine o'clock in the morning and that's not the time to go to a ball in any season; secondly, we're in the middle of summer, and that's not, I believe, the season for dancing. Paris is empty, or nearly so."

"Where is everyone, then?" I exclaimed, in aguish.

"How do I know. At seaside resorts, spas, traveling."

"Which shall we choose? Where shall we go?" I sighed, discouraged. "The world is so large!"

"Let's begin with the coast of Normandy; then we can go to Italy, and when winter arrives, the displacement will do you good."

"Oh, let's go! Let's leave this evening."

"All right," said my mother. "We'll go."

The dear woman thought I was in love with some unknown woman glimpsed momentarily, whom I wanted to find again. She judged that there was no reasoning with me, and was, in any case, glad of the diversion from my illness; she set forth with me, bravely. Would she not have gone around the world to spare me chagrin?

A month later we were at Baden, having exhausted all the Norman and Breton beaches. I was no further forward than on departure; my ideal apparently did not frequent our coasts.

"But where did you see this woman?" my mother asked.

I dared not reply that I had never seen her for fear that she might not be so sympathetic to my fantasy, or might think me completely unhinged.

"I saw her in Paris," I said. "I think she's a foreigner."

It was on the basis of that feeble clue that we had chosen Baden, where foreigners were then abundant. She was no more in Baden than on the beaches.

I wanted to go to Norway, on the pretext that she was blonde. She was not in Norway either.

Far from extinguishing my infatuation, these eternal disappointments excited it to the highest degree. That chimerical pursuit, that hope renewed every day, did not lack a certain dolorous charm. My poor mother, however, was beginning to tire of it.

"But you're ruining me, child," she said to me. "No fortune is sufficient for this emulation of the Wandering Jew."

That life was, in fact, insane. My mind extended toward my obsession, I was devoid of pity for my dear and excessively devoted companion. I followed the thousand caprices of presentiments that were never justified. I came back precipitately to a town we had left, claiming that the unknown woman must have arrived just as we were leaving, or I called off a planned departure at the last moment, on some analogous pretext.

Finally, after a mad race through Italy, we came back to Paris, where my mother, on my insistence, was obliged to renew her connections and launch me into society.

The winter passed in a whirlwind of parties; the unknown woman did not show herself.

When spring returned, the tenacious hope that had sustained me suddenly abandoned me; I fell into complete dejection. I was still as infatuated as ever, but I now felt certain that the woman of whom I dreamed would remain a dream.

I allowed my mother to take me to her château in Touraine. Did I not need calm and solitude to weep over my imaginary beloved and my undiscoverable amour?

I had not seen Les Trembles since I had grown up. The property, where I had spent my childhood, was situated close to Loches, in superb countryside. It was a large house in the middle of a huge park, which sloped downwards toward a luxuriant valley. Each angle of the main residence was rounded out by a white turret with a pointed roof, that gave the so-called château a feudal aspect. The interior was vast and comfortable; there had once been great receptions there, feasts and hunting in the woods. Since being widowed, however, my mother had broken off her worldly relationships.

In that retreat, my folly gripped me more fully. It took a bleak resignation there, which, strangely enough, vanished as soon as I crossed the threshold. One of those sentiments that often imposed themselves upon my feverish brain, and which I took to be a form of second sight, persuaded me that something of the one whom I desired so ardently was in the atmosphere of that house. The vision appeared to me there more distinctly than anywhere else; it seemed to have found its true frame.

She's been here, that's certain, I said to myself, with bated breath. *This time, I'm not mistaken.*

My amour, which lived on so little, threw itself avidly upon this new pasture. I searched the house from top to bottom for the illusion that had me in its spell; I ferreted around continually, on the lookout for any clue, any vestige.

One chamber, in particular, attracted me invincibly. It was one of the most beautiful in the house, situated in one of the corners of the château, opposite my mother's, which occupied the other corner; there was a dressing-room in the turret. The first time I went into that room, the almost imperceptible perfume that floated in its atmosphere caused a frisson to run through my veins.

"It's her room!" I exclaimed, as I stood on the threshold, pale and trembling.

You can imagine the ardor with which I visited every corner of it. All the drawers were opened, and all the items furniture. I was hoping to find some forgotten item—a piece of ribbon or a hairpin—but they were all quite empty.

In the dressing-room, the perfume was better preserved, and I breathed it in delightedly; there was something warm and soft about it, a mixture of iris and verbena, which awoke something in me like the memory of a better life. I plunged my gaze into the large Venetian mirror place on the dressing-table for a long time. Oh, why had it allowed the dear image that it had possessed to escape?

I returned to the room. On a little table-desk a blue morocco portfolio had been placed, marked with my mother's monogram. I opened it without finding anything therein, but the blotting-pad had retained the imprint of a few lines of bizarre angular handwriting. I ran to a mirror to try to read it in the reflection, but I could not do it. By dint of gazing at it, however, I discovered that the characters were different from ours. It was not French; it was Russian!

I had not been mistaken, then, in searching snowy lands!

There was a black fur rug beside the bed. How charming her little bare feet must have been, plunged into that somber carpet!

I went to kneel down beside the bed, which I covered with kisses—stifling a few sobs, I believe, in the folds of the covers.

I wanted to take up residence in that room. I said as much to my mother, who, accustomed to yielding to all my caprices, had my luggage transported there. I had sworn to myself not to mention my crazy reveries to her again, so I kept my discoveries to myself. I could have asked her a few questions, to clarify my suspicions, but I was too frightened of seeing my scaffolding of illusions crumble beneath the impact of some brutal reality.

A young groom crossing the nuptial threshold surely has no emotion more poignant than the one that gripped me the first time I was due to lie down in that bed—which, I was convinced, had been hers.

I shall not say anything about the insomnias, the fevers and the insane dreams that assailed me.

I was soon in a state of extraordinary excitement; my health, generally rather frail, deteriorated seriously; I grew thinner and paler; a continuous languor and fatigue overwhelmed me. My mother was overcome by anxiety; she strove in vain to extract me from that torpor, to drag me outside.

The physicians she summoned recognized the commencement of a consumption.

What? Was I really going to die at the age of twenty-two, of an agony created by my brain, for a woman who probably did not exist?

I was definitely incurable mentally, and perhaps physically too. I could do nothing to react against that morbid state, and I allowed myself to become resigned; I waited for death in that room, which I stubbornly continued to consider as hers.

One day, I had gone to look for one of Cooper's[4] novels in the library, and was reading it vaguely, lying on a chaise longue. Suddenly, as I turned a page, I had a terrible shock. I had just seen, between the pages, like a forgotten bookmark, a photograph, a portrait of a woman...of her!

My heart was beating as if to burst, my ears were buzzing, I could no longer see. This time, I was not mad; it was not a dream, a chimera; it was her. She existed, just as I had imagined her!

I sank, with an indescribable ecstasy, into the contemplation of that charming image, without at first seeking an explanation of how it came to be there. It really was the clear and profound gaze that my own gaze had been seeking for so long. I recognized those opulent curls, that childlike smile, that expression, imposing and playful at the same time. She was facing the camera, her chin in her hand, a fur pelisse slipped over her bare shoulders. I turned the little piece of cardboard over; the photograph had been taken in Vienna.

---

[4] James Feminor Cooper's novels were very popular in nineteenth-century France.

Suddenly, I started calling for my mother in a voice that caused her to come running fearfully. She was dumbstruck by the expression of joy radiating from my face.

"Who is this?" I said, handing her the portrait.

My mother suppressed a slight shiver. "Gregorovna!" she cried. "Where did you find it? I've searched so hard for this portrait."

"Who is she, Mother?"

"A very great lady, my child."

"You know her?"

"Yes."

I threw myself into her arms, weeping with joy. "I'm saved! I'm cured!" I cried. "It's her, the woman for whom I've searched so hard, adored so much."

My mother sat down on the chaise longue and drew me to her; there was something constrained in her attitude; then she smiled.

"How strange!" she said.

"Oh, I implore you, tell me about her!"

"It's Countess Gregorovna Samanov, the sister of one of my husband's friends."

"I knew that she was Russian. Where is she?"

"Doubtless in Moscow."

"We'll go. She's been here, hasn't she?"

"Yes, for a fortnight—why, she stayed in this very room."

I had a gleam of pride in my eyes. "How is it that I don't know her?"

"You did know her; you often saw her when you were young; she was already grown up; you remember her beauty without remembering her."

"Ah! Now I understand the persistence of my desire!"

"We spent several months in her house in St. Petersburg," my mother continued. "You fell gravely ill there, and nearly died. Yes, I remember now; you only wanted her; the bitterest drug you'd take from her hand. The horrible fever excited your young brain in a disquieting fashion; your speech frightened us; she alone could calm you down, merely by her presence; she seemed to dazzle you, to fascinate you.

"She was, indeed, very beautiful when she went into your room in the evening, radiant with gems, enveloped in the gentle gleam of satin and superb gowns. She would be going to a ball, a reception, or to the court, but before she went, she wanted to see you briefly. She would sit by your bed and talk to you softly while putting on her gloves, then brush your forehead with a kiss and tell you to sleep well, and she would flee, with a rustle of silk.

"You would close your eyes immediately, and we would think that you were asleep, but as soon as the carriage came back, you sat up, fixing your eyes, brilliant with fever, on the door, which she would soon open to ask how you were in a low voice. On the worst nights, she would sit up with me watching over you, for you always called out to her in your delirium.

"The doctor smiled and said to her: 'Even Marcel is in love with you.' You were five."

I listened, palpitating with emotion, to the words that my mother slowly let fall, and I sought in vain to reawaken the memories that she was evoking; only the charming vision appeared, more brilliant than ever, against a background of dense shadow.

"Why have I never seen her again?" I demanded. "Why have you never mentioned her to me?"

My mother's brows furrowed slightly. "We lost touch, and it never occurred to me to mention her."

"Oh, but it's necessary to find her again!" I cried, kneeling before my mother. "Now that I know the remedy for my illness, you can't let me die."

My mother looked at me with an anxious expression.

"We're going to Russia, aren't we?" I said to her.

"All right," she replied, after a momentary hesitation, "but at the very least, it's necessary that I warn the Countess, and find out where she is."

"A letter? Oh, that will take too long. Send a telegram instead."

"All right—a telegram."

The telegram was sent the same day, and we received the reply the following day: *What a charming surprise! Am in Moscow, where I await you impatiently. Gregorovna.*

A mad joy took possession of me. All my sufferings disappeared in consequence; my strength suddenly came back. I was cured. My mother observed the phases of that resurrection attentively, but she retained a certain anxiety and constraint.

When I questioned her she said: "But you don't have any doubts, child. Are you so very sure that she will love you? That she is free?"

A love like mine admitted no obstacles. I hastened the preparations, and we left.

The further we went, the more difficulty my mother had dissimulating an increasing anguish. I hardly paid any heed to it, too deeply absorbed by the plenitude of my happiness; I savored it silently, meditatively, my eyes half-closed, rocked by the jolts of the railway carriage.

We arrived in Moscow in the evening; one of the Countess's carriages was waiting for us at the station. During the short journey from the station to Gregorovna's house, I could not say a word; my mother held my hand in hers and squeezed it nervously. She was almost as emotional as me.

It was as if in a dream that I perceived a sandy courtyard, tall trees, a glazed, brightly-lit peristyle, and trod the carpet of the stairway between tropical plants. A perfume of verbena went to my head; a voice, which seemed to me to be as gentle as music and as terrible as the trumpets of judgment, resounded. A rustle of silk, swift and impatient! The Countess ran toward us, and embraced by mother.

"It's him! It's Marcel! Ah, embrace me, my dear child!" she said, turning to me.

I stood there, as if stunned; everything whirled around me.

"Damnation!" I cried. "My life is ruined—I was born too late!" And I fell unconscious on to the bosom of the Countess, who received me in her arms.

What can I tell you, my dear friend? Gregorovna was over fifty; the ash of time had tarnished her blonde curls; her gaze, still beautiful, no longer had any but fading gleams; her calm lips no longer spoke of love.

She was already a woman when she leaned over my cradle like a fairy and engraved forever in my young soul the image of her beauty, then in its full splendor. But I fell from the height of my dreams, thunderstruck; the woman I loved no longer existed.

She was full of forbearance on learning off my madness, and who knows whether a regret similar to mine might perhaps have brushed her heart? She had always remembered the pretty infant who had shown her such a keen affection, and had suffered so much when deprived of the sight of her.

I guessed, by virtue of a certain mutual reticence, that my father had been smitten with her, and that it was because of that nascent passion that she had broken off relations with us, in order to avoid causing my mother chagrin, but that my mother had been unable to help retaining a certain rancor toward her for having involuntarily disturbed her happiness.

Today, the Countess is a second mother to me, but I suffer horribly in her company. Her intelligence, her tastes and her character prove to me in the most evident fashion that she really was the only woman that I could love.

Cruel irony of fate! We were predestined for one another, but our lives did not coincide. You will understand, now, why everything is indifferent to me, why life is nothing to me but an arid desert; it is because I shall never be in love.

THE INN OF THE FLOWERING REEDS

One morning in the fifth moon of a recent summer, an elegant boat went slowly up the river Ogava and emerged from Tokyo, the capital of Japan, which was called Yeddo under the viceroyalty of the Tycoons.

Two boatmen, one standing in the bow, the other at the stern, were steering the vessel, occasionally saying a few words to one another necessary to the maneuvering over the heads of the two young lords seated in the middle of the boat.

One of those young men was leaning distractedly over the water, dipping a fingertip therein as if he were trying to trace a line on the river's surface; the other, lying down with his hands behind his head, was gazing at the sky.

The air was delightfully cool; the sun, still obscured, was thus displayed like a ruby lost in muslins, and pink clouds rolled over the horizon, like silk cushions push by the arm of a sleeper waking up.

On the banks of the river, the city seemed a city of vapors, and the confused rumor that escaped from it was lost in the morning racket of aquatic birds, assembled in thousands in the tall rushes and reeds.

Suddenly, the man lying in the bottom of the boat sat up and looked at his companion, laughing. The latter turned his head, and also began laughing.

"Well, Boitoro?" he said.

"Well, Miodjin?" said the other.

"Why are you laughing?"

"Why has my laughter, like a willow leaning over the water, found a reflection on your lips?"

Miodjin bowed his head, blushing slightly, and nibbled the end of his fan.

"It's me, then, who has to begin the confidences?" Boitoro continued, unsurprised by his friend's disturbance.

114

"What confidences?" murmured Miodjin.

"What point is there in our remaining silent any longer?" said Boitoro. "For a year, our secret has not emerged from our two hearts, but our hearts have heard one another regardless; our actions speak in default of our lips and, with common accord, we follow the same path without our being declaring the objective toward which we are heading. Let's see—at this very moment, why is this boat taking us out of the city?"

"Because today is the sixth day of the month, the day of the Festival of Banners, and we're fleeing the town to avoid the tumultuous crowd that is cluttering it," said Miodjin, smiling.

"Where are we going?"

"To the Inn of the Flowering Reeds, where one finds peaceful retreats and charming landscapes."

"Is that all that you hope to find?" said Boitoro, incredulously. "You aren't expecting to see, like last year, disembarking at the inn's water gate, two beautiful young women accompanied by their mother, their older brother and a few servants? You've only been waiting impatiently for this day for so long in the hope of seeing once again the lacquered bridge that curves over the pond, the centenarian cedar that shelters the inn and the jovial face of the landlord?"

"Why do violence to those tender thoughts, which our souls veil jealously?" said Miodjin. "Why drag them into broad daylight, like nocturnal birds that light confuses? We've kept quiet for a year—why talk today?"

"Because we're no longer children, Miodjin, and we've been dreaming like that long enough. A seed buried in the ground hides its mysterious work for a time; then the stem appears and deploys its foliage; love is like the plant, and the one that has been germinating in our hearts is only waiting for a ray of sunlight: the warm gaze that will cause it to flower. Last year, joyful and foolish young students, we were not yet men and we did well to hide the sentiment that were carried away, as thieves hide a treasure; but today, our studies are terminated, we are free; it is necessary to act in concert, and promptly, lest others might take from us those we love."

"You're right, my friend," said Miodjin, with a hint of melancholy. "I'll do as you wish."

At that moment, the boatmen stopped rowing.

"There's Fuji-Yama," said one of them.

The young lords fell silent and stood up to admire the superb Mount Fuji on the horizon, completely disengaged from the mists that rise from the rice-fields in the morning. It rose up majestically, draped in its mantle of snow, slightly tinted with pink by the rising sun; and, amid the velvety green hills undulating at its feet, it was reminiscent of a prince in the midst of the lords of his court, prostrate before him.

"Futen, the god of winds, who lives at the summit of Mount Fuji, has blown away the clouds that surrounded his dwelling," said Miodjin.

"Yes," said Boitoro, making a shade over his eyes with his open hand, "the weather is very clear; we shall have a little breeze during the day, and the heat will be tolerable, for one can make out the buildings of the monastery situated half way up Fuji-Yama."

The boatmen began rowing again, and the vessel soon drew nearer to one of the banks and went into a little inlet shaded by superb vegetation, which rounded out in front of the Inn of the Flowering Reeds.

The water-lilies, irises and the slender reeds, launching forth like firework-sprays, specked with flowers in the form of stars or delicate feathers as light as a duckling's down, only left a narrow passage for the boats that brought clients to the inn. The building was only partly visible beneath the long flat branches of the centenarian cedar that extended over it, and through the thicket of climbing plants entwined around its slender wooden pillars. On the angle of the large roof, which advanced over an exterior gallery, a pheasant was smoothing its gilded feathers in the sunlight; the surrounding foliage was thick, impenetrable to the gaze.

In response to a shout uttered by the rowers, a young maidservant, clad in a blue cotton dress and coiffed in a large hat of bamboo straw set back over the ears by a string, emerged from the house. The landlord came forward in his turn, fan in hand, bowing as he walked.

"Ah!" he said. "What a happy event! What an honor it is for my inn to be visited by such noble lords!" And, lifting his robe slightly, he crouched down on his heels in order to attach the boat's mooring-rope to a stake.

The young men leapt on to the ground and went into the inn, where they took off their swords and their heavy black-lacquer hats, decorated by a single small gold ornament of a butterfly or flower; then, having drunk a cup of sake, they both went into a shady pathway.

"Suppose they don't come!" said Boitoro.

"I'm sure that they'll come," said Miodjin.

Boitoro looked at his friend with a surprised and curious expression.

"Yes, I'm sure of it," Miodjin went on. "I heard one of them say to her sister, near the Pavilion of the Thousand Bells, 'When we come back next year, that young fisherman will have grown by a sasi.' I even know the name of the older of the two young women; she's called Yamata."

"What!" cried Boitoro. "The older one? The one that I love? You knew her name and you left me in ignorance for a year? But do you know the name of the other, of your beloved?"

"No," said Miodjin, who had suddenly gone as pale as the pebbles of the pathway.

The Pavilion of the Thousand Bells was a small belvedere built on the river bank in a gap in the foliage. It consisted merely of a roof, supported at each corner by a bamboo pole; the floor, rather worm-eaten, was higher than the ground, and it was necessary to take a large stride to climb on to it. On the side of the river there was a low balustrade. There were no bells on the edge of the roof that might have explained the pavilion's name, unless they were those suspended by the climbing plants that mounted an assault upon it, but there was a charming view over the river from that spot, all the way to the distant mountains.

The two young men had stopped there, and were watching the river, for no boat coming from the city could land at the inn without passing before them. Boitoro had lit a little pipe, whose silver bowl was smaller than a thimble. Miodjin, leaning on the balustrade, was attempting to hide his anxiety and sadness, but his companion noticed his pallor.

"What's the matter, my friend?" he said. "Do you feel ill?"

"Don't you feel the same?" said Miodjin, in a slightly tremulous voice. All my blood is flowing back to my heart, and a keen anguish grips me as the moment so long awaited draws nearer."

"I'm certainly emotional," said Boitoro, "but my emotion is joyful; my blood is running more rapidly in my veins; I feel light and happy, while you seem to be suffering."

"A thousand anxieties are besieging me," Miodjin went on. "We love, but are we beloved? Might not those for who we are waiting with so much confidence have disposed of their hearts a long time ago? I have sad presentiments; just now I thought I saw a fix grimacing behind the trunk of a cedar."

"A truce on bleak omens!" Boitoro exclaimed. "Here comes the boat so dearly desired."

A large boat was indeed advancing around a bed in the Ogava, and something like a musical hum could be heard. The two friends leaned over the water and tried to make out the people in the boat. As yet, they could only perceive a bright mass whose vivid colors cast undulating reflections in the river. Only the boatmen could be seen clearly, standing in the bow, their silhouettes outlined against the sky. Soon, however, they were able to make out the floating pennants with which the vessel was decorated, the pink parasols in bamboo-fiber paper and the beautiful costumes of the women sitting at the rear.

The sun's rays played over the group, striking scintillations here and there, and making a thousand sparks danced over the water stirred by the oars.

Suddenly, Miodjin cried: "It's them!"

"Yes, yes!" said Boitoro, shading himself from the sun with his fan. "Yamata has her back to the cabin wall."

The boat soon glided past the Pavilion of the Thousand Bells. Two young woman and one of mature age were seated in the rear, surrounded by the silky waves of their robes. Large pins of blonde shell were inserted in their black hair, making a kind of crown of spokes; their creamy complexion was slightly rose-tinted by the translucency of their parasols.

One of the young women raised her head to look at the pavilion, and smiled on perceiving the two young men. Teeth like grains of rice were seen shining momentarily.

In the prow of the boat an elegantly-dressed man was bent down, tying his shoelaces; the light was reflected from his black lacquer hat in the form of a shield. Servants were busy with baskets laden with provisions. Inside the cabin, visible through large openings, a singer of national legends, doubtless hired to charms the excursionists with her musical talent, was squatting on the floor, making the strings of her biva resonate, singing a popular ballad in a shrill voice.

Over the silent water, in the tranquil air, the words of the song vibrated clearly:

"'Here,' said the fairy to the old man, 'are two baskets, one heavy and one light; take away whichever you prefer.'

"'For a poor man like me,' said the man, 'the lighter will still be heavy enough.' And he took the less ponderous.

"As the fairy had instructed, he did not open the basket until he was back home. It was full of beautiful clothes.

"His shrewish wife asked him where they came from, and when he had told her, she thought that she too might well encounter the fairy.

"So she went to the hill, and did indeed see the fairy coming. 'You maltreated me,' the latter said, 'when I came to your home in the form of a sparrow; nevertheless, choose between these two baskets.'

"The woman took the heavier one and returned proudly to the house, but when she opened it, two frightful red monkeys leapt out of it and fled, pulling faces at her."

The boat disappeared behind the water-lilies and irises, into the little inlet that rounded out in front of the inn. The singer fell silent.

Boitoro left the pavilion precipitately and ran toward the jetty. Miodjin followed him at a distance and hid behind the trees; he saw his companion advance toward the newcomers and bow to them graciously.

"Aha!" cried the brother of the young women, good-humoredly. "We rediscover the same company as last year; the day will be joyful."

"I had an idea that we would see you again," said the mother, whose broad face expanded in a benevolent smile.

"The hope of finding you again brought us back to this shore," said Biotoro, darting a glance at Yamata.

"Is your friend not with you, then?" asked the younger woman, lifting the broad sleeve of her robe up to her mouth, and hiding herself slightly behind her sister's shoulder. "I thought I saw him in the pavilion."

She was dainty and petite, with the lively and curious expression of a bird. Her blue dress patterned with gold thread, gathered over her hips, an enormous knot bulging behind her waist, she held her pink and blue parasol delicately above the large pins in her hair. Her sister had a graver beauty, softly veiled by melancholy; her long dark-irised eyes allowed a burning and dolorous gaze to escape; her sad smile was full of charm.

Miodjin had come forward on hearing the young woman ask about him; his gaze met Yamata's, but the latter immediately turned her eyes away.

"There he is!" whispered the younger woman to her sister.

"Shut up, Mizou," Yamata murmured. "Put a veil on your joy."

Mizou pouted mutinously, and deployed her fan in order to look askance.

"Come on, Futen," said the mother, addressing her son. "Ask these young lords to be so good as to join us to spend this day in the country, since we have had the good fortune to meet them again."

"My venerable mother, the noble Yakouna, has said aloud what I was thinking quietly," Futen replied, bowing to the two friends with a smile.

"Well, that's agreed," cried Boitoro, "And may Heaven ensure that this is not the only day we spend together!"

Futen capered joyfully and ran into the woods.

Soon, the entire company plunged into the shade with little cries of joy, and that fluttering bird-like gait that the inhabitants of cities adopt on arriving in the country.

They searched for a pleasant place amid the grass, to eat lunch. Each of them cried that he had found the most delightful spot, and then ran from one to another, gaily.

Boitoro had caught up with Futen, the brother of the young women; he was a cheerful fellow with a round face, scarred by smallpox, thick lips and a mischievous gaze beneath his slanting eyelids. He had lifted up his robe and tucked one of its flaps into his belt, in order not to be inconvenienced by the brushwood in his gamboling; his brown muscular calves were bare.

"You have no brother, Lord Futen?" said Boitoro, walking beside the young man.

"I have no brother; I'm the head of the family," Futen said, putting on a comical air of importance.

"And you find the exclusive society of women pleasant?"

"A fish swims in the river where it is born! But I pray every day to the Sun goddess to send my brothers-in-law to my taste."

"Given the beauty with which your sisters are endowed, Ten-Sio-Dai-Tsin will have little to do to answer your prayer."

"Oh, you don't know them," Futen exclaimed, biting his lip in order not to laugh. "They're coquettes, capricious and expensive enough to frighten the most generous of husbands."

"Well, I would be happy to submit to the caprices of Yamata," said Boitoro, uttering a sigh.

Futen suddenly became serious. "If it's to the head of the family that you're speaking," he said, "let's not joke any longer. You would like to marry my sister. First of all, who are you?"

"I shall speak on my behalf and that of my friend Miodjin, who loves your younger sister," said Boitoro. "We are not related, and yet he is my entire family, as I am his; both orphans, we became acquainted on the school benches and became friends. He is a samurai, like me; our fortunes are sufficient and we have been masters of them for some months. For a year we have been secretly in love with your sisters, and we have come back here to arrange marriages."

"Well, I'll think about it," said Futen—and he resumed his cheerful expression and started running through the trees, challenging Boitoro to catch him.

A place for the meal had been chosen, and the servants surrounded the read mats that formed a kind of wall. They also spread out mats on the thick grass and set out the provisions there on little low tables of black lacquer decorated with gold. Kettles, blue porcelain bowls with flower patterns, arm dishes furnished by the innkeeper, rice and sake soon covered the ground.

After having set up her music-stand, ornamented by two large red acorns, and leaned her silent biva against the stand, the singer of legends walked around collecting flowers. The new friends were chatting in groups, but the mother of the family soon clapped her hands and cried: "It's ready! It's ready!"

And everyone gathered, crouching down, armed with sticks of lacquer or ivory, held in one hand, maneuvering them like pincers, and attacked the meal.

Boitoro was very cheerful; he was laughing and joking with his future brother-in-law while devouring the beautiful Yamata with his eyes. Mizou too seemed happy; she gazed at Miodjin covertly, with half-smiles—but he, pale and silent, kept his gaze obstinately lowered and scarcely ate anything.

Yamata, too, was not eating.

Futen had whispered a few words in the ear of the singer of legends, who had tuned her biva and as now singing verses that she improvised. Those verses related to everyone's secret preoccupations; they spoke of young people sitting on the grass, dining together for the first time. Thinking about the family meal that brings together those who love one another on a daily basis, they drank sake from cups swathed in straw, but thought that it would be sweeter to empty the pretty jug with two spouts from which one drinks of a wedding-day.

"Who can tell what will happen?" she said, in conclusion. "That depends on the god of winds; he will blow this way or that, bringing together or separating."

That allusion to Futen's name, which was also that of the spirit of the winds, was transparent; everyone looked at Futen, smiling.

"Come on," she cried, gaily. "We must offer a few libations to that capricious spirit, in order that he might blow as everyone desires. Receive this, Futen." And he emptied a full cup of sake in a single draught.

Everyone began to laugh, except for Yamata and Miodjin.

The meal went on for a long time, and then they danced around the remains. Futen proposed the rice dance, but he was the only one who knew the numerous and complicated steps; they became confused, ran out of breath, and everyone ended out lying in the grass drowsily.

At dusk, the boats were illuminated and they returned slowly toward the city. The two boats glided side by side, their large round lanterns swaying. The singer of legends strummed the strings of her instrument distractedly.

In the direction of the city a great glow expanded into the sky; Tokyo was lighting up. As they drew closer, a rumor swelled, compounded of voices and music. Fireworks exploded in the sky continually.

"The festival is still going on," said Futen, standing in the prow of the boat.

The banks of the river were dark, however. The shops, warehouses and offices enclosed in the regular files of buildings, raised up on piles, were not lit; the uninterrupted festoon formed by their roofs was outlined in black against the bright lights of the neighboring streets.

"We'll escort you home," said Boitoro. "That way, we'll know where you live."

"Try not to lose us in the crowd," said Futen, "and beware of thieves!"

And they prepared to launch themselves into the midst of the crowd, as if they were jumping into the agitated waves.

In every direction, the multiform and multicolored lanterns that decorated the houses radiated their light and caused the embroideries and rich fabrics of the strollers' costumes to shine. Suspended from the summits of long bamboo poles aligned on either side of the streets were slender pennants of silk or gilded paper, hoops made of horsehair or feathers, or pompoms; elsewhere, there were fish made of lacquered straw, attached by the gills, swaying at the tops of masts. Long floating banners displayed themselves and hid by turns, according to the caprice of the wind, with armories, flowers and fantastic animals embroidered in their folds, or were extended, motionless, on frameworks of reeds, either displaying giant individuals: gods, sovereigns and illustrious warriors, or sentences, satires and famous verses in golden characters. Sellers of works of art in bronze or enamel had mingled their shiny displays with rare weapons, helmets and entire suits of armor, which took on the strange appearance of giant insects.

At every moment, bands of young boys passed by, carrying large sabers made of lacquered wood on their shoulders. Large blades in silver cardboard, curved in a bizarre fashion, were planted at intervals in the ground, fixed at the hilt. A few passing children bowed to these blades, representing the weapon of Sioki, the beloved hero of the people, whose image was reproduced in all sorts of poses on thousands of banners.

The sound of countless footsteps formed a continual susurrus like that of a waterfall, and over that bass-line rose the laughter, the songs and the jovial tumult of the crowd.

The new friends took more than an hour to travel the distance separating them from the house; on another day, they could have done it in ten minutes.

They bowed to one another amicably, promising to see one another again soon, and then they separated.

"Well?" said Boitoro to his friend, when they were alone. "Our affairs are making good progress; why do you seem so dejected?"

"You know that I like to keep my impressions to myself," said Miodjin. "It seems to me that I would lose something of my joy if I allowed it to evaporate in the open."

The following day, early in the morning, the two friends went out into the country to look for a pretty bush, similar to a buckthorn, whose foliage always remains green.

When they had found the bush, each of them took his saber and cut a branch. After a moment's reflection, however, Miodjin threw his back into the bush.

"Why did you do that?" asked Boitoro.

"Because it would not be seemly to ask for the two young women at the same time," he said. "When the fate of the elder is settled, it will be time to think about the younger."

"That's true," said Boitoro, lowering his head. "My poor friend, your happiness will therefore be delayed."

"I can wait," said Miodjin, with a sad smile.

They went back to the city and went to the house where the young women lived.

Boitoro borrowed a stool from a nearby merchant and set about fastening the green branch above the entrance-door of Futen's house. Then they drew away and both went to stand watch at the street corner.

Soon, a servant who was coming out of the house looked up, and saw the suspended branch, which caused him to go back in precipitately. A few moments later the family came out in their turn, looked at the branch for a few seconds, and then went back in.

"Alas!" groaned Boitoro, who never took his eyes off the house. "Shall I be refused?"

But the door opened again; a maidservant carrying a green lacquer footstool appeared, followed Yamata, pale with emotion. Supported by the maidservant, the young woman slowly climbed on to the footstool, detached the branch, and took it into the house.

"She accepts me! She accepts me!" cried Boitoro, running across the road in order to go into his fiancée's house.

Entirely devoted to his happiness, he did not notice Miodjin's distress. The latter, instead of following him, leaned against the wall, his eyes full of tears.

The day fixed for the wedding of Yamata and Boitoro dawned, and the guests, in their most brilliant clothes, went to the bride's dwelling. She received them in her bridal dress with a sad smile, very pale.

Boitoro was grave and happy. Futen had put a temporary brake on his noisy gaiety. The mother of the bride shed a tear. Miodjin, who had come in spite of a strong fever, fluttered around young Mixou with a sort of affection.

When everyone had arrived, the ceremonies began; they assembled in the interior courtyard of the dwelling, in the middle of which a large fire was blazing.

Two young women, dressed in azure robes embroidered with large golden butterflies, advanced gracefully. The young women represented a couple of those lovely insects, all wings and love, which symbolized conjugal felicity. Each held a handle of a large basket full of children's toys, which they threw into the fire one by one.

"The playful child is no more," said one.

"The girl is transformed into a woman, as the chrysalis becomes a butterfly."

"The dolls have had their days; henceforth you will cradle your sons."

"You will smile at your husband; you will supervise the household."

And the toys fell into the crackling flames one after another. When the last one was gone, the two butterflies clapped their hands, and cried: "Let's go! Let's go!"

Then the mother of the family burst into sobs. Mixou lifted her large, heavily-embroidered sleeve to eye level and Futen lowered his head, while Yamata hid her face in her white veils. That nuptial costume, the color of mourning, signified that the young woman was henceforth dead to the family, that she would belong entirely to the husband who would become her master.

Then the guests went into the street and formed up in procession behind the fiancée, going to her husband's house.

Boitoro and Miodjin had slipped away unseen, and the spouse was already at home, installed in the room of honor, when the cortege arrived. He welcomed his wife with the most profound marks of esteem and joy, and then invited the guests to drink sake and amuse themselves; but the butterfly-girls escorted the fiancés to the images of the domestic gods hanging on the wall. They had to crouch down there, facing one another, and drain to the last drop a small metal vessel full of sake. That vessel, which one of the young women held by a long handle, had two spouts. Each of the fiancés drank from the one at lip-level.

"It is thus, side by side, that you will drink life," said the butterflies.

"The same liquor, sweet or bitter, will quench your thirst."

"Everything is henceforth common between you, joys and pains."

"Drink, drink! The first drops are intoxicating."

"Let nothing trouble the beverage, let nothing embitter it or turn it to poison."

"May it be, on the contrary, until the final drop, a philter of love and happiness."

The spouses rose to their feet; they were united for life.

All the witnesses then spread out through the rooms to admire the bride's superb trousseau, which was displayed there, and the furniture she had brought: mats, umbrellas, mirrors, lacquer boxes and kitchen utensils. Then a meal was served in the gallery overlooking the garden.

Toward the end of the meal, when everyone was drunk, Yamata, who had kept her eyes constantly lowered, looked up and sought Miodjin with her gaze. She perceived him some distance away, almost facing her. The dolorous contraction and pallor of his face frightened her, and she made a sign indicating that she wanted to speak to him, but the young man did not see it. He had risen to his feet and headed toward the garden.

Yamata got up too and followed him. She looked for him for a few moments in the obscure garden; a stifled sob permitted her to discover him. He had thrown himself on the ground, face downwards, and was weeping, with his head in his hands.

"Brother, brother!" Yamata said, kneeling beside him. "You're weeping, alas! What's wrong? What's happened?"

The young man stood up abruptly.

"You, here?" he cried. "Oh, leave me alone! I'm no longer master of my heart; my dolor, too long contained, is overflowing; I can no longer hold it back, and you must not see it."

"Am I not your sister?" said Yamata, softly. "Do you have an aversion for me, that you do not want to permit me to share your woes?"

"You haven't guessed, cruel woman?" Miodjin cried. "You have the heart to come like this to insult me with your happiness?"

"My happiness?"

"You haven't understood, then, that for a year, I've loved you with all my heart, and that for a month, I've been suffering unspeakable tortures!"

Yamata uttered a muffled cry, and tottered momentarily.

"He loved me!" she murmured.

"Boitoro loved you too, and he was more worthy of your love than me; I veiled my thoughts in order not to sadden his joy. But now, you love him; you're his wife; my heart can burst and let all its blood run out. Go away! Let me weep, let me die!"

"Alas, alas!" cried Miodjin, bursting into sobs. "What have we done, Miodjin? I too have loved you for a year, but my younger sister was infatuated with you, and I hid my love in order not to spoil hers."

The two young people, stunned by that confession, looked at one another silently for a long time, in the semi-darkness, bewildered and unsteady on their feet.

Suddenly, Miodjin grabbed Yamata's hands. "Come," he said to her, in a low voice. "Come, let's flee. I'm your master, since you love me; here, it is hell for us; away from here, happiness is everywhere, since we shall be together. Come on, let's go."

"Do you think so, friend?" said the young woman, through her tears. "It's too late; we're doomed; we might as well be dead. I'm Boitoro's wife!"

"Why did you do that? Why did you accept him?"

"Oh, for a thousand reasons that now seem to be a thousand traps. I had let my sister see that I loved one of the strangers encountered at the Inn of the Flowering Reeds. What do I know? I persuaded myself that it was her that you wanted; I was afraid of awakening suspicions by refusing Boitoro; besides which, another husband would have been imposed upon me—he was, at least, your friend."

"And you think that I can let my heart be crushed like this, without a rebellion?"

"A protest would warn them about the harm they are doing us, and in order to be happy, they must be unaware of it. We are the victims, friend; let us submit to destiny, let us not become executioners. My sister adores you; he seems to love me profoundly. Let us not make them suffer what we are suffering. Let us sacrifice our vain complaints to their happiness, since our own misfortune is irreparable."

"No, no!" cried Miodjin. "Why should they be happy rather than us? Come, let's flee this place. You love me; after those words, all others are empty of meaning for me."

Yamata pulled away her hands, which the young man was still holding in his.

"Miodjin," she said, "will you have less courage than a woman?"

He bowed his head silently and put his hand over his eyes. After a few moments he said, in a calmer voice:

"That's good, my sister. You have the soul of a hero; I shall not be less than you. I am on the edge of a bottomless gulf, into which my share of happiness has fallen; the feeble hope that remained to me has just falling into it in its turn. I submit; command me. What must I do?"

"You must marry my sister," said Yamata, trying to make her tear-softened voice firmer. "You must make her happy for me, as I shall love my husband in memory of you."

"I'll obey if I have the strength to go on living," said Miodjin. "I shall complete the sacrifice that tender friendship has imposed upon us. Tomorrow, I shall hand the emblematic branch over her door."

"Thank you," she said. "You are a man. Heaven will reward us, in another existence, for having been able, out of devotion, to renounce our terrestrial happiness. Adieu, my brother, adieu!"

"Adieu! Adieu!" murmured Miodjin, while the distraught Yamata fled, weeping. And when he could no longer see her white veil though the trees, he threw himself down on the grass again, to stifle the heart-rending sound of his sobs.

THE MARVELOUS TUNIC

A Chinese Story

One morning, in the coldest winter that the inhabitants of Nan-Kin could remember, a company of young men was going through the noble city toward the suburb of Tsie-Tan, with a loud noise of words and outbursts of laughter. It was broad daylight, but none of the shops was open yet; the streets were deserted, and such a cold snap retained in their beds those sleepers who, in order to rise at such an hour, would have had to stay up all night.

That was the case with these young men, who were making their heels click on the paving-stones of the streets and conversing loudly without any respect for the sleep of others; they had been drinking and amusing themselves all night on the occasion of the marriage of one of their friends. Warmed by rice wine, they did not feel the cold, against which they were, in any case, protected by the warmest of most beautiful of furs. Some had their silk mantles lined with fox-fur, white astrakhan or Chinese rat, the others in the skin of lynxes, deep or pelicans. Only one, as if he were a prince, wore sea-dragon—that marvelous fur that has no equal. All of them had furry black satin boots and variously-embroidered velvet hoods over their skull-caps.

The young men reached the suburb of Tsie-Tan, while continuing to laugh and chat.

"Hush, my friends, we're nearly there!" said the one marching in front, his finger on his lips.

The young man in question was the least sumptuously dressed of the joyful band, but he was the most charming in terms of his face and bearing.

"Ruby-Heart's right," said another. "Let's adopt the silent manner of fish gliding in the white river."

They fell silent and set about marching alongside the wall with exaggerated precaution.

"This is my uncle's house," said Ruby-Heart, a hundred paces further on

"Hush!" said the entire band, in chorus, producing a sound like that of wind in reeds.

Ruby-Heart beckoned to a slave, who was following the young lords at a distance. The slave advanced; he was carrying a roll of papers of various colors and a pot of glue.

The papers were unrolled and, with stifled laughter, the young fools approached the house pointed out by Ruby-Heart.

It was sufficiently beautiful in appearance, but dilapidated and poorly maintained. The green enamel of the small roof, turned up at the corners, which formed an awning above the door, was peeling, and had gaps in places. The walls were cracking and it was no longer possible to discern what color it had been painted beneath the thousand mud-splashes that covered it, Rust was devouring the iron tortoise that served as a knocker; it was evident that the proprietor refused his abode the repairs that it was demanding imperiously.

A poster, a beautiful bright red in color, soon appeared over the dirty hue of the door. Large elegantly-traced characters were carefully aligned in columns.

Every being and thing, they said, *bears the name that suits it; never has a mouse been known to call itself a horse, or a dung-heap to take the name of a perfumed flower. Why, then, is San-Ko-Tcheou, the venerable owner of this house, not named the Miser, the Skinflint, the Moneybag-Slave, or some such analogous title.*

A blue poster was extended below the red one.

Listen to an amusing story, this one said. *A venerable miser of the suburb of Tsie-Tan was invited to dinner by the lord of an important house. The miser accepted the invitation, and when the day came, ate with a hearty appetite and drank*

so much that he had to be carried home. The guests present at the dinner hastened, one after another, to return the lord's generosity; the miser was invited every time, and dined in succession in all the homes of the noble lord's guests. Since then, many moons have gone by, and every morning the noble lord interrogates his slaves.

"Has no invitation come from the venerable miser?"

"No, Master."

And the lord frowned. Sometimes he had his slaves beaten, but they swore by the household spirits of their ancestors that it had never come. Has anyone in the Middle Kingdom ever heard of such a neglect of convention?

The young man whose shoulders were enlarged by the soft thickness of the Sea-Dragon leaned over Ruby-Heart's shoulder and reread the second poster.

Friend, Friend," he said, in a low voice, "we must love you, to expose ourselves like this to being forced to eat your venerable uncle's cuisine."

"Certainly," said Ruby-Heart, "the common run of the mendicants and vagabonds who emerge from the Plumes de Poules[5] in the morning is preferable to a man whom avarice has diminished to the extent of my unfortunate uncle; the stew that means to prisoners that their hands are freed momentarily—or, better still, the one made by poor Koo-Li, who had the virtue of not eating before having served the meager pittance of which he only had the residue."

"Hey, hey!" said one of the young men. "You're scaring us, but we'll be brave. What will one not do to oblige a friend."

"I don't want you to die," said Ruby-Heart, laughing. "Don't forget to dine copiously before answering my uncle's invitation."

---

[5] "This is a sort of public shelter where mendicants and beggars sleep. It consists of a single room, whose floor vanished beneath a mass of chicken-feathers." [Author]

134

"All right, all right! We'll dine beforehand," said the young men, stifling their laughter

"Let's get away," said one of them. "They're beginning to open the shops, and the sub's making the frost on the roof-tops glisten."

Ruby-Heart uttered a sigh and looked up at the red trellis of a window.

"You're going to wake up Reed-Flower with your sighs," said the young man in the fine furs.

"Oh, if I could only see the tip of his finger or the shadow of her slender hand on the paper of the window"

"Come on, patience! If our plot succeeds, Reed-Flower will soon be your wife."

All the young men drew away and, before disappearing round a street corner, cast one last glance at San-Ko-Tcheou's house.

A few passers-by had stopped in front of the papers, and were reading them, holding their sides with laughter. One of them lifted the door-knocker and let it fall noisily—and then they fled in all directions."

An old head, thin and angular, which seem to be carved out of centenarian ivory, slid out of a partly-open window and looked outside.

At the same time, a servant opened the door and scanned the solitude of the street with his surprised gaze. The servant was a young man, as thin as a stick of bamboo, tall, silent and dismayed. From the first moon of winter onwards, chilled to the marrow of his bones, he trembled perpetually like a damp dog—but don't even imagine that anyone can forget to warm himself.

San-Ko-Tcheou had got up. In response to his master's call, the servant had rushed, arms extended, as if something bad had happened to him, and received his orders without saying a word. He had only moved his large fearful eyes, and departed suddenly with the same gesture of despair. For him, life was something incomprehensible and terrible.

At the sight of the posters striping the door, he emerged from his mutism; with arms upraised toward Heaven, he uttered a long exclamation.

"What is it, Koo-Li?" said the old man, looking down from above.

"Come, come!" cried Koo-Li, who did not know what gesture to use to express his fear.

San-Ko-Tcheou drew back his head, closed the window and came down. The clink of keys, and the grating sounds of bolts being withdrawn were heard.

"What is it? What is it?" said the miser, appearing in the doorway. "Has someone stolen the tortoise, or some other external ornament?"

Koo-Li drew his master outside and half-closed the door in order that it might be more brightly lit; then he put his hands to his temples, as if he wanted to prevent it from blowing up in the face of such misfortune.

"Oho!" the miser exclaimed. "Do they take my house for a public pillar, or has some unrenowned poet chosen my door for a publisher? In that case, he'll pay me a royalty,"

And San-Ko-Tcheou, taking a enormous pair of spectacles from his overcoat, made of sheepskin worn all the way to the leather, set them on his nose.

As the meaning of the characters sunk into his brain, the miser's face became immeasurably elongated, as if he were being reflected in one of those polished copper balls that ornament balustrades.

"I'm being insulted, eh?" he murmured. "I'm being covered in shame and dishonored—me, a venerable man who is over sixty and worthy of respect. Miser! Skinflint! Just because I'm poor and thrifty."

The passers-by, increasingly numerous, stopped curiously San-Ko-Tcheou tore down the posters and was about to throw them in the river; but he changed his mind, thinking that someone might take a shot at him. He went back inside and closed the door angrily.

"What's happening, Father? Why do you seem so irritated?" asked a young woman, pale with cold, who came into the honor room from the other side as San-Ko-Tcheou reached it.

"Do good, then," cried the old man, animatedly. "Take in orphans as I have taken in Reed-Flower. Be polite to everyone, as charitable as Miaou-Chen[6]—did I not, last year, distribute a bowl of rice to an entire army of mendicants?—only to be treated as I am treated, to receive this reward!"

And he threw the two posters, which he had screwed up into a ball, into the middle of the room.

Reed-Flower picked them up and unfolded them. While she read them, trying to reconstruct the meaning in spite of the tears, Koo-Li threw a few glowing coals into a large copper heater half-full of ash. In such bitter cold, however, that meager fire was a bitter irony; it seemed to freeze itself in that large glacial room, which fifty heaters would have had difficulty warming.

The hall had once been decorated by San-Ko-Tcheou's parents, and still retained an air of elegance. A frieze of red wood, cut into pieces, ran around the walls near the ceiling, where beams that had once been painted and gilded intersected. The wall-hangings were an old fabric, entirely faded, although traces of embroidery could still be seen. Only the sculpted ironwood furniture had become more beautiful in growing older, but some items were unsteady.

In an alcove raised by a step was the bench of honor, on which visitors were sat; it was covered with a small flat mattress, like a pancake, which hid a ragged bamboo-fiber mat. It was in that corner, somewhat shielded from draughts, that Reed-Flower usually sat. She carried the heater there and set up an old screen, whose lacquer was flaking, in front of the opening of the alcove. A few dusty lanterns hung from the ceiling in places.

"Well, Father," said Reed-Flower, raising large oblique eyes fringed with superb lashes toward San-Ko-Tcheou, "it's

---

[6] "The Goddess of Compassion." [Author]

easy to put an end to this frightful scandal; it's necessary to render to your friends the politeness they have done to you."

"Is that what you think?" said the old man, shrugging his shoulders.

"Think of your dignity. Dare you appear in the street with the fear of being insulted by the passers-by?"

"Since I've torn down the posters, no one will read them."

"Perhaps they've already been read," said the young woman.

San-Ko-Tcheou lowered his head momentarily, but he was still not convinced. "Koo-Li," he said, "go prowl around the market-place, and try to find out whether people know about my misfortune."

Koo-Li raised his arms to the heavens and fled. The miser started striding back and forth in the room in order to warm himself up and calm his agitation—but the young servant was not absent for long. He came back in hurriedly, greatly alarmed, his garment stained with half-melted snow.

"Everyone knows," he said. "Wicked people! Koo-Li beaten." The poor fellow was miserly himself with words. He only pronounced those that were indispensable.

"What! You've been beaten, my poor Koo-Li?" said Reed-Flower.

Koo-Li nodded his head and mimed the snowballs that had been thrown at him.

"It's necessary to submit," said San-Ko-Tcheou, with a sigh. "They're capable of treating me the same way. Al these people want my ruin and my death."

"Come on, Father—you won't die of having hosted a dinner for once in your life."

"Oh, if I listened to you," cried the miser, "we'd soon be reduced to beggary. One might truly think that you believe me to be rich."

The young woman smiled, but made no response. She went to take red paper from a drawer.

"Come on," she said. "Write your invitations."

"It's a long time since I held a brush," said San-Ko-Tcheou. "My hand trembles. Write them yourself."

Reed-Flower sat down and gripped the brush between her small, long-nailed fingers.

The operation was laborious. As Koo-Li mixed the ink, it froze. The young woman read aloud the names that she was tracing on the red paper. Each name drew a sigh from San-Ko-Tcheou.

"That one's a glutton," he said. "He eats until he's stuffed; that one is as thirsty as the sands of the steppes of Tartary; as for that one, he throws handfuls of gold liangs around as if they were pebbles; the day I dined with him, no less than ninety-two dishes were served. Do you remember, Koo-Li?"

"Oh yes," said Koo-Li, his eyes upraised. He had shared the remains of the feast with the other servants, and had obtained a delightful indigestion that day—the only one he had ever had in his life.

"Let's not forget to invite your nephew Ruby-Heart," said the young woman. "He has a very facile tongue, and when he speaks, people forget to eat."

That reason seemed to decide San-Ko-Tcheou, who had initially shaken his head.

"A-Mi-To-Fo!" he cried, when the invitations were ready, "Here's a fine adventure! Isn't it enough to have to nourish ourselves? Is it necessary, then, to feed these young madmen, who, not content with the hunger of a lion, take drugs to sharpen their appetites? Oh, I'd like to see them all on the other side of the golden bridge of Pou-Tien."[7]

Koo-Li, shivering with cold, took the carefully-folded pieces of red paper and got ready to take them to the relevant addresses. His master held him back by a flap of his robe.

"Don't forget to set out the rat-traps," he said. "We're bound to trap half a dozen of the rodents, and that will supply a few fricassees."

---

[7] "The bridge leading to Hell." [Author]

A few days later, at the fifth hour of the evening, Ruby-Heart went into his uncle's drawing room. As a close relative, it was permissible for him to arrive before the other guests and to go in without being introduced.

Reed Flower was busy just then making repairs to an old silk tablecloth that had once been white but was now yellow and worm-eaten. She uttered a squeal on seeing a man come in, and swiftly hid her face behind the broad sleeve of her robe.

"Don't flee, I beg you, my pretty cousin," said Ruby-Heart, stopping on the far side of the table. "I've come early with the intention of talking to you momentarily."

"Are you scornful of me them, my lord," said Reed-Flower, still sheltering her gaze behind her raised arm, "that you speak to me like this, as one does to vulgar women devoid of modesty?"

"I'm speaking to you simply and with sincerity," the young man said. "I don't have time for the beautiful phrases and manners that custom commands. Know that for a long time my heart has only been filled by you, Reed-Flower, and I would like to know whether you would like to love me and approve the plans I have made, or whether I am only good for hanging myself from some scaffold with a silken rope around my neck."

"Alas, my noble relative, you're making fun of a poor girl who has no wit with which to defend herself. You've never heard mention of me, and I don't believe that I've committed the sin of letting my face be seen, so your love cannot exist, and the words you are speaking to me are offensive."

"I've seen your delightful face twenty times," said Ruby-Heart. "I'm a criminal, it's true, but I'm harshly punished by having seen you and not seeing you always."

"You know my face?" exclaimed the young woman, her surprise so great that she uncovered her forehead and eyes.

"You didn't suspect, during the winter evenings when you worked beside your lamp behind your closed window, that someone was spying, without paying any heed to the biting wind. Look, it's over there, on that side of the garden. I scale the wall that my uncle has fitted with iron spikes. I cling on, and I watch. Your shadow is projected clearly on the oiled paper of the window. I see your delicate features, your long lashes, your abundant hair, including the little wisp that curls over the nape of your neck. I follow the movements of your supple body when it bends down over the work; I see your dainty hand rising and descending, drawing the needle or pricking the fabric. Sometimes, you blow on your fingers, numbed by cold, and I curse the infamous avarice of your adoptive father. Sometimes, though, you place the lamp between the window and you, and I can't see you. On those days, I go away with tears in my eyes."

Reed-Flower, emotional and pensive, allowed her arm to fall, no longer thinking of hiding herself.

"Ah!" she murmured. "If I had known, during those long, sad evenings, that someone was thinking about me tenderly, I would not have felt the cold that was freezing my fingers or the ennui that was gnawing at my heart!"

The young man looked avidly at his cousin, whom he had, after all, only ever seen in profile. What new charm there was for him in her complexion and the somber velvet of her eyes!

"You're even more beautiful than I thought," he said, in a tremulous voice. "I dare not ask you to look at me, so fearful am I that my person might displease you."

"I owe you a confession in my turn," said Reed-Flower, smiling. "Look at this screen behind which I usually hide myself. There's a little rip here, which I made with my fingernail in order to look at you at my ease during the rare visits you make to my father."

"Is it possible that, while I was thinking about you night and day, you were also thinking about me?"

The young woman's only reply was a slight sigh, as she lowered her gaze.

"Someone's coming," said Ruby-Heart, pricking up his ears at the sound of footsteps audible in the street. "One more word; I have a plan to get my uncle to give me the sum of money indispensable for the initial expenses of a household; if I succeed, will you consent to become my wife?"

"Since you have seen my face," said Reed-Flower, lowering her eyes again, "I can have no other husband than you." And she went away, as rapidly as her tiny feet permitted—but she was anxious and sad, for she knew that it was less difficult to pry a star loose from the heavens that to extract any sum of money at all from San-Ko-Tcheou's coffers.

In spite of the cold, San-Ko-Tcheou came to greet his visitors on the threshold of the exterior door. Some arrived in palanquins, others on horseback or on foot. At each new arrival, the miser rushed down the three steps of the threshold and hurried forward. Then the Tchin-tchins multiplied, closed fists were raised to eye-level, spines curved and knees bent.

Lord Pen-Kouen, the man who wore such rich furs, was the last to arrive; servants preceded his palanquin, borne by eight men. For him, San-Ko-Tcheou advanced into in middle of the road; he helped him to get down, then set his knee on the ground and said: "For a long time I have been thinking incessantly about your perfumed name!"

Ruby-Heart greeted his friends with cordial joy and a knowing smile.

When they were all together, they were not long delayed in sitting down at the table, and the miser called out, in his quavering voice: "Come on, Koo-Li—the first course!"

Very flustered, Koo-Li appeared and set various bowls and trays on the table.

"Try this almond milk," said San-Ko-Tcheou, audaciously offering his guests the water in which a little flour had been mixed. "And then," he continued, with similar aplomb, pointing to mysterious fricassees, puréed deer's feet, cranes' stomachs and sugar-cane caterpillars, "would you prefer shark-fin pellets, frogs' heads in green turtle-fat, swallows' nests in candied sugar or these woodcocks garnished with peacocks' crests, or these goose-feet, or this porcupine?"

"What a princely menu, Uncle!" cried Ruby-Heart. "You're truly giving your guests a reception worthy of them."

The young men bit their lips in order not to burst out laughing, and avoided looking at one another, for fear that one might draw the others into an impolite hilarity. The miser continued his listing, and in his prodigality, gave several designations to the same dish.

Pen-Kouen proposed a toast, in order to be able to abandon his seriousness momentarily in the subsequent hubbub.

They rose to their feet and, each holding his cup in both hands, left the table and advanced into the middle of the room. The guests, divided into two rows, addressed the usual salutes, and then the cups were emptied. Either because of the tremors of suppressed laughter, however, or because of the disgust inspired by the bitter and dilute liquid they were obliged to drink, more than half of it was spilled on the ground.

They sat down at the table again. Koo-Li brought the second course.

"Is it so cold, then, that you keep your furs on?" asked Ruby-Heart, who never ceased fanning himself.

"He asks whether it's cold," said San-Ko-Tcheou, who was shivering with his knees pressed together, bent double, with his elbows digging into his sides.

"He's always warm himself, since he possesses a certain talisman," said Pen-Kouen, with a perfectly serious expression.

"See how he's sweating," remarked another.

While they were drinking the toast, Ruby-Heart had slipped outside briefly, and had placed a handful of snow beneath his skull-cap; water was indeed running down his forehead.

"Is it possible!" cried the miser, looking at his nephew in amazement. "Perhaps you're ill," he added, though. "You, who have such a prodigious appetite, haven't eaten anything."

"I'm as healthy as the Li-cou-li Tower, Uncle," said Ruby-Heart, "but I only eat rarely, for the taste; the talisman that warms me also nourishes me."

"What tale are you telling me?" said the old man. "You're making fun of me!"

"Oh, Uncle, how could you think such a thing? Have I ever failed you in any other fashion? Let's not say any more about the talisman. I withdraw my words if they've wounded you."

"Not at all, not at all—but what you say is so extraordinary that I'm entitled to be astonished." Looking once again at the sweat running down his nephew's forehead, he added: "It's incredible, though, how warm he is."

"He's very lucky," said Pen-Kouen, "for, in spite of our furs, we're frozen."

"Where is it, then, this talisman?" said San-Ko-Tcheou.

"It's simply this blue cotton tunic covering my shoulders."

"You want me to believe that that vestment nourishes you and warms you?"

"For six months, Uncle."

"And where can such things be obtained?"

"In the Kingdom of Flowerless Plants.[8] You know that those European barbarians possesses powers that tend to the marvelous. They doubtless know all the secrets of magic; their carriages move without horses, their ships without sails; they talk to one another from one end of China to the other by means of an iron wire; they manufacture an instrument that seizes and fixes your image in a minute with the eyes of children;[9] what else can they not do? Well, among other things, some of them possess these cloaks, which protect them from cold and hunger."

---

[8] "England." [Author]

[9] "Many Chinese people imagine that the objective lenses of cameras are made from human eyes." [Author]

"Indeed, indeed," said San-Ko-Tcheou, half-convinced, "these barbarians might well be demons; they have supernatural knowledge—but this seems a trifle implausible to me. To begin with, how did this cloak come into your possession?"

"It was about six moons ago," said Ruby-Heart. "I was passing through the crossroads of a small village on horseback. I heard shouting and a racket, and saw a large number of furious people belaboring a poor white-bearded man whom they had knocked to the ground, striking him with their fists and feet.

"'What has he done, then?' I asked.

"'He hasn't done anything,' they replied. 'He's a barbarian priest. We're going to kill him and chop him into little pieces.'

"I couldn't bear to see an old man treated like that, so I set about distributing a few strokes of the whip, and got closer to the poor fellow. 'Quickly,' I said to him. 'Jump up behind me, and hold on tightly.'

"In spite of his injuries and his age, fear made him nimble, and he was on the horse in the blink of an eye; I spurred the beast vigorously, which knocked a few people over and set off at a fast gallop.

I brought the poor priest here to Nan-Kin and put him under the protection of the authorities. 'My son,' the barbarian said to me, 'as I was about to leave him, I might perhaps die of these wounds I've received, but you've saved me from a crueler death, and I won't forget it. Ask about me tomorrow and on subsequent, and if my condition gets worse, come and see me. I swear to you that you won't regret your visit.'

"A few days later, he was in very poor way, and I went to see him as he had recommended; he only had a few minutes to live. 'Take this cloak, my son,' he said. 'I have no more need of it. You'll soon recognize its marvelous virtue, and congratulate yourself for having done a good deed.'

"In order not to annoy the dying man, I put the vestment—which didn't seem to me to be very elegant—over my shoulders. I thought it had belonged to some saint of the priest's religion, and that it was for that reason that he thought it so valuable, but it was just an insignificant rag to me, which I might as well throw away at the first street corner.

"I abandoned that idea very rapidly; there was a stifling heat at the time, but as soon as I put on the tunic I felt myself enveloped by a delightful coolness—for although the garment is warm in winter, it remains cool in summer. Gripped by surprise, I turned toward the priest to question him, but he had quit this world. I went away, ordering that the stranger be given a decent funeral.

"What more can I tell you, venerable Uncle? That day, I forgot to eat dinner; I spent an excellent night in spite of the heat, thanks to the tunic, which I never took off. The next day, I was sated before having eaten three grains of rice. I understood then what a treasure I possessed, and, full of gratitude, I had funerary tablets set up in my house to the barbarian priest who had enriched me."

"Give that garment to the unfortunate San-Ko-Tcheou, who is shivering with cold and expends enormous sums for your nourishment!" cried the miser, utterly convinced, whose little slanting eyes were sparkling with avarice."

"Give away my tunic!" said Ruby-Heart. "Do you think so? You have beautiful gold liangs in your cellar growing bored beneath the dust; you can buy furs and have excellent meals prepared for yourself."

"Me! I have liangs!" said the miser, shrugging his shoulders.

"While I'm poor," the young man continued, "and this miraculous vestment shelters me from all need. I would only give it up, temporarily, for three hundred gold liangs, to a member of my family or a friend, on condition it were bequeathed to me in his will."

"You're certainly not estimating it at its true value," said one of the guests, attracting a resentful glance from San-Ko-Tcheou with that observation.

"If you give me time to amass three hundred liangs," said another, "I'll buy it. After a year, I'd have earned twice that sum, and I'd be able to buy a house in the country."

"Personally, I wouldn't want the cloak," said Pen-Kouen. "I'm too fond of eating well and putting on rich garments."

The miser was busy with calculations.

Three hundred liangs, he said to himself. *We spend that in two years, food being so expensive; so, in two years, I'd have recovered the price of the cloak, and in the third year I'd begin o make a profit; that would, indeed, be a good deal—but Reed-Flower and Koo-Li would probably want to eat, and that would spoil everything.*

The guests, especially Ruby-Heart, were following San-Ko-Tcheou's meditation from the corners of their eyes.

"Can your talisman nourish several people?" he said to Ruby-Heart, suddenly breaking the silence.

"Twenty, thirty, a hundred men, an entire army, Uncle. It's sufficient to wear it for a few moments to have dined very well."

"And women?"

"Oh, I must confess, the talisman's virtue stops at women, and has no effect on them."

"Really!" said the disappointed miser. "That's a shame; I would have bought the cloak, but I have an adoptive daughter, as you know—Reed-Flower."

The young man's heart beat faster. "The young woman must be of an age to marry," he said. "She'll be leaving you soon."

"Marriage! You think so? What about the enormous expenses it involves—the trousseau, the ceremony?"

"That's true—and I understand you all the better, Uncle, as I haven't married myself in order to avoid all the expenses of a wedding. I know that there's a custom that permits one to marry without expense simply by taking the young bride away, after the father has consented before witnesses to give her to you for a wife, but how, when one has a little dignity, can one propose that to a family, admitting that one is so poor?"

"Well then, marry your cousin!" exclaimed Pen-Kouen. "That will work our marvelously; the venerable San-Ko-Tcheou couldn't ask for a better son-in-law."

"I've never heard mention of Reed-Flower," said the young man disdainfully. "I don't know what she's worth."

"Oh, she's accomplished in everything," said the miser, swiftly. "Gentle, pretty, modest, even-tempered, not too talkative—in sum, perfect."

"If she were all that, I'd gladly marry her," said Ruby-Heart.

"Well then, before this honorable assembly, I grant her to you for a wife."

Reed-Flower, who was following this scene excitedly hidden behind the screen, stifled a joyful exclamation.

"On the condition," San-Ko-Tcheou continued, "that you take her without any trousseau and that you sell me your tunic."

"Agreed, Uncle," said Ruby-Heart, who had difficulty concealing his delight. "In my turn, I assume, I can dispense with the customary gifts?"

"So be it," said the miser, nodding his head.

"This very evening, I'll leave you the marvelous tunic and take Red-Flower away."

"No, no," said San-Ko-Tcheou, seized by a doubt. "Before concluding the bargain, I want to submit the tunic to a little test."

All the guests exchanged anxious glances, but Ruby-Heart, although full of anxiety, put on a brave face.

"As you please, Uncle," he said.

"This is it: you'll spend the night under my roof, in this room, where you'll permit me to lock you in. When the heaters are extinct and morning approaches, the cold here is so extreme that rice wine freezes in the gourds. You'll lie down there, under the bench of honor, with neither blankets nor cushions. If you haven't frozen to death tomorrow morning, I'll buy your cloak in complete confidence."

The young man, whose heart was burning with love, felt capable of confronting a polar chill; it was, however, with a slight tremor in his voice that he replied: "That's fine, Uncle; I'll comply with your orders."

Ruby-Heart's friends delayed their departure for as long as they could, in order to shorten their companion's ordeal; their presence, the heaters and the lights warmed the glacial chamber slightly, but they could deduce what it would be like abandoned to itself.

"Take care," said Pen-Kouen to Ruby-Heart in a low voice. "Several people have died of cold in the streets in recent days, you know, and it's like the streets in here; I'm frozen in spite of my furs."

"I want to attempt to adventure," the young man replied. "Just think—if I'm still alive tomorrow, Red-Flower will be mine."

"Be brave, my friend," said Pen-Kouen, shaking his hand.

Everyone was obliged to retire, and Ruby-Heart remained alone, with no fire and no light, as the large room was invaded by the cold.

I'm in a pretty pickle now, he said to himself. *I wish to Heaven that the barbarian priest's cloak were as I'd described it.*

The north wind was blowing under all the doors, making an extraordinary music. The full moon, shining in a clear sky, illuminated the room through the oiled paper of the windows.

Ruby-Heart went to the bench of honor and curled up in a corner, but the cold seemed to be intensifying by the minute, and the suffering it inflicted upon the unfortunate young man became intolerable. It seemed to him that he had been plunged into icy water; his knees were knocking, and his teeth chattering so violently that he stuck two fingers into his mouth, fearing that they might break.

"Alas, alas!" he murmured, "I shan't have the gold liangs and I shan't go to sleep on my bride's heart, for I'll die here."

A dangerous numbness gradually took possession of him.

Suddenly, he stood up and shook off that torpor; he had just had an idea. He slipped underneath the heavy ironwood table on which the meal had been served and lifted it on his back. Thus laden, he started running round the room at a rapid pace.

Soon, his blood began to circulate again; he felt warmth and life returning gradually. He continued marching ardently; from time to time he stopped to draw breath, and then set off again. When the table wearied him too much, he set it down and took a chair in each hand; then he ran around the room, shaking them. He continued that exercise until the moment when, dawn having broken, he heard his uncle's footsteps on the staircase. Then he put everything back in place, lay down on the bench of honor and pretended to be asleep.

San-Ko-Tcheou approached his nephew without making a sound; the latter was breathing noisily.

"That's incredible," he murmured. "He's not dead." He felt the moist hands, the forehead damp with an incontestable sweat. "That's marvelous!" he exclaimed. "There's no more room for doubt."

Ruby-Heart woke up, cracked his fingers one after another, rubbed the pit of his stomach and stood up.

"Good day, Uncle," he said.

"Here's your three hundred gold liangs," said San-Ko-Tcheou, "and you can take my daughter away."

A few moments later, the young couple, drunk with joy, left the miser's house.

A short while after that adventure, Koo-Li, thinner and more nervous than ever, came to find Ruby-Heart at his home. He looked at him for a long time, terrified, before daring to speak.

"Why, you don't seem to be very well, my poor Koo-Li," said the young man, laughing. "Have you had some indigestion since I last saw you?"

"Oh no," said Koo-Li. "Nothing to eat for a week; at meal-times one puts on a cloak—but me, I eat rats."

"Would you like something to eat?"

"Oh, yes," said Koo-Li.

"What did you come to tell me?"

The thin child took on a lamentable expression and trembled in every limb. "No fire and no dinner for a week," he said. "Noble master is dead."

"Eh? Great Poussah!" exclaimed Ruby-Heart. "Is it really imaginable that he persisted stubbornly in not eating?"

Grief-stricken, he went to his uncle's house right away, and, in his capacity as sole heir, had the cellars opened. As he had anticipated, they were cluttered with bags of gold and silver.

San-Ko-Tcheou had a sumptuous funeral, which would have drawn tears from the dead man's eyes had he been allowed to know what it cost. Ruby-Heart was determined to conduct himself as an affectionate relative and a grateful heir—but when his tears were wiped away, he returned to his beloved Reed-Flower, and to his happiness, now completed by a fortune.

Koo-Li entered the young couple's service; he grew so fat that at the end of a year, his oblique eyes, once so large, looked like two mere brush-strokes in his face.

THE FORBIDDEN FRUIT

A Sketch of Chinese Mores

It was in Canton. A new year was beginning, the ninth of the reign of Emperor Tao-Kouang. A dense and joyful crowd almost hid the ground in the Street of the Lantern-Merchants completely, even though it is the broadest in the city.

Beneath the perpendicular rays of the sun—for it was noon—the bright colors of new skullcaps, the gleam of fresh silks and the scintillation of large gems were reminiscent of the waves of a river strewn with flowers, between the yellow facades of houses decorated with pennants all the way to the roofs, at the corners of which green dragons were bursting into laughter.

On the first day of the year, ambulant vendors set up in the Street of the Lantern-Merchants and display dazzling marvels there all along the houses, which people contemplate or buy. There are delicately-sculpted jades, as translucent as a princess's fingernails, and grotesque and charming bronze monsters with large, staring painted porcelain eyes. Then there are lacquer boxes, little gold figurines, historic or fabulous paintings framed in bamboo and pearls, nettle-cloth imported from Nan-Kin, a large quantity of sumptuous items of furniture and magnificent costumes, sold by rich people who disdain objects more than twelve moons old, and a thousand other things.

That year, the flood of merchants and the richness of the merchandise were such that the oldest inhabitants of Canton had never seen anything similar; children cried out in astonishment, raising their arms to the heavens; women, timid and excited, bit their fingernails while inclining their little heads, ornamented with plumes, to the left. But the crowd was so dense and so agitated that one could not admire the same thing for long, and more than one customer who was haggling idly over a fan ornamented with characters suddenly found himself, with the fan in his hand, before a display of old coins and ancient weapons, pursued by the howls of the frustrated merchant.

That vast mass of pedestrians was undulating softly, swaying without jolts, for everyone was allowing himself to be driven along without resistance. Everyone was mechanically obedient to the slightest impulse, originating from near or far; anyone who had formed an audacious resolution to steer toward a goal, or merely to go in one direction rather than another, would have run a considerable risk of losing the better part of his costume, and even one or two of his limbs, on the way.

That double misfortune evidently threatened the rich and honorable bookseller Sang-Yong, the hero of this story.

That young man of thirty years and seven moons, irreproachably dressed and with an amiable expression, seemed to be prey to an obsession; brisk and prompt in spite of his already-respectable paunch, he was exerting all his strength, burrowing through the crowd with his elbows, fists and head, toward the displays of costumes where the discards of important individuals were sold. He cast an avid glance over wools and silks of all colors, and then, as if discouraged, drew away.

Just as he was about to reach the last and most sumptuous of the clothing boutiques, two men on horseback appeared at the corner of Drum Street, driving back the crowd with clubs and shouting at the top of their voices: "La! La! La!" They were the forerunners of a magnificent procession, which was about to cross the Street of the Lantern-Sellers laterally. The illustrious Mandarin Tchin-Tchan, the governor of Canton, was making his new year's visit to the Viceroy Koua-Pio-Kouen.

As soon as the crowd was sufficiently divided, as if cut into two stumps, numerous domestics carrying little roasted pigs on the ends of long wooden pikes advanced rapidly, crossing the street; then a portable chair appeared, magnificently decorated and open on all sides, in which Governor Tchin-Tchan was sitting, clad in yellow, immobile and imposing. Behind him marched porters carrying lanterns, banners and parasols. The Cortege went into the Street of the Apothecaries, and the crowd closed up again.

Sang-Yong had gazed at the illustrious mandarin with a strange enthusiasm; someone herd him whisper, very quietly, to himself: "No, the Son of Heaven doesn't look more handsome in one!"

When the procession had disappeared, the bookseller continue to head for the last clothing boutique. He succeeded in getting close to it, having been spun around several times, and began to inspect the display with an expression that strove to seem indifferent—but that ruse did not deceive the merchant.

"What are you looking for among my marvels, which you seem unable to find?" he asked. "Chance has obviously not guided your eye to the object you desire."

Sang-Yong looked around rapidly, as if to make sure that no one was listening.

"Have you a yellow robe?" he asked, very swiftly and quietly.

The merchant raised his arms to the heavens. "A yellow robe!" he cried, in a fearful voice. "Do you dare to ask? Only the Emperor, and those who represent him in the various capitals of the Middle Kingdom, have the privilege of wearing robes of that color. Do you know to how many strokes of bamboo your back would be exposed by wearing the smallest fragment of yellow cloth, and to what punishment I would be liable myself if I consented to sell you one?"

Greatly alarmed, Sang-Yong tried in vain to impose silence on the merchant.

"Do you not think, in any case," added the other, speaking even more loudly, "that if I were not stopped by the fear of punishment, I would be by the respect I owe the Son of Heaven and the Mandarin Tchin-Tchan?" Suddenly lowering his voice, however, he said: "Come back here when the bell has sounded the order to extinguish the lights. I'll take you to my house, and you shall have a yellow robe, as fresh and resplendent as the Emperor's."

Sang-Yong nodded his head and went away full of joy.

"At last!" he murmured, hiding his hands in his sleeves. "That which I desire will soon be accomplished."

He spent the rest of the day buying large mirrors of polished steel and having them transported to his house.

Sang-Yong had been favored by the Spirit of Fortune; his bookselling business had succeeded beyond his hopes; he was endowed with a jovial character, good health and a considerable appetite, which he satisfied daily with the most delicate foodstuffs. Moreover, he was unmarried, preferring to have in his apartment the oft-renewed joyful Flowers of the suburban Flower-Boats, rather than a monotonous and sullen spouse. He was not happy, though. A singular idea had one day taken possession of his mind and had not let go. He had admitted to himself that for all his fortune and appetite, he would always remain a vulgar merchant; that his lack of education would prevent him from reaching any high rank—and he would have given all of his fortune and appetite to be a mandarin.

He nursed that thought for a year, eating less and laughing less, his face veiled by constant anxiety; then he thought about his idea logically, and asked himself what the mandarins he envied had that he did not.

The absurd response presented itself to his mind: They wear a yellow robe! If you wore a yellow robe, you would receive, according to the law a hundred strokes of bamboo on the shoulders.

He could find no other motive for his ambition, and from then on, a fatal desire slid into his heart. "I need a yellow robe," he repeated to himself, night and day. "I'll lock myself in my room, which I'll have garnished with limpid looking-glasses; I'll light a great many lanterns; I'll put on my yellow robe every evening and look at myself in the mirrors, and I won't receive any strokes of the cane."

Often too, he said to himself: "I'm mad! What use is a yellow robe to me?" Nevertheless, he searched for one was an incessant obstinacy.

When he eighth hour sounded be found himself, full of excitement, in the place that the costume-seller had indicated. The latter, who was waiting for the bookseller, started walking silently, and Sang-Yong followed him. They went through narrow muddy streets, and finally went into a dirty and ugly little shop. The yellow robe was beautiful, almost new; the merchant wanted two ounces of gold for it, which were handed over without any objection, and Sang-Yong went home very satisfied.

That same evening, by the light of fifteen lanterns, four or five well-polished looking-glasses showed him the dazzling image of the satin robe, on which the Dragon with Five Claws was displayed, embroidered in red on the breast—and the small rotund person of the bookseller, with his triple-chinned face crimsoned by good cheer and the abuse of rice wine, made an amusing contrast with that pompous garment.

Sang-Yong, ecstatic and radiant, marched back and forth in his room with dignity; he made his costume rustle and squeak, and, as it caught the thousand gleams of the lanterns in its folds and reflected them in yellow radiance, he said: "I'm very well; I'm a mandarin."

He looked at his own image in the four or five mirrors, and added, gravely: "Here are other mandarins, no less handsome than I am, who have come to visit me; let's make the welcome according to the consecrate rituals."

Then, steering toward each mirror in turn, he put his hands together and raised them to the level of his breast, according to the rule of salutation called the Kong-Tchao; then, accomplishing the second salute, known as Tso-Se, he bowed deeply, with his hands joined; then he bent his knees without placing them on the ground, as the Tsa-Sien orders, and finally knelt down, obedient to the custom of Tsien.

But these modes of reverence might not be respectful enough for such respectable individuals, he thought; *let's per-*

form the Ko-Tao, which requires one to strike one's head on the floor after kneeling; the San-Kao, which demands that one rubs one's hair three times in succession in the dust of the parquet; and let's not forget the Sou-Kao, which is merely the San-Kao repeated twice.

And the honest bookseller, kneeling in front of the mirrors, did indeed salute his imaginary guests. He did not go to bed until he had heard the fourth round of night-watchmen pass by, who were banging little pieces of wood together noisily; and when, vanquished by sleep, he threw himself down on his bed, he had a dream in which he saw himself received by the Emperor, in the most magnificent room of the Palace of Peking, and carrying out, before the Son of Heaven, who was scarcely more brilliant than himself, the most solemn of salutations: the San-Koui-Kiou-To.

For three moons, Sang-Yong was not separated from his brilliant costume; when business affairs obliged him to appear in his shop, or when the excursions necessary to preserve his health and to maintain his appetite, which had finally returned, took him through the streets of the city, he threw a second robe over his shoulders, black or grey, but beneath that scorned vestment, he wore his yellow robe, whose sumptuous folds he could hear quivering as he walked, and which he often palpated delightedly.

One spring morning he went out before the tenth hour, for the sky, admirably pure, invited long walks. He went through the old Tartar city, where he lived, and, after having gone through the Southern Gate, entered the Chinese city, which was separated from the ancient city by a long lateral wall and was forbidden to barbarians. He son reached the limits of Canton and head toward the River of Pearls. In spite of the late hour, the northern bank of the river was cluttered and noisy; the crowd was very active there, buying and selling.

A thousand boats were floating lightly on the water, avoiding one another with skill and agility; large boats laden with vegetables and fish, or carrying anxiously-lowing cattle, waited for long rafts that drifted slowly, weighed down by cargoes of bamboo, giving them free passage. The high bulbous hulls of anchored war-junks, like the breasts of storks, their sails open and extended like the wings of cockchafers, were immobile, their variegated flags undulating in the wind. There were also merchant vessels from the north, painted white black and red; their prows bore sculpted fish-heads with enormous stupefied eyes, surmounted, by way of brows, by long menacing horns, and their matting sails, broadly deployed, resembled immense fans.

Sang-Yong paused, considering that agitation silently, and thinking about the fine effect he would have on the crowd if he suddenly appeared in his magnificent robe—but a few police soldiers, walking along slowly with pikes in their hands, reminded him about the terrible blows of the cane. Having searched briefly with his eyes he signaled to a boatman, who made haste to bring his boat to the shore.

"Cross the river, going slightly upstream," said the bookseller, when he was comfortably installed beneath the plaited awning.

To avoid the crowd of merchant ships, the boat went past the floating city of Flower-Boats, which formed streets, squares and crossroads full of ever-quivering reflections.

Sang-Yong sighed as he gazed at the green trellises of the bamboo houses, the joyous pennants, the hanging lanterns and the ornaments of gilded paper and peacock feathers, and especially the little terraces where he had so often smoked long opium-pipes. *How pleasant it would be to sit there, clad in yellow, in the midst of a despicable circle of merchants!* he said to himself.

After having passed the Flower-Boats the boat landed on the other side of the river. Sang-Yong plunged into the countryside; he skirted the long pagoda of Hai-Tsioun-Tsée, the red-lacquer palisades of elegant summer dwellings, engulfed by clumps of flowers, and finally reached a little wood of young cedars, where he stopped to savor the mild freshness of the air. He was alone, invisible.

He thought that the light of day had never admired him in his superb costume; violently, he threw off his black robe and appeared in all his magnificence. The sun darted its rays through the branches in order to see him more clearly; the birds sang his glory; the cedars quivered in amazement.

Suddenly, two little bursts of laughter rang out, clear and joyful, a few paces away from Sang-Yong; the bookseller's entire yellow-clad person took on a fearful expression so comical that the young laughter, if he had been the subject of it, would have redoubled its rapidity, like a cascade whose slope increases. He soon perceived, however, that no one was paying any heed to him; the voices laughed, spoke, and then laughed again.

Tranquilized, he drew nearer to the place from which the noise was coming, for he would have sworn that the laughter was coming from pretty mouths. He suddenly found himself confronted by a palisade of painted bamboo, which the cedars had initially hidden from him, and beyond which flourished a garden of marvelous elegance.

The pathways, irregular and twisting like lianas, were paved with smooth stones, various in shape and color, which formed pleasant designs. Porcelain lions were sitting, mouths agape, at the entrances to little marble bridges crossing artificial lakes. In the midst of artificial rocks of bizarre and implausible aspect, slender cascades glided over the moss and ran from every direction into the lake. In vases imitative of dragons, elephants and fantastic monsters, moonflowers and yellow daisies bloomed, preciously cared-for, while large peonies, justly known as the empress of flowers, burst forth in the flower-beds, dazzling the eyes. The trees were sparse and carefully pruned; there were bloody dragon-trees and pale lemon-trees, and also a few perfumed orange-trees that were beginning to flower; the wind caused rose-petals to fall into the lakes, and agitated the light plumes of black bamboos gently.

Sang-Yong contemplated that garden with admiration; it seemed to him that it must have been designed as a small-scale version of the imperial gardens of the Forbidden City.

The voices, which had drawn away momentarily, came closer again; the bookseller saw a young woman appear, who was walking with difficulty, her arms extended in order not to lose hr balance, amusing herself by kicking a large shuttlecock into the air with the tip of her little foot, which she never allowed to fall to the ground. She wore a double robe of bright green damask embroidered with gold, and as she played, sometimes allowed a glimpse of pink satin trousers. Her face was carefully made up; pearls and flowers mingled with the three dangling braids, one down her back and the other who over her breast. A young maidservant was following her, carrying a parasol. The two young women were laughing together, in a familiar fashion, at the evolutions of the shuttlecock, but their gaiety suddenly turned into great annoyance; the shuttlecock had fallen into one of the little artificial lakes.

"Oh! Oh! A-Tei!" cried the young mistress, on seeing her shuttlecock in the water. "My mother will find out that we've been outside our private garden. You're a naughty girl to have brought me here."

The young woman tried to reach the shuttlecock with her fan.

"Be careful, be careful," said A-Tei. "If you fall in the water, I won't be able to fish you out, and you'll be much more easily seen than the shuttlecock. What shall I tell your venerable mother, who won't fail to ask me: 'Where is the noble Princess Blanche, villainous A-Tei? What have you done with Princess Blanche? Come here that I may whip you.' Don't drown, Mistress; I've no desire to be whipped."

"You're laughing," said Princess Blanche. "I don't want anyone to laugh while I can see the shuttlecock in the lake."

"That's all right, naughty Mistress; I'll throw myself in the water, and the shuttlecock will sink."

"You've given me an idea," said Princess Blanche. "Let's throw stones at the shuttlecock."

160

"The stones will fall to the bottom, but the shuttlecock, which has blue and green feathers, will come back to the surface to tease us."

"You think so, little one?"

Behind the palisade, Sang-Yong was burning with desire to go to the aid of the two young women. He hesitated, not knowing in what fashion or according to what custom he ought to introduce himself. He thought of putting his black robe on again, but he could not bear the idea of appearing so badly dressed to such beautiful individuals; he therefore decided to remain dressed in yellow, assuming that the women would not have the perspicacious eyes of police soldiers, and in order to attract attention he sang, to an elegant rhythm:

"Two beautiful young woman are embarrassed because their shuttlecock has fallen in the middle of a great lake, but the Mandarin Sang-Yong, who is walking in the little wood of cedars, offers to put an end to their grief."

Princess Blanche swiftly hid her face behind her fan. Less timid, A-Tei looked at Sang-Yong.

"Should we reply to him?" she asked her mistress.

"What does he look like?" said Princess Blanche.

"He's a noble young man in ceremonial costume; his face is slightly comical, but not lacking in pleasantness, and I'd gladly take that face for a husband."

"Silly girl!" replied Princess Blanche. "But one can't dispense with replying politely to a noble mandarin; tell him my name, since he had given his, and tell him that I thank him for his offer, although I can't accept it."

A-Tei turned to Song-Yang. "Honorable Mandarin," she said, "my mistress orders me to tell you that her name is Princess Blanche, that her mother's name is Tsing, and that her father is the illustrious Tchin-Tchan, governor of Canton. My name is A-Tei; I'm seventeen years old and I'm not married. We thank you for your offer and we accept it gladly."

At the name of Tchin-Tchan, San-Yong's face had gone pale.

"A-Tei, A-Tei," said Princess Blanche, "that's not what I instructed you to say."

"Forgive me, Mistress. I'll explain that I made a mistake,"

"And advise him to go away," added Princess Blanche, "for it's not seemly that a man should be walking so near to two young women."

"Honorable Mandarin," said A-Tei to Song-Yang, "my mistress orders me to have you come in, in order that your generosity can retrieve the shuttlecock from the water."

"Little wretch! It's me who'll have you whipped!"

"Oh, Mistress, he's so pretty…!"

Princess Blanche peeped between the blades of her fan, while A-Tei opened a little hidden door in the palisade; she burst out laughing on perceiving the worthy booksellers jovial clownish face. *A-Tei has singular tastes*, she thought.

When Song-Yang had come in, he addressed a thousand salutations to the young noblewoman, who ordered her maidservant to return them; then he broke off a bamboo stem and tried to catch the shuttlecock. At first, he only succeeded in pushing it further away, but by chasing it in that fashion he moved it nearer to the other bank. He went over one of the little marble bridges and seized the plaything delicately between two fingers.

A-Tei clapped her hands, saying: "That's a very dexterous mandarin."

"It's necessary to thank him," whispered Princes Blanche, "and get back very rapidly to the interior apartment, begging him never to come back to the little wood of cedars."

"My mistress asks you to come back to the little wood of cedars tomorrow, in order that we can enjoy the honor of your company again."

"I'll have your tongue cut out," murmured Princess Blanche, drawing away rapidly.

Sang-Yong had begun to salute again; when he raised his head, the young noblewoman had disappeared, but he could see the mischievous face of A-Tei through the branches, which was smiling at him from afar.

The bookseller was drunk with joy. In spite of his black robe, which he had to put on again, he thought he was a veritable mandarin; his conviction was scarcely shaken when, on returning to the city, he saw the large sign shining over his shop, on which could be read, in golden letters:

When honorable people want to buy books, they should pay heed to the sign of this shop; the merchandise here is sold at a true price; neither children nor old men are deceived in the shop of Song-Yang, who sells books of every kind.

Song-Yang shut his eyes in order not to be distracted from his dream; he groped his way across the threshold of his house, cluttered with volumes, and ran to lock himself in his room, between the four obliging mirrors. There, all day long, he thought about the beautiful Princess Blanche, and when night fell, he dreamed that he married the daughter of the illustrious Tchin-Tchan, after being appointed governor of Canton himself.

The next day, before the tenth hour, wearing his magnificent yellow garment under his black robe, making the soles of his shoes ring triumphantly on the flagstones, he set off for the little wood of cedars, and his joy was extreme—but the Spirit of Good Fortune had abandoned the bookseller Song-Yang.

To avoid the crowds in the Street of Lantern-Sellers he had gone via the Street of Coppersmith. A pleat of his robe caught on an iron cauldron hanging from a merchant's door, and the cauldron rolled into the street with a deafening racket, dragging a great many sonorous utensils after it. The merchant appeared on the threshold shouting: "Stop, thief!" Behind the merchant came a little bright yellow dog with a pointed nose, upright ears and a curly tail, which started yapping madly.

Sang-Yong, already frightened by the noise of the cauldrons, could not help making a forward movement when he heard the dog. Without knowing why, he began to run; the bright yellow dog ran after him, barking frantically. The merchant followed the dog; then all the merchants and all the dogs in the street appeared at the doors, the former shouting in Song-Yang's ears, the latter howling at his ankles.

Soon, the unfortunate bookseller had a long shrill cortege of animals and people at his heels. Bewildered and dazed, he kept running; police soldiers brandishing their pikes joined in the pursuit without knowing the cause of the frenzied race, and Song-Yang thought he was going mad.

Suddenly, the clamors resounding behind him changed their nature; people were no longer shouting, but laughing.

"Look, look!" someone said. "He has a yellow robe."

The unfortunate felt his hair prickling, and his pigtail quivering behind his head. While trying to bit his legs, the frightful dogs had seized the fugitive's topmost robe in their little blue-tinted maws; they had ripped it, pulled it away, and torn it to pieces, shaking their heads violently in all directions, and Sang-Yong had appeared in all his splendor—alas!

It was then that he understood the necessity of flight; he launched himself forward in terror, arms extended, mouth open, and would never have stopped—but the River of Pearls suddenly barred his way; barking and howling, the crowd surrounded him; the police soldiers arrived in their turn, shouting: "Don't let that man dressed in yellow escape, who is insulting the Son of Heaven in the person of the illustrious governor Tchin-Tchan!"

And Song-Yang was seized, tied up, dragged away; his mind was so disturbed at this point that he demanded what they wanted with him, but the words "yellow robe," still bandied around on every side, soon made him conscious of his crime and his situation. Then, apparently calm but inwardly desperate, cursing ambition, robes of every color, the noble Princess Blanche, the Street of Coppersmiths, merchants and dogs, he seemed to feel the terrible blows of the bamboo cane already falling on his shoulders, and he let himself be taken without resistance to the feared house of the Lord Chief Justice.

On the evening of that day, so fatal for the bookseller Sang-Yong, the illustrious Tchin-Tchan, governor of Canton, was walking with his daughter and the mischievous A-Tei in the magnificent garden that flourished alongside the wood of cedars when he was brought a bamboo scroll, on behalf of the Lord Chief Justice, tied up with a yellow ribbon.

Tchin-Tchan unrolled the scroll saying: "It's doubtless a sentence that only requires my signature."

And Princess Blanche, being curious, read over her father's shoulder as they walked along:

The bookseller Sang-Yong, caught in the streets of Canon clad in a costume whose color is reserved for the Son of Heaven and the high functionaries of the Empire, is condemned to receive a hundred strokes of stout bamboo.

Then followed the relation of the circumstances in which the crime had been discovered.

"There's a singular story," said the Governor, when he had finished reading. "Why has that honest tradesman rendered himself guilty of such a misdeed, with no advantage for him? Didn't he know the penalty he was incurring?"

Beside him. Princess Blanche was writhing with laughter. Tchin-Tchan turned to her abruptly.

"What! Wicked child!" he cried. "You rejoice in such a immoderate fashion with regard to a poor man who is going to receive a hundred strokes of stout bamboo?"

"Don't scold me, venerable Papa," said Princess Blanche, for I can tell you myself why that humble bookseller was thus disguised as a mandarin."

"Really? Give me pleasure by telling me what you mean."

The curious A-Tei had drawn nearer to her mistress; the latter gave her a knowing glance.

"The Mandarin Song-Yang is merely in love with A-Tei," she said. "He mistook her for a princess, and, in order to win her heart, made himself a mandarin."

"The story is funny," said the governor, who could not help laughing, "but the unfortunate fellow must pay for his impudence nevertheless."

"What!" cried the saddened A-Tei. "Is the amiable Sang-Yong really going to receive a hundred strokes of bamboo?"

"He will receive them," said the Governor. "The law is precise. My poor A-Tei, if he survives his punishment, you'll have a well-broken husband."

"Does one sometimes die of a hundred strokes of bamboo?" asked Princess Blanche.

"Quite often."

"Oh, dear Father," she said, coaxingly, "you can't let a man be killed who has made you laugh."

"You're the one who laughed."

"You too, Father, and you even laughed in spite of your efforts to hold it back. Can you really want to make A-Tei die of grief?"

"It's true that I'll die if he dies!" cried the maidservant, bursting into sobs.

"The law doesn't care about A-Tei," said the governor.

"But here in Canton, you are the law," said Princess Blanche. Making a moue, she added: "I would never have believed that your heart was so hard, and I'm going to throw myself in the lake; I couldn't live with the idea that I laughed at a man who was killed by strokes of the cane."

"But, wicked child, you know full well that mercy for a criminal doesn't depend on me alone," said the Governor.

"Good! We know full well that the Viceroy does everything you want."

"Well, we'll see," said Tchin-Tchan, smiling. And he tore up the bamboo-fiber scroll.

Joyously, Princess Blanche threw her arms around her father's neck and caressed his beard gently.

"Mistress, Mistress!" whispered A-Yei. "Am I really going to marry the bookseller?"

"It's absolutely necessary," said Princess Blanche.

166

"What happiness!" murmured A-Tei, whose face was blooming like a peony at sunrise.

The young maidservant in now the richest merchant's wife in Canton; she sells books of every kind at true prices, and Sang-Yong, sitting beside her every evening in his interior apartment, has no regrets for his bachelor freedom. He has burned the yellow robe that was nearly so fatal for him, but he keeps its ashes in a vase of precious jade, for it is to the robe that he owes the graceful wife who embellishes his home.

THE PRINCE WITH THE BLOODY HEAD

A Legendary Story of Annam

The low branches of the mangrove-trees, garlanded with lianas, form a kind of hammock above the marsh, and it is there that the buffalo-herdsman is lying nonchalantly, one leg dangling down, caressing with his bare foot the long ribbons of grass that are trailing on the water.

In a soft and mechanical voice, the young man is singing, matching his song to the vague rhythm to which he sways while making the water splash.

Some distance away, wallowing in the mud, their pug-nosed and velvety muzzles extended toward him, his animals seem to be listening, in spite of the proverb that says: "Music is not made for the ears of buffaloes."

The words spill from his lips as follows:

"Save yourself, Lord Tiger, save yourself! In spite of your claws, in spite of your terrible teeth, your death is certain. Here comes the elephant, king of the forest; crushing the brushwood as he advances, and he will break your back.

"Poor goat with the graceful horns, what good does it do to flee and bound madly? The tiger is hungry, he has to eat.

"The bird with multicolored wings flies high, far from ambushes, singing his joy with all his might. Alas, the serpent, coiled around the tree, fascinates the bird and swallows it with its gaping mouth.

"Beneath the grass and the dead leaves, by virtue of being humble and small, the tiny worm escapes all danger. But no—from the heights of the air the bird has seen it; it plunges down and devours it.

"Only the herdsman of buffaloes is small enough and sufficiently ignored not to awaken any covetousness!"

Inundated with light and heat, in the ardent serenity of midday, nature is fermenting and quivering. Beneath the inertia of things, life swarms and pullulates; there is sound in the silence. Overriding everything, however, a continuous buzzing resonates. Reluctantly, the young herdsman listens.

What is it? One might think that it were the distant rumble of chariots of war, the cadenced footfall of marching horses, and the dull clash of weapons.

Not, it is not that.

On the other side of the pool, a frangipani blossoms marvelously; on the bare branches, there is nothing but flowers, little yellow and white flowers, adorably perfumed; and the tree, reflected in the troubled water, is no more there than smoke; but an entire population of bees, insects and butterflies is swirling in the flowery branches, with what tumult and what joy! They gorge themselves, get drunk, go crazy; wings vibrate or palpitate; droplets of gold, emerald and flame melt on to the embalmed petals, biting them, sucking the honeyed saliva, kneading the tender pulp swollen by a bitter milk; at times the tree seems to shake, rejecting certain insatiable individuals; but they rush back again, still avid, with a more sonorous vibration.

The herdsman smiles and half-closes his eyes.

The gourmand bees mounting an assault on that tree seem to be mimicking the sound of chariots of war reverberating in mountain gorges. But why is he thinking about war? The bees are not thinking about that. Like them, he wants unconscious happiness in unconscious nature. Unknown, lost in the ensemble of things, is he not like an insect? Less than that?

And he repeats the last verse of his song:

"Only the herdsman of buffaloes is small enough and sufficiently ignored not to awaken any covetousness!"

But now, with a start, gripping the branches with his hands, he sits up, his eyes wide open.

A brutal rustle of foliage, close at hand, has frightened him. Is it an escaping buffalo? Some beast of prey with designs on his herd?

A brief whinny replies to him, and immediately, brushed by the branches, a warrior appears, followed by another.

169

The horses, moist with sweat and out of breath, leap into the marsh, drinking the water avidly. They have gone in breast-deep, and ripples are running along their sides.

One of the warriors tucks the sleeve of his silken tunic under the scales of his armband, revealing a bloody wound.

In spite of the weariness that is overwhelming them and the dust tarnishing their armor, these two warriors have a singular grace, an imposing majesty. One might taken them for adolescents, but there is no way to be sure, their helmets half-masking their faces.

The buffalo herdsman watches, his eyes wide and his lips agitated by a tremor. Under the rain of sunlight falling between the leaves, that sparkle of armor seems to fascinate him—especially those bare arms, so smooth and so pure, where the blood, trickling in red threads, glides all the way to the slender fingers, which shake it off. He would like a golden cup in order to collect that blood—which must, he thinks, be infinitely precious.

Leaning over the water, the warrior washes the wound, presses that dolorous opening cruelly in order that the blood might carry away the venom if the arrow was poisoned; then his companion bandages it with a strip of cloth from his belt.

Then, in order to breathe more freely for a moment, they take off their helmets and reveal their proud faces; one of them—the one that is wounded—is extremely beautiful.

The herdsman lets slip an exclamation, revealing his presence. They look at him now; another exclamation replies to his.

"Royal sister, look—do you recognize him? The escapee, the fugitive, the one believed to be dead?"

"I recognize him.

And he murmurs, with his hand over his eyes: "I'm dreaming; I can't see you there, before me; you're phantoms."

"You know our names, as we know yours, Prince Lée-Line, you who left our palace empty, deserting life."

With his extended hands, he pushes the vision away. "Midday burns," he says, "The blood is pounding in my temples; my dazzled eyes see flames! You're not real!"

But the wounded warrior-woman cries: "A herdsman of buffaloes!"

Then he gets to his feet, mastering his amazement. "Yes," he says, "A herdsman of buffaloes! In that oblivion, I was swallowed up, forgotten—and I too, perhaps, forgot."

"Better to die."

"I was going that way, but without haste. Has death forgotten? Who can tell? I wanted, with all my heart, to reject my dreams, my suffering, not to take them with me; to die, I was only waiting no longer to be alive."

"What did you dream, then? What did you suffer, to be as cowardly as this in the face of destiny?"

"I fled to silence my desires and to hide my tears. How can I tell you today that the tears have submerged the desires?"

"Do you not know who is questioning you?" cried the younger of the two women, who, in a fit of anger, urged her horse forward."

"Ba-Tioune-Tiac, Royal-Flower, is before me," Lée-Line replied. "And you, Ba-Tioune-Nhi, Golden-Stem, are her sister.

But Golden-Stem frowned. "That's all you know? You have truly fallen so low? You are blind to the point that the glare of an unparalleled glory cannot ignite any gleam in your eyes?"

"For more than three years: shadow, silence, desert!"

She leaned swiftly toward Royal-Flower, removed her left leg-guard and pulled back the silky cloth. "Well, look!" she said

The slender and muscular leg appeared, above the foot wedged in the stirrup, and it did not seen bare, for a green tattoo covered it from the ankle to the knee. A monster, clad in scales, was coiled there, twisting its body, unsheathing the five talons of its claws, darting its forked tongue out of its menacing mouth; it was the terrible dragon, the emblem of supreme power.

"How can that be?"

Golden-Stem cried: "She is the king of Annam!"

And Lée-Line, suddenly pale and seized by a tremor, prostrated himself.

She is the king of Annam!

They are now in the shadow of a tent, a warm and gilded shadow; the interior walls are of yellow silk, for it is the royal tent.

All around, the immense camp is deployed, but its rumor is muffled as it approaches the wall of canvas that forms the sacred enclosure; it fades away entirely in traversing the empty space that isolates the master's tent.

All three of them are there, lingering in a silence full of memories. On a bed made of mats and rugs, is the queen—or, rather, the king, for there is no feminine word to signify the supreme leader. The excruciating wound in her arm has enfevered her. Golden-Stem, standing up, renews the fresh water and balms incessantly. On a cedar-wood stool encrusted with nacre, Lée-Line, overwhelmed by emotion, is weeping softly, his head in his hands.

Royal-Flower allows her gaze, heavy with thought, to weigh upon him, and finally says, in a slow voice, as if she were concluding her reverie aloud:

"After so many days we see you again; you emerge from the oblivion of death; and the mind is frightened before you, as if in the presence of a phantom. It really is you, however; our eyes have not yet unlearned your form. Like us, you are a branch of the ancient dynasty of Hung; the same orchard has seen our childhood grow and our youth flower—until the moment when a gust of wind blew down the enclosure. Then you disappeared, and all trace of you was lost. Explain that inconceivable exile now, Prince Lée-Line, and why you, who shone among the illustrious, have become the peer of Miao-Tseu savages, sons of the uncultivated fields."

"Everything that we are belongs to the Master," said Lée-Line, drying his tears. "You question me; I must respond. It is necessary for me to dig, like the earth of a grave that is to be opened, into the oblivion amassed over my despair; it is necessary for me to extract it from mystery, to tear apart its shroud of silence, alas, to bring back that which was buried into the light, with the terror of discovering it once again alive! You want it; it must be....

"Yes, we were, as you have said, flowers of the same bush, drinking the same sap, bathing in the same sunbeam. Do you remember the increasing ardor that burned us as we discovered life, the beauty of things, the wisdom of thinkers, the divinity of poets? It was like a new birth, the hatching out of our intelligence. Flowers at first, bound to the natal branch, we became butterflies, free wings taking flight in the light, and, with a mad intoxication, we took possession of the spring."

"Yes," said the queen, "oh yes, I remember! Everything has been dark since that dawn, since a storm dispersed our wings, petals torn from flowers! Centuries had passed, during which the masters of Annam, the Chinese conquerors, have oppressed us in the name of the suzerain Emperor; but we were used to the yoke and it seemed light to us. Then a new governor appeared, who, in a tyrannical frenzy, set about turning the land upside-down; everything that was noble and virtuous, everything that was elevated by spirit and courage, was cast down, humiliated, ridiculed; dementia reigned with debauchery and terror; the Chinese became hateful...."

"To the Chinese, however, we owe the most beautiful aspects of ourselves," Lée-Line continued. "In enslaving us, they delivered our minds from ignorance; they are the creators of our soul. The wave that had submerged us rolled over all the marvels: poetry, music, all the arts, writing, science, the rites! To see it mingled with putrid and poisonous mud! What a disaster! But that alone would not have cast me down...another grief, more profound...."

"Another grief?"

"I speak to obey," said Lée-Line. "It will be necessary to forget my words and not be angered by them."

"I will forget!"

The Prince turned his gaze away and said, in a duller voice: "Your father announced that he had chosen for his son-in-law a man of noble race loved by the people: the illustrious Khisak! That news fell upon me like a thunderbolt. I was a tree burned to the very roots, yet still standing. I wanted no more than to complete my dying. It was easy; I had only to offer my throat, to disapprove by a word or gesture of the tyrant's actions, and the blade would fall upon me. Alas, I was afraid of eternity!

"I had been told that the ills of the body end with life, but that our soul carries mental pains with it, to suffer them again in time without end. The cruelty of my grief frightened me, clarified the danger; the dread of dying, before having killed me despair, took possession of me, maddened me! At the court, death hovered above all heads. I fled the court, and the city, in order to hide myself, to lose myself in the crowd, to disappear, to be less than the least, infinitesimal among the infinitesimal...."

"A herdsman of buffaloes!" exclaimed Golden-Stem, sarcastically.

The queen remained silent, her eyes troubled, looking into the distance of her thoughts.

A trumpet sounded in the camp; a faint, shrill song as clear as a sunbeam, which seemed to pierce the satin wall.

Glory to the queen! it cried. *Let us be her rampart; let us watch over her!*

As if stung by that royal fanfare, just pride recovered its glare; her eyes cleared, Ba-Tioune-Tiac became once again the sovereign will with the impassive mask.

"Speak, Golden-Stem," she said. "Inform him of the history of Annam in these last three years."

And Golden-Stem spoke:

"I see again," she said, "the hall of the red columns, where the golden dragons unfurled, and the guards with gri-

174

maces on their painted faces; they head their broad-bladed lances in two hands, points downwards; I see the courtiers again, peacock plumes in their bonnets but mourning in their faces, standing in front of the throne, lined up all the way to the steps climbing up from the garden, and behind them, on the gravel of the broad driveway, borne by two stone lions, the gong of justice, which no one any longer struck.

"The man who was sitting on the throne and, in the name of the Son of Heaven, the Emperor Kouan-Vou-Ti, governed the land of the Giao-Gi, would have been reproved by tigers as too cruel; nevertheless, he usurped human form.

"That day, to the drunk, the infamous, the monstrous To-Ding, the newlyweds, the virtuous Khisak and the beautiful and pure Royal-Flower, were to offer presents and make their submission, in accordance with the rites.

"Before the throne, a lake of blood on the paving-stones barred the route; the young bride who was advancing suddenly saw her fearful face mirrored therein.

"A frightful wager had just been concluded. The courtiers of debauchery and crime, sprawling on their cushions, were still laughing, and threading pieces of gold on the ribbons of their belts.

"Disemboweled women were lying there. On seeing them, Khisak could not suppress a movement of anger and revolt; he frowned, and clenched his fists.

To-Ding's face reddened, and a horrible laugh bared his teeth. "Do you think you are the royal censor," he cried, "to dare to show me any other expression than that of humility and respect? You can combine it with that of dread, for your long head with its narrow eyes, its sparse gray hair and the wrinkles of pride that have engraved a false renown on your forehead do not please me, and any head that does not please me rolls in the blood.

"It was in the midst of a livid silence, which suspended all respiration, that Khisak's response—his final words—resounded. 'The man who dies, as you will die, on the dung-heap of his crimes,' he cried, 'may dread his end, for his soul falls into the body of a swine, but the souls of sages fly to the company of the immortals!'

"'Fly, then!' howled To-Ding.

"And immediately, at a sign that he made to the executioner, Khisak's head rolled in the bloody pool.

"Royal-Flower did not cry out or make a gesture, but her lip trembled and her gaze was terrible. I went to her to sustain her, to share her fate, for the lowered blade, from whose point a red serpent was escaping, might have been raised again.

"Oh yes, I see that assembly again, frozen in a stupor of terror! All those faces of cowardice, those grimaces that believed themselves to be smiles, and, at the feet of the bride, the noble head with the eyes enlarged, whose open mouth seemed to be screaming an order.

"Indignation choked me; I could not contain it; it was about to overflow in insults and sobs, when Royal-Flower seized her husband's head by the unknotted hair and fled, uttering a clamor so superhuman that many members of the audience fell to their knees.

"The infamous To-Ding had risen from the throne and he left the room, hastily returning to the interior of the palace, as if he too were fleeing.

"I snatched the still-tarnished blade from the executioner's hand and I followed Royal-Flower.

"She had already arrived in the broad driveway, in front of the gong of justice, still holding Khisak's head by the long hair. Suddenly, that head whirled and struck the sonorous disk violently.

"Oh, the lugubrious and sonorous sounds!

"At each impact of the skull they swelled, rumbling, sending forth echo after echo, the noise of a landslide, a cyclone, unleashed waves. It was a prodigy. The heavens spoke, and the entire city heard.

"They came running from every direction; the guards threw down their weapons, the slaves prostrated themselves, the people extended their arms.

"The widow, with her husband's head, was still striking, and in the formidable tumult one believed that one could hear the plaints of the oppressed, the cries of fury, the cries of vengeance.

"To-Ding emerged from the palace, the whip of command in his hand, in the midst of the Chinese warriors of his escort. He believed that he would impose respect by his presence, reduce that populace to silence—but when he appeared at the top of the steps, such a clamor of hatred burst forth that the tyrant went pale, and took a step backwards.

"Royal-Flower ceased striking the gong. From among the weapons that had been thrown on the ground she picked up a bow, took an arrow from a quiver and fired it at To-Ding. Heaven guided her arm, for the arrow hit the monster, who fell on to one knee.

"'Go, my faithful sister, and cut off his head,' Royal-Flower shouted to me. "The blade for that action is in your hand.'

"As prompt as her will, I obeyed my sister; I climbed the steps in two bounds and, also aided by Heaven, struck off the head of To-Ding with a single blow.

"Annamite mandarins had seized the Chinese warriors who tried to help their master by the throat; they knocked them down and held them down while I showed the crowd the grimacing head of the tyrant.

"Royal-Flower set her foot on the body of that swine, which disgorged a red cascade from the top of the stairway. She made a gesture with her hand, and a profound silence was established.

"'See, people,' she said, 'what two women have been able to do. The noble Khisak is avenged, and you have been delivered from the odious tyranny that has crushed you for such a long time. That which your hundred thousand robust arms have not even attempted, our fragile hands have accomplished. Are you not ashamed? Do you not want to complete the work, to take your share of glory?'

"One single voice proclaimed: 'Yes, yes, we want that. Speak! Speak again!'

"'Well then, throw away, forever, the stumps of the broken chain; become free again; expel the invader, the voracious Chinese, from the palace, from the city, from the kingdom; render to the land of the Giao-Gi the independence that has been stolen from it. Do not hesitate; do not delay; today, at this very moment, before this impure blood that soils our land, choose a leader, who will avenge our ancestors and lead you to victory.'

"'You! You alone!' proclaimed the crowd. 'Be the king; be the master; we will obey you; we will follow you.'

"She remained silent momentarily, her eyes raised to the heavens; then she said, in a firm and loud voice: 'The gods order me to accept. They will guide me and sustain me. I shall be your will and you shall be my strength. The king of Annam swears to you now: He will deliver you, and conquer his kingdom!'

"And Royal-Flower extended her hands, as if to take under her protection all those prostrate people.

"Oh, the beautiful days of battle! The blessed victories! The glorious marches! Royal-Flower, in her armor and the helmet with the golden wings, seemed the spirit of the war. When she appeared, her bow on her back, her blade in her hand, guiding her ardent horse with her knees, the army, fanaticized, felt invincible. In less than a month, all of the Chinese who had not perished were driven beyond the frontiers; sixty-five cities submitted to the king; the elephant that carried us in triumphs walked on silk and flowers.

"Then, with independence recovered, there were happy days; the people were cured of all ills; prosperity returned under the peaceful reign, full of equity and wisdom.

"She is the king of Annam! And no sovereign ever merited the love of his subjects as much as her!"

"You have done that?" sobbed Lée-Line, his forehead in the dust at Royal-Flower's feet. "You have done that, saintly heroine! And I, wretch, was weeping for you in solitude, instead of being there to serve you, to die for you!"

"Get up, Lée-Line," said the king. "Get up, to serve me. I name you supreme leader of the army; the foremost of the kingdom after Golden-Stem, who is like me. You have not had days of pomp and glory; ripened in dolor, like a larva enclosed in a stifling cocoon, you have seen nothing and known nothing of life. You have returned when the sky has darkened, alas. Let your courage sustain mine!

"Listen: after three years of mute humiliation, formidable China rose up against us again. Civil wars had absorbed the enemy's forces, but the revolutionaries, the terrible Red-Eyebrows, have been vanquished; the Emperor Kouan-Vou-Ti then turned his gaze southwards, and he ordered the reconquest of the beautiful land of the Giao-Gi, so long his vassal. Last autumn, war was reignited: a war of skirmishes, ambushes, ruses and endless fatigue. I have not weakened; the autumn and winter have passed; the Chinese have gained nothing from us—but the blood of Annam is running out and theirs is inexhaustible; we are like a lake confronted by an ocean.

"Bad omens have marked the beginning of spring. The plowshare broke when, in accordance with the ritual, I hollowed out a furrow for the sowing of the first seeds; a devouring drought is blasting the crops and preparing famine. Alas, the distracted gods are no longer sustaining me; anguish clutches my heart; my arms are breaking under too heavy a burden...."

"I will be your rampart and your strength," said Lée-Line. "I want that, and you have proved yourself that will can do anything."

The faint fanfare sounded an alarm, and the curtains of the tent pated abruptly as three armed mandarins appeared. They were the bravest and most faithful ministers, Koo-hoang, Nhat-ham and Hop-pho.

Royal-Flower stood up, proud and calm, her brow intrepid.

"Speak!"

"The Chinese have crossed the Annamese frontier."

"They are covering the mountains of Langson, filling the valleys."

"Lu-Lan, one of their most valiant leaders, is marching at their head."

"The gods are marching with us," said the king, "and as always, they will lead us to victory. Do your duty, Lée-Line, prepare everyone for a great battle. Tomorrow, at dawn, we shall deliver a decisive combat. Leave me alone with my sister now; we shall spend the night in prayer."

The rumble of war chariots, echoed by the mountain gorges, the cadenced tread of marching horses, the clash of weapons, orders howled by hoarse voices, precipitate gallops over the green slopes of hills; then the furious melee, beneath the fluttering standards and the bristling of lances.[10]

The Chinese ocean has overflowed into the valleys of Annam, but the liberator of the kingdom stand before it like a dike, preventing it from going any further, driving it back. She leads the army's center; Golden-Stem commands the right wing, Lée-Line the left wing.

And the burning hours go by, the battle persisting without respite. There is confusion, carnage, the delirium of despair.

Lée-Line achieves prodigies, however. Gradually, the enemy retreats before him, harassed by his two blades, which seem to be furious serpents, every bite of which opens a bloody fountain.

But how many dead there are, alas, how many voids in Royal-Flower's heroic army! One against ten at the beginning of the battle, the soldiers of Annam are no longer more than one against a hundred. And yet, at present it is they who are marching on Chinese territory; they are driving the warriors of the Son of Heaven back into the narrow gorges.

---

[10] "This battle took place in year 42 of our era." [Author]

The latter, wearied by having killed so many, seem to be giving way, to be fleeing. Their leader, Lu-Lan, wounded in the face, the gesture and the voice, draws them backwards, and soon they all draw away and disappear, abandoning the field of combat.

"Lée-Line! Lée-Line! Royal-Flower is calling for you; she's wounded, mortally wounded!"

Golden-Stem has caught up with the prince, who was pursuing the enemy, and Lée-Line, with a dolorous start, stops short, turns around, and comes back at a gallop.

The queen is still on horseback, so pale that she seems an ivory statue. Her breastplate had been removed in order that her breast might be compressed beneath the folds of a sash. In the ardor of combat her hair has become unbound beneath the helmet; heroism and fever make her eyes resplendent.

"Thank you, Lée-Line," she said, "I owe you these last hours of victory. It's thanks to you that my blood, like a royal seal, has put its mark on enemy soil. The end is nigh, however, and this is the final adieu."

"The adieu! No, not between us; here I am, and where you go, I shall go."

Their horses touched. Lée-Line supported the fainting queen with his arm, and she placed her weary head on the warrior's shoulder.

"Life has separated us," she said, "but death will reunite us. Look into my heart; the wound, in opening my breast, has laid it bare. Look, and you will see your image there; it was the temple in which I kept your memory, O companion of my spring."

"Oh, let us not stay on the earth!" cried Lée-Line. "It is not our place; the herdsmen of buffaloes has become the equal of the gods."

"Your eyes shine like bacons at the entrance to the celestial realms; they announce to me the delightful calm after the storm."

"Beware!" cried Golden-Stem. Anger trembled in her voice. "You're still the king of Annam; you're not yet free. Before dying, awaken to your glory."

And she whipped the horses, to tear apart the adieu that was commencing eternity.

"All is not finished, then!" said the queen. "What's wrong?"

Scouts were there, having come back in haste, breathless.

A few minutes' march away, a formidable army was advancing. General Ma-Vien, the most illustrious of the Chinese leaders, whose daughter had married the Heir of Heaven, was at its head. The entire horde that they had vanquished was merely the advance guard of the real army.

"A few hundred soldiers, wounded and exhausted, are all that remain to us," said Golden-Stem.

"Oh, I don't want to fall into the hands of the enemy!" cried Royal-Flower. "I ought to die on the soil of Annam, reconquered by me, and lost again today, alas! It is that sacred soil that must drink my blood. It is into the natal air that I must exhale my last breath. Save me, Lée-Line, protect my flight; be the peer of the gods; block the route to that entire army, and give me time to reach the river of Cam-hé."

"I will do that," said the prince. "Take all these hesitant soldiers; they will be your escort. Alone I shall defend this defile, long enough for you to reach the river; and afterwards, I swear, I will rejoin you. You have taught me by example that will can accomplish anything."

"Adieu, then," said Golden-Stem. "You will find me again too."

"Soon!" cried the queen. "The recompense awaits us."

And the horses fled at a gallop, while Royal-Flower, turning in her saddle toward Lée-Line, pointed with her finger at the heavens....

In the dense shade of centenarian banyans with colossal branches, the priestesses march two by two, their faces grave, allowing the hems of their long gray tunics with ample sleeves to trail over the disjointed paving-stones of the roadway. To the right and the left they slowly climb the stone staircases that lead to the platform of the pagoda.

A large bell is rumbling and tolling at irregular intervals.

The roofs of the temple are visible in tiers, three red roofs of decreasing breadth, the corners of which are turned up like wing-tips. Sculpted on the ridges are the dragon Long and the bird Foo-Ouan. Taller than the edifice, the giant trees extend their bushy branches.

Two black elephants, in painted terra-cotta, equipped with natural tusks, flank the door of the sanctuary, which hollows out a somber square like the mouth of a cavern. The priestesses appear momentarily white against that shadow, and then plunge into the darkness

Inside, the light of day does not penetrate. Large torches and silk lanterns illuminate the red drapes that veil the four faces of the altar, the sumptuous folds of which fall from obscure heights. To the right and the left, small chapels, closed by translucent blinds, allow confused glimpses of gilded statuettes, and between the chapels, on the walls, tigers, giant tortoises and winged horses are sculpted.

A woman whose face is noble beneath her long white hair, the superior of the nuns, is crouching on a mat in front of the altar. All the priestesses arrange themselves in a semicircle around her and crouch down, each upon a mat.

The bell stops ringing, leaving the last vibrations to tremble for a long time. The superior makes a gesture, and the red curtains, rolling up, rise up again toward the invisible ceiling.

On a marble pedestal, two colossal statues appear, of two kneeling women, their hands extended toward the heavens. One is clad in a robe of yellow satin, the other in a robe of red silk. An extremely tall miter, overladen with golden glowers, coifs each of them. To either side, inscriptions reveal the names of the goddesses: *Ba-Tioune-Tiac; Ba-Tioune-Nhi*.

On the table of offerings, covered by precious vases and lighted torches, the servants heap fruits and flowers; others throw odorant wood on to the embers of large bronze cassolettes, whose smoke rises in thin, oscillating threads.

A large book set on a lectern is open before the superior.

"Today, the anniversary of the great battle," she says, "I must tell you the story of the saintly death of the Prince with the Bloody Head."

And, her body swaying slightly, to the rhythm of a chant, she intones in a monotonous voice:

"A hundred thousand warriors! A hundred thousand warriors! They cover the summits, the slopes and the valleys.

"The sons of the Dragon have come to devour Annam. They want to seize the two sublime women who have inflicted so many defeats upon them and expelled them from the beautiful kingdom they had conquered.

"A hundred thousand warriors! A hundred thousand Chinese warriors! They reach the narrow defile that it is necessary to pass through in order to enter the sad kingdom of Annam.

"A single man is there, who bars the route: one single living man. But an entire host of dead men are still defending their king, for, stood erect again, they obstruct the route, and confront the enemy with frightful faces.

"The living man is Prince Lée-Line, who has sworn to stop that entire army long enough for the two royal sisters to reach the river Cam-Hé.

"A hundred thousand warriors! A hundred thousand Chinese warriors! The Prince launches arrows and strikes some of them dead—and the dead enemies that are heaped up also bar the route.

"Thousand of arrows fly toward the Prince, but they do not reach him; he seizes them in flight and sends them back to the enemy, so that he never runs out of arrows.

"'It's a prodigy!' cry the attackers—and the prodigy lasts until dusk.

"Then, full of anger, General Ma-Vien advances himself, passes over the dead men, and comes to do battle with the Prince.

"'I can die now,' says Lée-Line. 'I have kept my oath; the two sisters have reached the river.'

"He fights on nevertheless—but Ma-Vien strikes him with his blade, reaching his heart; then he cuts off his head,

"A hundred thousand warriors! A hundred thousand Chinese warriors! The entire victorious army has passed over the Prince's corpse; it draws away over the slopes, through the valleys, and disappears.

"Then the hero stands up. He picks up his bloody head and replaces it on his bloody neck.

"And at a rapid pace he marches, marches toward the river Cam-Hé.

"Large drops of blood fall along his route; his bloody head weeps great red tears—but as soon as one of those drops touches the ground, a winged horse takes flight, bearing it into the heavens, leaving in the place where it fell a block of stone in the form of a winged horse.

"The Prince with the Bloody Head has reached the river Cam-Hé. A host of weeping men and women is kneeling on the shore, contemplating two dead women, lying on a raft of flowers that is slowly moving upstream.

"They are weeping; they have recognized the king of Annam and her heroic sister. They strive to draw the bodies to the bank, but they cannot do it; the strength of so many arms is impotent.

"But the Prince with the Bloody Head advances and immediately, of its own accord, the raft of flowers approaches and touches the bank.

"Then the Prince lies down at the feet of the two saints, and his bloody head rolls from his shoulders.

"In the very place where the miracle took place, the Pagoda of the Two Princesses was erected, which still shelters us today, and where my voice is singing for you.

"The proud columns raised by the Chinese leader, which said: *Annam will perish on the day when they are overturned*, have long since disappeared.

"But the names of Ba-Tioune-Tiac and Ba-Tioune-Nhi are still in all hearts, still on all lips. The two heroines, become goddesses, watch over Annam without ever tiring.

"For it is today one thousand eight hundred and fifty-seven years since the Prince with the Bloody Head came to fall at the feet of the glorious sisters."

A DESCENT INTO HELL

One day, the beautiful Miou-Chen awoke from a long sleep. She was in a wild forest, lying on lotus flowers; a tiger the color of jade was asleep at her feet.

While she scanned her surroundings with a surprised gaze, she saw a young boy with shiny brown skin coming through the trees, who was carrying a flag that was flapping in the air and brushing the foliage.

The child approached and, setting the flagpole on the ground, bowed to her.

"I have come to you by command of the Lord of the Hells," he said. "The great Jade King admires your wisdom, and if your courage is unfailing he will consent to let you pass through the gate of the terrible city of Fou-Tou-Tchan and visit his realm."

Miou-Chen rose to her feet without trembling, and gazed at the narrow strips of blue sky through the dark foliage.

"Wherever I am, so long as my virtue does not weaken," she said, "the Master of Heaven will protect me."

"Come, then," said the boy, lifting up his bloody banner. "The King of the Ten Hells is waiting for you at the golden bridge of Pou-Tien."

He cleared a path through the branches noisily, and Miou-Chen followed him.

They emerged from the forest and entered a solitary valley. After having walked for some time, Miou-Chen perceived a man sitting on the ground at the entrance to a cave, and stopped in surprise, for the man was surrounded by a band of demons who were attacking him, while scorpions scaled his body. To his left were beings with the bodies of leopards and frightful faces, stirring red-hot chains and shaking furious serpents. A frightful she-devil, her breasts pendulous, her head shaven and her muscles stripped of flesh, was holding a frog by the foot, and was jiggling it in front of the victim's eyes, laughing stupidly and toothlessly. To his right, two young women of superhuman beauty, magnificently ornamented, but allowing foxes' tails and deformed feet to be glimpsed beneath their robes, were displaying the gleam of their beautiful smiles and seductive gazes, while their rosy lips murmured soft words.

Miou-Chen said to the King of the Hells' envoy: "Who is that unfortunate man?"

"That man is the sage Ma-Min. The great Jade King has sent his devils to tempt him."

Then Miou-Chen drew nearer to the sage. "O Ma-Min," she said, "I see your immaculate thought rising from your forehead like a vapor and forming a glorious cloud that will raise you up to the realm of the immortals."

Then the young woman continued on the route toward the Hells. She arrived in the province of Sée-Tchoen, and reached the golden bridge that ends at the Gate of Hell. As she was about to cross it, she was forced to retreat by a tumultuous host of men and beasts, which was running from the other end of the bridge.

As she stood there, astonished, her young guide said to her: "You see here those who are returning to life in a new form. These superb kings were once poor and virtuous; these deformed beggars were once full of pride; these reptiles crawling and hissing have been envious and crafty men; these birds were young fools with light and careless hearts; as for that herd of donkeys rushing and braying, they're mostly former functionaries devoid of probity."

When the noisy troop had drawn away, Mious-Chen went over the bridge and found herself in front of the arched gate—yellow, like an imperial gate—of Fou-Tou-Tchan, the Severe City. To either side of the entrance two demons, one with the head of an ox, the other with the head of a horse, were posted as sentinels; a third being, the color of soot, whose head was made of iron, was sweeping the threshold. As the young woman approached it drew aside and the gates opened. She went in; the two heavy battens closed behind her, with a plaintive clang.

She went along the broad streets of the City of Justice, following the crowd of the newly dead, whom soldiers were driving toward the Palace of Supreme Judgment. At the corners of the crossroads she saw, along with heaps of useless debris, old torn-up account-books and instruments of torture worn out by over-use and no longer good for anything. Further on, however, active blacksmiths were hammering their anvils and twisting iron.

The boy who was guiding Miou-Chen went into the hall of a vast palace, and the young woman followed him. Then she perceived the Jade King on his throne. She admired his head-dress fringed with pearls and his face, the color of a ripe orange, exhaling honesty and equity. Facing him, on a platform, stood the ultimate tribunal, where the great judge Loun-Yo was seated, beneath two banners flamboyant with stars, assisted by numerous servants riffling through and setting in order the dossiers of the summoned dead. All around the hall were the mandarins of Hell: Fou-Chou, the bearer of the three-pronged lance; Pen-Tchan, the gourmand, the pou-sah of good cheer; Ti-Tsan, the priest of the infernal cult; and Ta-Tcha, the nocturnal spy who records insomnias and criminal dreams.

The Jade King bowed to Miou-Chen and said to her: "Would you care, young woman, to descend with me the seventy-two stairs of Hell?"

She made an affirmative gesture and the king got up from his throne. Then Miou-Chen saw a yawning gulf in the middle of the hall, and the first steps of a stone stairway. The king began to descend; she followed him, pale and trembling, and plunged into the heavy darkness of Hell.

Soon, howling and sobbing rose up like a bitter wind. The young woman saw a precipice beneath her, populated with serpents, dragons and furious monsters; a narrow bridge traversed it, guarded by the demon of that hell, assisted by a warrior with the head of an ox, bearing a placard one which was written: *Good and Evil*. The damned were driven toward that bridge and, stumbling, full of terror, they fell, with cries of horror, into the gaping and avid mouths.

"This is the first region of penitence," said the king. "You can see the ambitious, the cruel and those swollen with pride."

And he continued the descent.

She then saw a pale and motionless demon sitting on a throne of ice, its body covered in snow, and, as if caught in crystal shackles, the reddened heads of condemned individuals, whose teeth were chattering with a sinister sound, passing at regular intervals over the hard surface of the pool.

Miou-Chen wept, and her tears froze on her lashes.

"These men are the avaricious and the implacable rich, who allowed supplicant mendicants to die at the doors of their palaces," said the Jade King.

They reached the third hell, where women attached to stakes were being tortured. Several demons with bloody bodies were tearing out their entrails and replacing them with hot coals, then sewing up the skin again.

"Those are adulterous wives. Let their guilty entrails be subjected to burning remorse."

And the king plunged on toward the fourth region. There was a vast sea of blood therein, in which a host of men and women were fighting, while the gondola of that hell's devil sailed its thick waves. That devil was entirely clad in white and wore an immense conical hat on its head. When the damned approached to climb into the boat, it gouged out their eyes, ripped out their tongues, and writhed with laugher as it repelled them with kicks.

"You're witnessing the torment of debauchees and women of loose morals," said the king. "That white devil is Ti-Fan, who presides over storms."

Miou-Chen went down a few more steps and saw the fifth hell, the floor of which is paved with trenchant blades, over which the demons cause iniquitous judges and calumniators run incessantly.

The sixth hell was the most terrible. The devil that ruled it, with his one-eyed face the color of ebony, bristling with red hairs, was the most redoubtable of devils. Under his orders, the damned, imprisoned in wooden troughs are slowly and methodically sawed by toothed implements.

On penetrating into that region, Mious-Chen sighed, and put her hand over her eyes, but the Jade King said to her: "Don't groan like that, young woman, for these men are parricides."

They went rapidly down the lugubrious stairway and reached the seventh hell, where the victims were howling in boiling oil. They were poisoners.

The young woman, her heart full of sadness, shedding floods of tears, arrived in the eighth circle, and saw that an enormous cutlass, rising and falling, was slicing the bodies of thieves and murderers into a thousand pieces.

In the ninth infernal region iron mills were crushing arsonists, while furious dogs were licking up the blood and tearing shreds of flesh from the victims.

She finally reached the last of the ten hells, where the teeth are broken in the mouths of liars and their tongues are torn out with red-hot pincers. There, she threw herself to her knees and, wringing her arms, cried: "A-Mi-To-Fo!"[11]

Then, lost in ardent prayer, she remained motionless for a long time.

Then, slowly, a rain of lotus-blossoms descended to the ground; from circle to circle, the demons' cries of rage were heard, and the sound of instruments of torture breaking; the damned, delivered from their suffering, intoned songs of joy, the sound of which flew toward the western sky.

Miou-Chen is venerated today in China and Japan, under the name Kouanine or Kouan-Chi-In. She is the Goddess of Mercy.

---

[11] "O Great Buddha!" [Author]

THE BOATWOMAN OF THE BLUE RIVER

In those days, Nanking was still the capital of China; the Ming dynasty was flourishing. It was during the reign of the Emperor Hoai-Tsong. The city, which was seven leagues around, was enclosed by formidable ramparts, so high that it was always pitch dark beneath the triple vaulted gates that pierced it at intervals. Those gates were surmounted by fortresses and high towers, the edges of whose roofs disappeared beneath the multicolored fluttering of pennants and flags.

Sentinels stood watch on the walls; soldiers proudly camped by the gates, leaning on their lances, questioning all comers.

The walls of the city contained mountains, lakes and rivers; the streets, broad and straight, bordered by superb palaces, were traversed by triumphal arches with sculpted and turned up roofs. In the distance, the tall tower of Li-cou-Li, the marvel of marvels, was visible. That tower, constructed two thousand seven hundred years before on the order of King A-You, had only three stories at first; two hundred years after its foundation, the Emperor Kien-Ouan repaired it and had the relics of Fo sealed within its walls. The Mongols burned it a thousand years later, but Yong-Lo rebuilt it, dedicated it to the Mother-Empress and called it the Tower of Gratitude, Li-cou-Li. It rose to a great height, with nine superimposed galleries; its walls, lined with yellow, red and white porcelain, shone like a pheasant's wings; the nine roofs, laid with green tiles, resembled emeralds, and the wind made charming music by agitating the thousand tiny bells suspended from every story, large statues were erected on the terraces of gods and spirits, and at the top of the tower a golden sphere scintillated like the sun.

In that era, shady gardens surrounded the tower of Li-cou-Li, hiding peaceful dwellings with very high roofs, constructed in cedar-wood. Bamboo palisades pierced with trellised gates only closed by latches surrounded those cool gardens; on stone pillars near each gate, two chimerical dogs or two dragons in bronze or varnished wood were set.

One evening in the fourth year of Emperor Hoai-Tsong's reign, shortly before sunset, a young man lifted the latch of a gate and came out of one those gardens. He saw the deserted square and walked rapidly, staying close to the palisade, without paying any heed to the dangling branches that brushed his face.

The young man was tall and well-built, handsome of face; his dark eyes, very long, elevated toward the temples, were full of pride; his eyebrows were slender and as smooth as velvet; his mouth resembled a flower. He was dressed in a black satin robe with a floral pattern in gold thread, tightened at the waist by a blue silk belt; his skullcap was also blue.

He reached another enclosure and stopped.

No sound was audible save for that of birds singing in the trees. The setting sun was already reddening the sky. The face of the Li-cou-Li Tower was resplendent.

The young man tried to peer into the garden through the branches, but the foliage formed a thick curtain and he could not see anything. Then he clapped his hands together, weakly at first, and then more forcefully.

At that signal, the head quivered and a young woman showed herself, only allowing her pretty head to be seen, which made a hole in the foliage.

"Is that you. Li-Tso-Pé?" she said, with an affectionate smile.

"Lon-Foo," said Li-Tso-Pé, rapidly, "go to the tomb of your ancestors; I'll join you there; take the Street of the Iron Lions; I'll take another route."

"I'll run!" said Lon-Fo, frightened by the expression of sadness imprinted on Li-Tso-Pé's face

The young man drew away at a rapid pace and went to the cemetery. He arrived well before the young woman and sat down on a tomb, at the foot of a stone horseman.

Horsemen similar to the one by which Li-Tso-Pé had stopped were visible on other tombs in all directions. The four feet of the horses were fixed in the ground, half-disappearing in tall grass. The warriors were represented in battle dress, brandishing their lances. Long avenues bordered by stone dromedaries, elephants or lions, facing one another, could also be seen. All these statues stood out in black against the pale pink and blue sky, and long oblique shadows extended over the ground.

Soon, a slender and graceful form slipped through the forest formed by the massive or slender legs of the stone animals; it reached the tomb close to which Li-Tso-Pé was sitting, and sat down beside him.

"Here I am," she said. "There is anguish in my heart, for I saw that your face is sad."

"Listen, Lon-Foo," he said. "My stepfather wants me to marry the daughter of a great magistrate."

"Is that possible?" cried Lon-Foo. "Doesn't he know, then, that your father and mine decided that we would marry one another? Has your mother forgotten her first husband to the extent of no longer remembering that solemn promise?"

"Since she has remarried, my mother is submissive to her new master; she has, however, tried to plead our cause—but my stepfather does not want to hear any of it."

"Can he force us to commit a crime against filial piety? Rather than disobey my dead father, I would kill myself instantly upon his tomb."

"It's certainly better to die than to fail in one's duty, but nothing is desperate yet. Listen—I've made a plan. I'm going to flee the country this very evening; I'll remain far away, without sending any news, until the woman intended for me finds another husband."

Lon-Foo made no reply, but began to weep.

"Alas," said Li-Tso-Pé, "this separation is a misfortune, but it will save us from a greater misfortune. We must try to harden our hearts. I'm going to leave you, therefore, Lon-Foo."

"I'm accustomed to seeing you. How can I bear your absence?"

"Would you prefer me to be another woman's husband, Lon-Foo?"

"Who can tell whether someone who leaves will ever come back?" said Lon-Fo, sobbing. "Who can tell whether, when he comes back, the one who remains will still be there?"

"What do you want me to do?" said Li-Tso-Pé, moved to tears. "Speak; I will stay if you order it."

"No, no, go," said Lon-Foo. "Go; I shall be strong, and whatever happens, I swear to you on the household gods of my father, who lies here, that nothing can make me change."

"Farewell, then," said Li-Tso-Pé. "The daylight is fading; it's time to go home." The two friends shook hands and separated, sadly.

As the young woman was going back through the cemetery, a man praying over a magnificent tomb saw her, and seemed to be interested in hr. He noticed her tears and thought that she was weeping for a recently-deceased parent. When he left the cemetery the man sent away an escort that was waiting for him with a gesture. He had not lost sight of the young woman, who, absorbed in her grief, did not see anything. He followed her, and when she had returned to her home, the man wrote on a tablet: *Li-co-Li Tower Square, the house of the blue dragons.*

Lon-Foo was an orphan. Her mother had died bringing her into the world; her father had lost his life in a glorious battle. The young woman lived alone with her old grandmother and a few servants. Their fortune was modest, but more than sufficient for their needs. Lon-Foo was seventeen years old. Brought up by her grandmother, full of indulgence, she had enjoyed a liberty greater than that ordinarily granted to young Chinese women; she did little embroidery, preferring reading or playing in the open air. She spent a great deal time in the garden of the interior apartment where women have the custom of shutting themselves away, especially after the day when she had seen Li-Tso-Pé.

On the night of her fiancé's departure, Lon Foo did not sleep and wept incessantly. So, the following morning, when she looked at herself in her polished steel mirror, like the disk of the moon, she saw that her eyes were red and swollen; in order not to make her grandmother anxious, she wanted to get rid of the traces of her tears, and she washed her pretty faces several times over in fresh water.

While she was thus occupied, a rap on the gong at the entranced door caused her to shiver.

Who is that, so early in the morning? she wondered.

She came down precipitately from her bedroom to the ground floor. Her grandmother was already under the awning of the house, and two servants were running to the garden gate, but when they opened it there was no one there, merely a lacquer box placed on the ground. The servants picked it up and brought it to their mistress.

"What's this?" exclaimed the grandmother, raising her arms to the heavens. "How do we know that this box is for us?"

"There's a letter under the silk cord sealing the box," said a servant.

Lon-Foo took the letter, written on red paper, and unfolded it.

"To the beautiful Lon-Foo, someone powerful offers these valueless objects," she read aloud.

"God Fo!" said the grandmother. "Someone powerful! How can he know you?"

"I don't know," said the young woman. "It's doubtless a joke, and the box is filled with stones."

"Let's see," said the old woman, lifting the lid.

The two women uttered simultaneous cries of amazement; a marvelous pearl necklace from Tartary was rolled up in several coils at the bottom of the box, like a sleeping serpent. The pearls were as big as peas, all similar and of unparalleled purity. It would certainly have been impossible to find a comparable necklace in the whole of the empire. The box also contained hairpins garnished with rubies and a complete set of ornaments: bracelets, clasps and sheaths to protect fingernails, in green jade worked with exquisite perfection.

"How beautiful it all is!" exclaimed the old woman, clapping her hands. "I've never seen anything so magnificent in my entire life!"

Where can it have come from? wondered Lon-Fo, vaguely frightened. *It's certainly not Li-Tso-Pé who's sending me a necklace that only a queen could wear.*

The day passed in conjectures. Lon-Foo ended up imagining that pursued thieves had deposited the box in front of the door to defect suspicion. She therefore began, with her grandmother's help, to compose a letter in which she explained what had happened to the city's magistrates. She had not yet finished writing it when the gong sounded again, struck with violence, and at the same time, a host of pages, grooms and lantern-bearers invaded the garden and arranged themselves in two rows to either side of the pathway.

Amazed, the two women had advanced beneath the overhanging roof of the house. They saw a mandarin of the first rank approaching, in a fine costume of the court, followed by two men, one bearing a parasol of honor and the other a crystal seal on a silk cushion.

The mandarin came straight to the young woman and bent his knee before her. "Is your name Lon-Foo?" he asked, humbly.

"Yes..." stammered Lon-Foo, tremulously.

"Well then, young woman, happiest of all the women of the kingdom, privileged beauty to whom I may only speak on my knee, know that the man from whom you received presents this morning, the man who has sent me to you, is the man before whom everyone bows down and trembles, the master of our lives and yours, the Emperor of China."

"The Emperor!" cried the grandmother, collapsing into a chair.

"Yes, the Son of Heaven himself!" said the mandarin. "He has seen Lon-Foo returning from the cemetery, and is informing her that he wants to take her for a wife, and that tomorrow, a magnificent cortege will come to fetch her in order to take her in great pomp to the imperial palace." The high functionary added: "I hope that when she is the favorite wife of our master, the beautiful Lon-Foo will not forget the messenger who first brought her the god news."

And after further salutations, the mandarin drew away, without the astounded Lon-Foo having said a single word.

The joyous bewilderment of the grandmother was so profound that she did not notice Lon-Foo's sadness and alarm. She sent servants in quest of all her acquaintances, to tell them the good news, and the house was soon full of people. Lon-Foo allowed herself to be complimented without appearing to perceive those who were clustering around her; she did not speak and did not look at anyone. People thought that her new situation had already made her proud and scornful.

When Lon-Foo retired to her room that night, she let herself to fall into a chair and remained motionless for a long time, her gaze fixed on the floor.

Suddenly, she got to her feet, and emerged from the stupor that had numbed her.

"It's necessary to act right away," she said. "I'm still free; tomorrow, in the palace, I shall be a prisoner."

She opened the door of her grandmother's bedroom slightly and listened. She heard a strong and steady respiration; her aged relative was asleep. She went along the landing and listened again. A profound silence reined within the house. The servants were also asleep.

Then Lon-Foo went back into her room, opened a few chests, took out her savings—a very small sum—and threw a dark-hued robe over her shoulders. She put out the light and went quietly down the stairs. The door of the house was sealed internally by an iron bar, which the young woman was unable to displace, but she opened a window and jumped down into the garden. The bamboo fence was only closed by a latch.

Lon-Foo opened and closed the gate; then, half-hidden by one of the dragons covered with dark blue enamel that flanked the entrance, she looked at the little house and garden for one last time.

"Oh, my dear Li-Tso-Pé," she said, shedding tears, "perhaps I shall never see this corner of earth again, where I have been so happy, but it is Heaven that has protected us by ordering your departure! What dangers would be amassed today over the head of the Emperor's rival!"

Lon-Foo crossed Li-cou-Li Square determinedly and plunged into a street. The darkness was profound; the sky was covered, and no light was shining at any window. The young woman did not know where she was going; she walked rapidly, feeling the all with her hand, occasionally stumbling, but never stopping. She soon went into a tangle of narrow backstreets that were not yet asleep; the noise of voices and laughter could be heard; threads of light filtered under doors; the oiled paper of windows was vaguely lit. Slightly frightened, Lon-Foo went forward hesitantly. Nevertheless, she hazarded a glance through a crack into one of the houses in which there were muffled noises; she perceived drunken men sitting at tables. The young woman leapt backwards, and fled more rapidly. Suddenly, at a street corner, she saw the lanterns of a police patrol shining.

Alas, she thought, *what would become of me if I were caught by those soldiers, and how would I explain my presence out of doors after the second curfew has sounded?*

She had backed up against a small dark house, and thought she could hear a hoarse voice inside, which seemed to be counting money. Lon-Foo knocked on the door resolutely, preferring to fall into the midst of a gang of thieves than into the hands of the police, who would take her home.

The door opened; the young woman went in hurriedly and closed it behind her.

"What are you doing?" cried an old woman sitting on a pile of rags and shapeless debris. "Women of ill repute don't

199

come into our home. I told you not to open the door." She was addressing an old man whose weather-beaten and wrinkled face looked like an old baked apple, and who was looking at Lon-Foo in bewilderment.

"I open it when someone knocks," he said.

"Don't worry," said Lon-Foo, "I'm from a good family; I left my father's house to flee the ill-treatment of a stepmother. I only knocked at your door to avoid the police patrol."

"Oh well, wait until it's passed by," said the old woman, with the indifference of someone too overburdened with worries to take an interest in the troubles of others.

"Wait until it's passed by," repeated the old man.

Then they both resumed counting the copper coins, which they moved about on the floor with their fingernails, and no longer paid the slightest attention to Lon-Foo.

The young woman looked around. A round paper lantern, badly torn, set on the floor between the old couple, illuminated the only room that made up their dwelling in a bizarre fashion. The ground formed the floor, the roof-tiles served as a ceiling. There was no furniture, but strange heaps of rags and debris of every sort seemed to be serving as chairs and tables; a few cracked porcelain bowls were placed on one of them.

When she raised her eyes to the wall, Lon-Fo could not suppress a cry of fright, for she thought she saw a row of hanged men that the light of the lantern was causing to tremble and twitch. She could distinctly see the feet of some of them, shod in old boots of threadbare satin, and others with their heads covered with hats, pulled down to the chin. On looking more closely, the young woman perceived that there were no legs in the boots, not heads beneath the hats, and that the hanged men were simply old costumes, faded, discolored and tattered, but very carefully disposed along the wall. Lon-Foo smiled at her surprise. A flaking sign, which was hung above the door of the house by day, told her that her hosts were old clothes merchants; she brought her gaze back to the inhabitants of the miserable dwelling.

They were still moving the copper coins around.

"You can count them a thousand times," said the woman, finally, "but the total won't increase."

"It's still a quarter of a liang short," said the man.

"Yes, and tomorrow, the owner of the house will throw us out and take our merchandise."

"He'll throw us out!" repeated the man, anxiously.

"I'll make up the sum," said Lon-Foo, then, taking a silver coin from her belt, "on condition that you let me spend the night here and that you exchange my silken garments for the costume of a woman of the people."

The couple raised their heads to look at Lon-Foo, whose presence they had forgotten; a smile contracted the old man's face, but the woman shook her head.

"You're making fun of us," she said.

"Not at all," said Lon-Foo, throwing the silver coin into the midst of the copper coins. Do you have the costume I need?"

"You're a good young woman," said the old lady, getting to her feet swiftly. "It's Heaven that sent you to us."

She went to unhook several costumes and show them to Lon-Foo. The one she chose was almost decent, composed of wide trousers in brown fabric, a blue cotton tunic and a vast straw hat that could easily hide her face. Then the old woman scattered a packet of rags in a corner of the room and covered them with a fragment on rush-mat.

"That's all I can offer you to sleep on," she said to Lon-Foo.

The young woman lay down on her rustic bed.

Son, the light was put out, and nothing more was heard in the obscurity but the sonorous snoring of the old couple.

Lon-Foo did not sleep. At first light she got up, took off her silken garments and put on the costume of the woman of the people; then she left the house without making a sound.

The neighborhood was still deserted; a few emaciated dogs, ferreting in the gutters, were the sole population of the wretched streets. The young woman hastened out of that sordid quarter and reached a broad avenue going down to the river. Soon, the Eldest Son of the Ocean was rolling its azure waves before her.

The morning sky threw silvery reflections over the water; an almost-insensible breeze caused a frisson to run over the surface of the water and deformed the image of a pagoda situated on the bank. Aquatic birds were piping and fluttering their wings in the rushes; cranes were launching themselves from the tops of trees uttering long cries, and the high mountains on the horizon were vaguely profiled among the pink and lilac mists of the Orient.

Lon-Foo sat down on the grass at the edge of the Blue River, deep in thought. What would become of her, all alone, so young, knowing nothing of life? She knew how to play with a shuttlecock, cultivate flowers and raise rare birds, but she had no aptitude for any kind of manual labor appropriate to her new condition.

She took her little purse from her sleeve and emptied it into her lap. A few gold liangs clinked gaily. It was something, but very little if she wanted to live on that sum until a change of reign. She counted her liangs several times and smiled as she remembered her hosts of the previous evening counting their copper coins over and over again.

At that moment, Lon-Foo heard footsteps close by. A man advanced to the edge of the river and hailed someone. A cry responded to his appeal, and a boat glided through the rushes to land in front of him.

The man leapt into the boat, which drew away from the bank and crossed the river.

Lon-Foo followed it with her eyes. It was one of those vessels known as *chan-pans*, surmounted by a little cabin covered with a bamboo mat—a cabin that served as the boatman's lodgings. Lon-Foo noticed that the person steering the boat was an old woman.

She's dressed as I am, the young woman said to herself. *I am therefore, costumed as a boatwoman. That, moreover, is a profession that would suit me very well.*

After having deposited the passenger on the other bank, the boat returned to a station near Lon-Foo, who stood up and gestured to the boatwoman.

"You want to go across?" said the old woman.

"No," said Lon-Foo. "I want to ask you a question. Where can one buy a boat like yours?"

"A new one?"

"New or old, it doesn't matter."

"If I could get a good price, I'd gladly give up mine and go to live with my children," the boatwoman said. "I'm getting old, and the damp isn't good for me."

"You'd really sell me your boat!" cried Lon-Foo, joyfully. "What price do you want?"

"Three gold liangs," said the old woman, at hazard.

"I'll give them to you."

The boatwoman opened her eyes very wide, and when she saw the liangs shining, she grabbed them swiftly, leapt on to the bank and, after several bows, went away rapidly. She feared that the young buyer might change her mind; she had sold hr boat for nearly triple what it was worth.

"You'll find a few provisions and two measures of rice in the cabin, which I'll throw in as well!" she called, from a distance.

Why flee so quickly? Lon-Fo wondered. *I would have liked to ask her for some indications as to how to steer the boat.*

At that moment a peasant arrived on the water's edge and jumped into the boat.

"Let's go, quickly," he said. "I'm in a hurry, take me over to the other bank."

Rather embarrassed, Lon-Foo descended into the chanpan with great precaution, then sat down and picked up the oars, but she was so inexperienced in their use that the boat swayed, made a thousand zigzags, and made very little headway.

"Have you lost your mind?" shouted the peasant, angrily. "Do you want to tip me in the water?"

"I'm not awake yet," said Lon-Foo.

She reached the other bank, however, and the peasant, after having cursed the boatwoman violently, went off without paying the price of the crossing.

These insults made Lon-Foo want to cry, but she soon pulled herself together.

Bah! she said to herself. *If that man knew that I'm sought by the Emperor, he'd throw himself at my feet with his forehead in the dust.*

Throughout the day, the young boatwoman had even more difficulty steering her boat through the vessels of every kind that furrowed the river; she almost capsized several times, but by dusk she knew as well as anyone how to guide a *chan-pan* over the Blue River.

Worn out by fatigue, she slept in the rustic cabin made of sheets of bamboo more soundly than she had ever slept in her own pretty bedroom.

During this time, the Emperor Hoai-Tsong, irritated by encountering obstacles to the accomplishment of his will, had become violently angry. He had maltreated his ministers and threatened several of them to cut off their heads if Lon-Foo were not found within a determined interval. The palace and the city were thus in an extraordinary state of agitation; rewards were promised to anyone who could provide information as to the whereabouts of the young person. Couriers left for all the provinces, and the entire Empire was soon searching for the beautiful Lon-Foo demanded in marriage by the Emperor.

Rumor of the adventure reached the ears of Li-Tso-Pé, who had gone to defend the frontier menaced by the Mongols. The young man, bitten to the core by anxiety, immediately left his post and took the road to Nanking again.

Meanwhile, people were on the trail of Lon-Foo; her clothes had been found in the clothes merchant's house, and he had given a description of the costume she had taken. It was also learned that an old boatwoman of the Blue River had suddenly been replaced by a young woman of extreme beauty.

The Emperor was therefore informed that the woman he sought was undoubtedly the young boatwoman whose origin was unknown.

Hoai-Tsong wanted to convince himself, and he went to the river bank in disguise, to the spot that had been indicated to him.

As the Emperor approached the *chan-pan*, Lon Foo, lying in the shade of the cabin, was singing in a low voice a song that she had composed while thinking about Li-Tso-Pé. The Emperor listened, and this is what he heard:

"Since you left me, I no longer live on the land. Day and night, the limpid water of the Blue River rocks me.

"The autumn wind has changed the greenery to gold. Where has the time gone when we chatted through the branches, while the yellow leaves fell lightly?

"Can all the Emperor's treasures outweigh duty accomplished? Can all his power efface a promise made to the dead?

"Where are you, then? What are you doing while my tears, drop by drop, fall into the river?"

"Good," said the Emperor, when Lon-Foo had ceased singing. "I know now why she disdains me, and has fled,"

He climbed into Lon-Foo's boat and lifted her up urgently. "Young woman," he said. "Would you care to take me to the other shore?"

"Certainly, Lord," Lon-Foo replied. "Is it not my profession to cross the river at any hour?"

"This profession does not seem worthy of you," said the Emperor.

"It suits me very well and I would be incapable of following any other," said Lon-Foo, taking the boat away from the bank.

"Those pretty white hands, like jade, are not made for gripping coarse oars. That ravishing face ought to dread the stings of the sun," Hoai-Tsong continued. "It is in the shelter of the imperial palace that it ought to bloom; it is a scepter of gold and precious stones that this delicate hand ought to hold."

On hearing these words, Lon-Foo went very pale, and looked fearfully at the man sitting facing her.

"You're mocking me, Lord," she said, in a tremulous voice. "A poor peasant like me! I would be an ink-stain on the white satin."

"What good is there in hiding any longer, Lon-Foo?" said the Emperor, suddenly. "Why did you flee two months ago? Why have you hidden when I was turning the whole empire upside-down searching for you?"

"God of Heaven! You're the Emperor!" cried the young woman, letting go of the oars and putting her hands together.

"For everyone else, I am the Emperor," said Hoai-Tsong. "For you, I am merely a friend."

"Have pity on me, great Emperor!" cried Lon-Foo, throwing herself on her knees.

"What!" said Hoai-Tsong. "Is that the way you greet me?"

"I am not worthy of this favor," the young woman said. "The honor you do me crushes me. I implore you, do not concern yourself with me any longer."

"I heard the song you were singing just now," the Emperor said, frowning. "Your fiancé is far away, you said; he would be dead if I knew his name; erase that name from your memory and wipe away your tears; I will take you to my palace and place you among my wives. Resistance is futile; I am the master."

"Alas," Lon-Foo murmured, "I am lost!"

The Emperor made a sign. Immediately, the banks were covered with people; joyful music suddenly burst forth; junks decked with flags, opening their great bamboo-matting sails like wings, advanced from all sides, laden with mandarins and high functionaries in ceremonial costumes.

On seeing herself the prisoner of that crowd, submissive to the Emperor, Lon-Foo raised her eyes to the heavens desperately.

"My dear Li-Tso-Pé," she cried, "Pray to God that our souls will be joined one day, for in this world we shall never see one another again!" And with one bound she leapt into the river.

The Emperor uttered a terrible cry.

The junks arrived rapidly; several men threw themselves into the river and dived. Hoai-Tsong's eyes never quit the place where Lon-Foo had disappeared.

"There! Look there!" he said.

The divers reappeared, and then dived again.

Several minutes went by, which seemed like centuries to the watchers. The Emperor stamped his feet with rage and dolor.

It was not until an hour has passed that the young woman was brought back to the surface of the water. She was dead.

At the moment when Lon-Foo's corpse was deposited on the bank, a fully-armed warrior arrived on his horse at a fast gallop. He dismounted and cleared a path through the crowd. On perceiving Lon-Foo lying lifeless on the bank he uttered a scream and knelt beside the young woman.

"Oh, my love!" he cried. "You have kept your word; you have died in order to remain faithful to your promise, and here you are, like a spring flower surprised by white frost; I would not have been able to save you from the Emperor, but I have arrived in time to die with you; your hand is still warm, your soul is waiting for its traveling companion, fluttering nearby. Be not impatient, my tender Lon-Foo—here I am!"

For an instant, a blade was seen to gleam; then a stream of blood flowed over the ground.

"I ask but one favor of the Emperor, that he bury me next to the one who has died or me," said Li-Tso-Pé, as he expired.

The Emperor remained standing, his arms folded, biting his lips, hiding his anger and his dolor from that entire crowd. He looked at the cadaver of the young man who had been preferred to him, with hatred.

"Should we accede to the dead man's desire and have the two fiancés buried side by side?" asked a mandarin.

"No, I forbid it," said the Emperor, curtly.

Then he drew away and returned to his palace.

A short while after this adventure, the Mongols invaded Chinese territory. Hoai-Tsong, dethroned, was killed. He was the last sovereign of the Ming dynasty.

One can still see, in the old cemetery of Nanking, the sepulchers of Lon-Foo and Li-Tso-Pé. Each of the two tombs is shaded by a magnificent acacia. They are far apart, but the two trees have extended their branches, which have met up and are interlaced.

THE JEWELER OF FOU-TCHEOU

If you had ever been to China and if you had ever rested one day beneath a flowering peach-tree on the edge of a lake or a river, you might have seen suddenly flashing past, with a shrill cry, a dazzling vision that disappeared almost immediately. Was it a flame, a star, a living emerald? It shook its luminous and multicolored frissons. Your astonished eyes searched for it hither and yon, and came to believe that they had not seen anything. It was a bird!

Can you see it now, suspended from that tall gladiolus swaying gently over the water? Look quickly, for it is already thinking of departing again. You really did see it; it is a jewel, a living fire; in that ray of sunlight it scintillates like gems; its wings are emeralds and the feathers of its breast are tinted with the blood of rubies. It has a large white pearl on its neck and the crest of its head is an incomparable blue, soft, shiny and metallic. Its tail is a swallow's.

There it goes, abruptly quitting the gladiolus and gliding over the water, which it skims with the tips of its wings; then it comes back; but it has a prey in its beak, a prey as luminous as itself: a little shrimp, still damp, transparent, agitating in diamante convulsions. Now it is passing above you, and a drop of water falls on your raised forehead.

If, as you return to the city, you ask some boatman what the adorable little bird is that you have just seen, he will tell you that it is called Fei-tsoui, that it only lives on the water's edge and nourishes itself on fish; but if your face pleases him, and if, by virtue of your manner and your costume, he judges you worthy of his esteem, the boatman will tell you the legend of Fei-tsoui, a touching story well known on the river-banks of China, which young women cutting bamboo sing all along the river in a shrill and melancholy voice:

There was once in the province of Fou-Tcheou an honest jeweler who lived placidly with his wife and three children; his commerce was not very extensive, but he lived in comfort and was renowned for the perfection of his work.

One day, misfortune descended upon him; thieves broke into his shop and took everything it contained: the stones, the gold, the silver, the pearls, and only left the unfortunate man his tools, henceforth useless. The poor jeweler almost went mad with grief, for he found himself as deprived as a beggar, and his hair turned white in a few nights. He tried to find work, but all the positions were filed and there was no work for him. Then his wife took her three children and went to beg in the streets.

One day, the jeweler was walking sadly along the bank of the river, thinking about his misfortunate destiny. *Alas*, he said to himself, *I believe that I would be wise to go and hang myself from a nail near the door of some mandarin, with my pockets full of supplications asking for the charity of that mandarin on behalf of my wife and children.*

It was winter; the path was covered in snow, the trees bare and black with fringes of frost, the river immobilized by ice. In the distance, the jeweler saw something on the snow that shone in the pale sunlight; as he had not seen it very clearly he blinked his eyelids and shielded his eyes with his hand.

It's a jewel that has fallen there, he said to himself. *I'll try to find the person to whom it belongs; I'll return it, and he might give me a few copper coins by way of recompense.*

The jeweler hastened his step, but, when he came closer to the shiny object, he perceived that it was a dead Fei-tsoui.

Oh, he said, *it's only a bird that has died of cold or hunger, as my children and my dear wife will soon die. Poor little creature! Your destiny resembles mine; you ate copiously and were warm in your nest, but winter has come to freeze the river that nourished you and lay your warm nest bare, and now you're dead—but at least you retained your magnificent adornment to the end, while my fine clothes and my wife's have long since gone to the pawnbroker's.*

And the poor man picked up the dead bird and admired its brilliant plumage. Suddenly, he slapped his forehead. "What an idea!" he cried. "It's the Master of Heaven who sent it to me."

He started walking with long strides toward his dwelling, and on the way he picked up all the dead wood he could carry.

When he got home he lit his furnace, so long extinct, and then looked around, counting on Providence to procure him a piece of metal. He spotted the door-knocker, which was solid brass. With the aid of a tool he wrenched it off and melted it in the fire; he had soon thinned it out into slender strips, which he twisted in a thousand ways; he made a bracelet with floral designs on its plates, but instead of stones or metallic colors he garnished the sections with the feathers of the marvelous bird. Then he took the strange bracelet to a mandarin famed for his good taste.

The mandarin looked at it closely, admired it a great deal and bought it. The jeweler made other similar trinkets, which sold; he replaced the brass with silver and gold. Soon, the fashionability of these charming ornaments became general; the Empress wanted to have one and summoned the fortunate jeweler to Peking, where he made an immense fortune—but he never forgot the little bird dead in the snow.

The jeweler of Fou-Techeou has been sleeping in a cedar-wood coffin for a very long time, and his three sons, who continued his charming industry, have long since gone to join him, but the tradition has been conserved, as everything in China is conserved, of fabricating these feathery trinkets, and they are made today with the same perfection as they were then.

Between the fine gold partitions that design the contours of a flower, a butterfly or a fly, the resplendent plumes are so artistically framed that they seem like metal to the eye, but they are no metallic enamels, no matter how perfect they are, which approach that gleam, that freshness, that strange charm; turquoise seems an inadequate term of comparison for those

211

inimitable celestial blues; an emerald is cold beside the dark and bright glimmers of those green plumes; and there is no coral that attains the delicacy of those reds.

The most extraordinary and most unexpected particularity of these Chinese jewels, which awaken the idea of a frail and fleeting fantasy, is that they are possessed of an extreme solidity.

THE EMPRESS ZIN-GOU

It is evening; the imperial palace is asleep; the guards are on watch; all is tranquil.

Invisibly, however, a man has climbed over the wall, slipped through the courtyards and the gardens, and now, abruptly, he is penetrating into the apartment of the Empress, who is already asleep.

In the bedroom, perfumed like a temple, the lamps are burning, veiled with silk. The man advances without hesitation; the parquet creaks beneath his feet and the Empress wakes up with a start, but does not cry out.

She looks at the man, and recognizes him. It is the handsome general Také-Outsi-No-Soukouné. He is clad in battle-armor, all stained with dust and blood imperfectly wiped away.

With a feverish gesture, she tears apart the gauze mosquito-net and leaps toward him, tall, beautiful and graceful in her long, pale nocturnal garments.

"You, here," she exclaims, "far from the combat! What has happened? Defeat?"

Také-Outsi prostrates himself. "No, Princess," he says, "but worse than that."

"What? What, then?"

"The descendant of the gods, the sublime Emperor, your husband, is dead. He was fighting at the head of his warriors, leading them to victory. A Korean arrow struck him. He has returned to the celestial abode."

"Ah! My presentiments!" cried the Empress, clenching her fingers in her long, scattered tresses. "The supernatural advice that was given to me that the master of Japan ought not to march in person against that people. Tisou-Ai-Teno did not want to believe me, and he is no more! He has quit the earth, the heroic spouse the son of the Prince of Warriors, who, out of filial piety, assembled more than a thousand white birds, his father's soul having taken refuge in the body of a *sira-tori*, the heron with large wings! Where, in its turn, is the soul of the tender son? Alas, alas, where is it?"

Suddenly, however, the Empress calmed down, shook her proud head and made a sign to the general bidding him to get up.

"Then all is lost," she said. "Victory has escaped us."

"Nothing is lost, my sovereign," said Také-Outsi, who remained on his knees. "Everything is merely suspended. I brought the body of the Mikado back in my arms, and laid him in his tent, saying that he was merely wounded, that he would be healed. Then, confident in the guards, who would pay with their lives for the slightest indiscretion, I left in secret and, sowing my route with dead horses, arrived at your feet.

The handsome warrior raised his eyes toward the charming queen, who, her head inclined, was also looking at him. She read in that ardent soul heroism, genius, devotion, perhaps affection. And she, simultaneously omnipotent and weak, understood that, with the support of such a heart, she might become redoubtable, invincible. A strange and entirely new sentiment quivered within her, made of ambition and courage. As if the soul of her spouse had come to reinforce her own, she felt ready to confront any danger—her, the nonchalant coquette who trembled at the slightest anticipation!

"Thank you, illustrious leader," she said to Také-Outsi. "You have done what needed to be done. The Mikado still lives; he is only wounded. Tomorrow, we will go to join him in the camp. I shall replace him. We shall march to victory. You, Také-Outsi, shall be the support of the Empire; I give you the title of Nai-Dai-Tsin."

For several days, the illustrious Empress Zin-Gou has been en route. Také-Outsi accompanies her, and a new troop, which she is taking to reinforce the army, follows her.

The lancers march at the head, armored, with visored helmets extended over the nape and ornamented in front with a sort of copper crescent, lance in hand and a little flag planted behind the left ear. Then come the archers, their foreheads encircled by a strip of white cloth, then ends of which float behind, backs bristling with long arrows, each holding a great lacquered bow in his hand. A new corps of archers has joined that one, and the soldiers composing it carrying bows of singular form, with the aid of which one launches stones, and which is of recent invention.

The foot soldiers advance after them, armed with halberds, two-handed swords and axes; their faces are covered by grimacing black masks, bristling with moustaches and red eyebrows; their helmets are ornamented with copper antennae or large deer-horns; others hide behind hoods of mail, which only allow their eyes to be seen.

And above these marching troops floats a whole host of banners and insignia of the most various forms.

The Empress, on a fine horse whose plaited mane forms a sort of crest, her feet in large sculpted stirrups, marches in the lead, and they arrive thus at the edge of a river called Matsoura-Gawa.

Then the beautiful Zin-Gou orders a halt. She is still a woman, and a singular idea has occurred to her. She wishes to fish with a hook in that river.

Standing on a little mound, she casts the line and says in a loud voice: "If I am to succeed in my enterprise, the bait will be taken; if not it will remain intact."

A great silence reigns; all gazes are fixed on the light buoy floating on the water. There it is, oscillating and dancing; with a swift gesture, the sovereign lifts the line, at the end of which a smelt is wriggling, shining like a dagger.

Joyful acclamations burst forth.

"Forwards!" cries Zin-Gou. "The fleet awaits us, and victory is certain."

They arrive at the harbor of Kaifi-No-Oura. The fleet appears magnificent and formidable; the great junks resemble monsters, and their sails are like wings. The mariners cheer the imperial army, which responds with a long cry.

The sovereign dismounts; she advances to the edge of the waves and, taking off her golden helmet, lets down her long hair. To efface its perfumes, she bathes in the sea, then winds her tresses and puts them up again in the form of a single chignon, such as the men wear. Then she seizes a battle-ax, and embarks of the most beautiful of the junks.

There, to everyone, the warrior Empress appears as on a pedestal. She has put on armor of black horn, whose plates, joined by threads of crimson silk, hang down below her knees, over the ample trousers of white brocade with cloudy designs, tightened at the ankles. She had black velvet shoulder-pads and enormous, exceedingly majestic sleeves that hang down to the ground, forming a kind of cloak. They are made of a cloth sown with gold florets disposed in diamonds, and uniformly lined with satin.

A golden chrysanthemum shines on the breastplate of the armor; the tall conical helmet is retained by a silken braid knotted beneath the chin; the battle-ax is passed through the belt beside two sabers, and the warrior woman leans on a staff of ivory and gold as long as a pike.

The sails stretch in the wind, and the waves rock the ships, while Zin-Gou, her gaze lost in space, cries: "Look! Look! The sea-god Foumi-Yori-Mio-Zin will be our guide and march before us!"

She is alone in perceiving the god of the sea, but no one doubts her word.

The king of Korea trembles and weeps in the depths of his palace. His Estates are invaded, his soldiers defeated. Before the invincible Japanese army, no resistance is possible, and before going into combat he feels vanquished.

Already the conquerors have taken the city. The warrior Empress is at the palace gates. She is truly animated by the soul of a hero. She it is who, through tempests and obstacles, has led her army to so many victories.

She is the first to launch the assault, crossing the ditch and hammering at the royal door, crying in a ringing voice: "The king of Korea is the dog of Japan!"

The battens burst and collapse, and the conquerors pass over the debris.

Above the entrance she has her ivory and gold pike suspended, which will remain there for centuries.

It is the hour of carnage and pillage; the soldiers finally want payment for the blood they have spilled; they are only waiting for the sovereign's order.

But here comes the king of Korea, his head bowed, his hands tied behind his back, advancing through his court of honor, strewn with the dead and the wounded. He has chained himself like a prisoner, and he is coming to humiliate himself, to submit, to surrender....

"I am your slave!" he cries, with a sob, falling at the feet of the beautiful warrior woman.

Then, beneath the rude breastplate, the woman's heart awakes and is moved. Zin-Gou lifts the poor king to his feet, unties his bonds.

"You are not my slave," she says. "You shall remain king of Korea, but you will be my vassal."

And she forbids the pillage of the city. They will only take possession of the king's treasures, reserving for her the paintings and the works of art, all the beautiful things created by China that Japan cannot make as yet.

Despair is succeeded by joy; the conqueror is acclaimed as magnanimous, who seeks her personal recompense in the eyes of the handsome Také-Outsi, increasingly troubled by admiration and affection.

Today it is more than thirteen centuries since the glorious Zin-Gou-Gvo-Gou returned triumphantly to her capital, gave birth to a son, and followed the course of a long and happy reign. And can one not say that in the modern Japan, so avid for progress, so different from the old, nothing has nevertheless changed?

The soldiers no longer wear the black helmet decorated with shiny horns; instead of the bow "of recent invention" that hurls stones, they have the most up-to-date cannon and rifles—but they are still the same intrepid heroes, disdainful of life.

The Mikado who reigns today, Mitsou-Hito, the Conciliatory Man, of the divine dynasty that, according to the official formula, reigns over Japan "since the beginning of time and forever," is the direct descendant of the illustrious Empress Zin-Gou. The cycle inaugurated by her accession to the throne is named Mé-Dgi, "the luminous reign," and it does, indeed, shine in a brilliant fashion. The present sovereign, whose victories astonish Europe, is certainly worthy of his forebears, and the Sun Goddess Tien-Sio-Dai-Tsin, his radiant ancestor, can recognize in him the son or her suns, and smile upon him from the heights of Heaven.

THE CELESTIAL WEAVER

A Japanese Legend

There was once in a suburb of Yeddo—today's Tokyo—a young peasant of exemplary conduct, but who seemed to be pursued by misfortune. His mother had died of grief on seeing the fields cultivated by her spouse become increasingly sterile.

He had followed his mother's coffin, weeping, and then had martyred himself with hard labor in order to support his aged father, but the father had died in his turn, leaving the son in such destitution that he did not have the money necessary to bury him; then he sold himself into slavery and was able, with the price of his liberty, to do his duty to his father.

Now he is going to the home of his master to fulfill the terms of his contract there. He is walking sadly, his head bowed, weeping for his lost liberty.

Suddenly, a woman of great beauty appears in his path. She approaches the young man and speaks to him.

"I want to ask you for a favor," she says. "I am alone and abandoned; accept me for your wife. I will be devoted and faithful to you."

"Alas," says the young man, "I possess nothing and even my own body does not belong to me. I have sold myself to a master, to whose home I am going."

"I am skillful in the art of weaving silk," says the unknown woman. "Take me to your master's house. I shall be able to make myself useful."

"I consent with all my heart," says the young man, "but how is it that a woman as beautiful as you wants to take for a husband a man as poor as me?"

"Beauty is nothing in comparison to the qualities of the heart," says the woman.

The soon arrive at the master's house, and the husband works zealously; he cultivates the flowers in the garden. When

219

he returns to his cabin to rest for a while, he always finds his wife occupied in weaving a magnificent fabric of silk and gold, and, increasingly wonderstruck, he admires the beautiful laborer.

One day, the master, who supervises the slaves personally, goes into the cabin and approaches the young wife. He stands there stupefied on seeing the superb piece of work that she is finishing.

"Oh, what splendid fabric!" he cries. "It is certainly inestimable in price!"

"It is yours if you wish," says the woman. "I will give it to you in exchange for our liberty."

The master consents to the bargain and allows them to depart.

Then the husband throws himself at his wife's feet and thanks her effusively for having delivered him from slavery.

But the woman is suddenly transformed; she becomes so luminous that the dazzled young man can no longer look at her.

"I am the Celestial Weaver," she says. "Your courage in labor and filial piety have touched me, and on seeing you unhappy I descended from Heaven to help you; everything that you undertake henceforth will be successful, if you never quit the path of virtue."

That said, the divine Weaver ascended to Heaven and went to take her place in the House of Silkworms.[12]

---

[12] "The constellation Scorpio." [Author]

THE PRINCESS'S SIXTEENTH BIRTHDAY

As it is winter and the weather is cold, panels of precious wood, scrupulously carved with incomparable art, have been closed around the Prince, and that makes the room in which he is sitting thoughtfully, with his arm on an elbow-rest clad in nacre, very small.

Several beautiful robes, coated with a down of silk, are superimposed, their variously-colored collars overlapping, on the Daimio's breast, and a kind of star can be seen, formed by five balls surrounding a sixth, embroidered in gold on his sleeve, near the shoulder. That is the well-known blazon of the very illustrious family of Kanga, which has no equal in power in all the isles of Japan but those of Shendai and Satsouma.

Yes, this Prince, who is meditating in the depths of his palace, is very powerful, very rich, very renowned; his people admire him and fear him, his vassals are ready to die for him, his slightest desires are laws for all those who surround him—and yet, today, he finds himself miserable, weak, poor, and deplorably lacking in imagination, because, for several days he has been seeing some surprise that he might give his daughter on the anniversary of her birth, and he cannot think of any.

It is true that the Princess in question, who will be sixteen tomorrow, possesses everything that it is possible to possess: she has marvelous birds, fantastic fish, extravagant dogs, chariots, oxen, horses, palaces—everything that she might desire, even marvels of which she never dreamed, brought for her from distant lands.

The Daimio admits, shaking his head, that he has spoiled that beloved daughter excessively, that he ought not to have heaped upon her thus, scarcely had she entered into life, all the riches of the world. What could he do now? His power is exhausted; he has nothing left to offer his child in order to astonish and charm her.

What point is there, then, in being a Prince?

For a long time, through the blurred transparency of the window, he lets a weary gaze wander over the bare garden, beneath the gray and mournful sky.

"What can she possibly still desire?"

Suddenly, he gets to his feet.

"Let's go see her," he says. "I might perhaps be able, without her knowing it, divine her caprice."

He strikes a gong suspended on a silken cord, held in the tips of its teeth by a bronze chimera.

Immediately, the panels forming the walls slide noiselessly, coming apart, allowing the sight of halls filled with samurai, pages, guards and servants. The samurai, noble vassals bearing two sabers, bow down profoundly, while the pages and servants prostrate themselves, foreheads to the ground.

"I'm going to my daughter's apartment," said the Daimio.

Then an escort forms up, and guards ran ahead, to warn the Princess's pages.

Fiaki, which means Sunbeam, was sitting in a tightly sealed room in her private palace, on a white floor-mat, and the pleats of her magnificent robes, with immense trains, were disposed symmetrically around her in fans, waves and hills. There were all sorts of fabrics there, of various very pleasant hues, but the most abundant fabric there was satin the color of the summer sky, with fine black embroideries depicting spiders' webs in which flower-petals were caught.

The young woman's face was as white as cream; her small mouth, slightly thick, enlivened with make-up, was parted slightly, revealing two rows of rice-grains; her eyebrows were shaven, replaced with two small black patches made with a paint-brush and placed very high on the forehead; following the fashion of princesses, her long hair, unbound, was flowing down her back, losing itself in the folds of her robe.

Maids of honor formed a semicircle around their mistress, and facing her, on the other side of a delicate sculpted balustrade, a dancing girl in a long robe, with floating sleeves imitative of wings, coiffed in a strange golden bonnet posed on the crown of her head, was dancing slowly, waving a fan. An orchestra of musicians accompanied her, playing a gotto, a biva, three kinds of flutes, a drum and a tambourine.

When the Prince came in, the symphony ceased, and Fiaki swiftly hid her mouth behind one of the spiders' webs on her sleeve, which was a modest and affectionate salute to her father.

He smiled with pleasure on seeing the beauty and grace of the child he idolized. She had risen to her feet, coming to meet him, and, like a sea agitated by a sudden tempest, the silk, satin and brocade behind her undulated noisily.

He lavished the most flattering pet names upon her—Mouroi, the Incomparable; Réifé, Supernatural Beauty; Réikio, the Perfume of Heaven—and then he asked her whether she was happy, whether anything had annoyed her, and whether there was anything she desired.

"Oh, illustrious Prince! Adored Father!" she cried, bending her supple body backwards in a pretty movement of sorrow. "How can one be happy when the earth is suffering? How can one smile when the heavens are weeping? The gods are very cruel to have created winter! Alas, there is not even snow to give the illusion of spring. It puts me in mind of a poor exiled plant, which cannot live and cannot die."

With a coquettish smile, lowering her long eyelashes with a modest expression, she added: "I've composed an *outa* on that subject, but even poetry cannot console me."

In an exquisitely mannered tone, she recited the short poem, beating the rhythm with the end of her fan.

The autumn is fleeing
With the flowers it bears away,
Has closed the door,
Forgetting me, half-dead
Before the frightful winter.

"I shall have that *outa* illustrated by the most famous painter in the realm," said the Prince. But I'm not a god, alas!"

Slowly, he went away, full of care.

"It's certain that her only desire is for spring," he said to himself. And he stopped, to listen to the bitter wind whistling outside.

The daylight was already dimming; the approaching twilight was about to take it unawares.

"Spring!" he murmured, sitting down again in the place he had left a little while before.

Abruptly, his sadness was transformed into anger. He summoned his prime minister.

The Nai-Dai-Tsin came running, bending his back, and while paying his compliments saw his master's somber expression, with augured nothing good. The Prince remained silent momentarily, as if he were hesitating to give an extravagant order, but after an irritated shrug of the shoulders he spoke in a harsh voice.

"Tomorrow is my daughter's birthday," he said. "At daybreak, I want—*I want*, you understand—the trees and bushes in the park, and all the countryside surrounding the palace, to be covered in flowers, as in the first months of spring. Go!"

"You will be obeyed, Master," said the minister, going out backwards.

Once he was outside, though, consternated and distressed, he allowed his arms to dangle in his long sleeves, which hid them. "It's exile! It's death!" he murmured. "Yes, death, for I don't have time to flee far enough. In the midst of prosperity, lightning has struck me!"

His legs became unsteady; he leaned on the woodwork.

"What have I done to be in disgrace?" he wondered, and after a severe examination of his conscience, he replied: "Nothing; it's for his daughter; he truly wants to command spring."

He stood for a long time with his mind blank, his head slumped on his chest like a lead ball, but he eventually shook that heavy head, and straightened up resolutely.

"Come on, let's be worthy of our race," he said. "The Japanese do not tremble before death; it will not be in vain that I have, since early childhood, taken lessons in suicide. Let's see—first the saber, to cleave the belly with a single stroke, from left to right; then the dagger that cuts the throat…."

He took out his saber, but the weapon remained at the end of his arm, the point resting o the ground.

"If it were possible, however, by some artifice, to simulate spring…instead of ruin and suicide what fortune! Let's no despair too quickly; there will still be time to die."

He started with fright on seeing that shadows had invaded the palace and the lights were beginning to illuminate.

"The immense park and the whole countryside!" he said. "And in only one night."

He went back to his dwelling at a run and summoned the council.

Without permitting his colleagues to sit down, he made them party to the extraordinary order given by the prince.

"This order must be carried out on pain of death, before daybreak," he said, indifferent to the fearful expressions surrounding him. "The Prince is in a terrible mood; there will be no mercy. Listen, and understand the idea I have had, which might save us. It is necessary that for a league around, men, women, girls and boys, nobles, merchants and peasants, with silk, velvet, satin and paper, set to work immediately to fabricate, as best they can, simulacra of flowers; that they cut up their clothes, massacre curtains screens, floor-mats, and anything that comes to hand, neglecting nothing; and then that all these flowers are, before dawn, tied, pinned or stuck to the trees, the bushes and the shrubs, the most successful on the borders of the paths, the coarser ones in the background; that painters are charged with directing the decoration and adding brush-strokes where necessary. I shall supervisee everything; I shall try to anticipate everything; our salvation is well worth that effort. Take the army, dispose of everyone; no one must eat or sleep tonight. Go! And if you value your lives, be as rapid as lightning."

Without saying a word, the ministers drew away—or, rather, fled.

Less than an hour thereafter, there was not a palace or a house in the city, not a cottage in the countryside, in which people were not feverishly occupied in fabricating flowers; and anyone who had looked from the heights of the Kanga palace, shortly after midnight, would have thought he recognized in the thousands of lanterns that were rolling, jumping and flowing over the ground, a frightful army of fire follets guided by foxes.

By that time, however, the illustrious Daimio was snoring behind a wooden screen encrusted with gold, and the incomparable Princess, by the light of a huge lantern muted by thin strips of nacre, was sitting up in bed riffling through a book, in search of a poem about spring to carry her into her dream.

Her maidservants were finishing dressing her the next morning when Fiaki heard the music of an orchestra and the singing of numerous voices bursting forth under her windows.

"Oh, that's true—it's my birthday today," she said, with a gesture of ennui. "Why was I born in winter?"

The shutters of the windows were parted.

"Look how beautiful the weather is, Mistress!"

Indeed, the sky, as if it were a mere courtier, had, for the occasion, put on a very soft blue, in which a cheerful sun floated, of a slightly pale gold.

Languidly, the Princess advanced on to the exterior gallery and leaned on the balustrade. But then, what a cry of surprise and joy! What had she seen there? Was it possible? Flowers—flowers everywhere! Spring had come!

She rubbed her eyes, thinking that she was dreaming.

"What!" she said, turning this way and that and running from one end of the gallery to the others, "The almond-trees!

The peach-trees red! The apple-trees white and pink! And the tall trees! What a miracle!"

Along all the avenues visitors were flowing, coming to pay their respects to the princess, lords on horseback, noble-women in chariots drawn by oxen, or in *norimonos*. The court emerged from the palace, gathered on the terraces. Fiaki hastened to go down.

The Prince, laughing with pleasure, greeted her at the bottom of the steps. With tears in her eyes, she threw herself into his arms, crying: "Father! Father! There is a god, you see!"

He proposed a walk in the park and the countryside, to admire the magical spring.

The Princess, utterly joyful, clapped her hands, and her magnificent chariot, in the form of a flag, blazoned with golden spheres in the shape of a star, drawn by two white oxen, advanced to the foot of the terrace; those of her maids of honor came next, then all the court followed, and the visitors too; it was a brilliant, joyful and interminable procession.

The Prince, on horseback, escorted his daughter; he had the prime minister by his side, grave an impassive in his triumph.

There was enchantment all along the road; the warmth of the sun, and the fine gilded mist that veiled nature slightly, rendered the illusion complete; they admired the richest spring, even more florid than the real spring.

"And what delicious perfumes are floating in the air! All these flowers embalming it!" said the Princess, who was leaning her pretty head out of the chariot continually, in order to get a better view.

The Daimio, very surprised, was indeed breathing charming odors.

That was because cassolettes had been hidden in the harness of the oxen, and the smoke they exhaled was confused with the vapor formed by the breath of the animals.

They went a long way into the countryside; Fiaki, her happiness complete, was untiring. She asked that they not return to the palace by the same route; was that possible?

The Prince, slightly anxious, looked at the minister; the latter remained impassive.

"Would the princess like to go back by way of the hills or the orchards?" he asked.

"By way of the orchards," the young woman replied. "It's longer, but it ought to be more beautiful."

They went via the orchards, and, indeed, it was even more beautiful than what they had seen thus far.

But one pink plum-tree attracted the particular attention of the Princess.

"Oh! I want to take away a branch from that tree!" she exclaimed. "I want a souvenir of this magical excursion."

The deception will be discovered immediately, thought the Prince, darting a glance of distress at the minister.

The minister had neither paled nor trembled.

"Let me have the honor of collecting it for you," he said, bowing to the young woman.

He spurred his horse, ran to the plum-tress, and came back with a superb branch. The Princess seized it, sniffed it, and plunged her face into it; it really was plum-blossom, perfectly fresh, moist with dew, and sweet-smelling.

The Master was secretly amazed; but then the maids of honor, seeing that it was permissible to pick branches, put their heads out of their carriages, demanding souvenirs for themselves.

This time, it was too much; the Prince made an angry gesture and was about to give the order not to stop; the minister reassured him, smiling with an imperceptible shrug of the shoulders; he knew women very well and had foreseen this too. He made a sign to the driver of an empty chariot to go fetch that which was demanded. The chariot son came back filled with flowers, which were shared out with joyful cries.

The minister had not hesitated to pillage all the palace hothouses; men mingling with the crowd were carrying all those flowers in brow canvas bags, keeping close enough to be there at any given moment. The Prince, who had not guessed that, was quite dumbfounded.

"You really are an amazing man," he said, as they went back into the palace. "You've done more than I could have hoped; you're an absolute magician. Perhaps you've done too much, and today's great joy in mingled with a muted anxiety; how will it be possible for us to surpass this next year?"

While the Master, remaining slightly in rear, was saying that to his minister, Fiaki got down from her chariot.

At that moment, the son of the Prince of Satsouma, who had just arrived at the palace with a brilliant escort, advanced to salute her. He was a young man full of elegance and beauty, and so brave that, in spite of his youth, people were already taking about him. At that moment, however, he was very emotional, and very pale, as if trembling with fear; the young woman, on the contrary, blushed, and, to hide that blush, buried her face in the flowers she was holding in her hand. The minister pointed out the two young people to the Daimio, calling his attention to the strange disturbance, which left the two of them nonplussed.

"When your daughter's seventeenth birthday sounds," he said, "Give that charming Prince to her for a spouse, and she will love him even more than she loves spring."

The Prince gave the minister a bronze trinket encrusted with gold.

"Here," he said. "This is the key to my treasures; take what you wish, and don't feel the need to be discreet."

SF & FANTASY

Henri Allorge. *The Great Cataclysm*
Guy d'Armen. *Doc Ardan: The City of Gold and Lepers*
G.-J. Arnaud. *The Ice Company*
Charles Asselineau. *The Double Life*
Cyprien Bérard. *The Vampire Lord Ruthwen*
Aloysius Bertrand. *Gaspard de la Nuit*
Richard Bessière. *The Gardens of the Apocalypse*
Albert Bleunard. *Ever Smaller*
Félix Bodin. *The Novel of the Future*
Alphonse Brown. *City of Glass; The Conquest of the Air*
André Caroff. *The Terror of Madame Atomos; Miss Atomos; The Return of Madame Atomos; The Mistake of Madame Atomos; The Monsters of Madame Atomos; The Revenge of Madame Atomos*
Félicien Champsaur. *The Human Arrow; Ouha, King of the Apes*
Didier de Chousy. *Ignis*
Captain Danrit. *Undersea Odyssey*
C. I. Defontenay. *Star (Psi Cassiopeia)*
Charles Derennes. *The People of the Pole*
Georges Dodds (anthologist). *The Missing Link*
Harry Dickson. *The Heir of Dracula*
Jules Dornay. *Lord Ruthven Begins*
Alfred Driou. *The Adventures of a Parisian Aeronaut*
Sâr Dubnotal *vs. Jack the Ripper*
Alexandre Dumas. *The Return of Lord Ruthven*
Renée Dunan. *Baal*
J.-C. Dunyach. *The Night Orchid; The Thieves of Silence*
Henri Duvernois. *The Man Who Found Himself*
Achille Eyraud. *Voyage to Venus*
Henri Falk. *The Age of Lead*
Paul Féval. *Anne of the Isles; Knightshade; Revenants; Vampire City; The Vampire Countess; The Wandering Jew's Daughter*

Paul Féval, *fils*. *Felifax, the Tiger-Man*
Charles de Fieux. *Lamékis*
Arnould Galopin. *Doctor Omega*; *Doctor Omega and the Shadowmen*
Judith Gautier. *Isoline and the Serpent-Flower*
Léon Gozlan. *The Vampire of the Val-de-Grâce*
G.L. Gick. *Harry Dickson and the Werewolf of Rutherford Grange*
Edmond Haraucourt. *Illusions of Immortality*
Nathalie Henneberg. *The Green Gods*
V. Hugo, P. Foucher & P. Meurice. *The Hunchback of Notre-Dame*
Michel Jeury. *Chronolysis*
Gustave Kahn. *The Tale of Gold and Silence*
Gérard Klein. *The Mote in Time's Eye*
Louis-Guillaume de La Follie. *The Unpretentious Philosopher*
Jean de La Hire. *Enter the Nyctalope; The Nyctalope on Mars; The Nyctalope vs. Lucifer; The Nyctalope Steps In; Night of the Nyctalope*
Etienne-Léon de Lamothe-Langon. *The Virgin Vampire*
André Laurie. *Spiridon*
Gabriel de Lautrec. *The Vengeance of the Oval Portrait*
Alain le Drimeur. *The Future City*
Georges Le Faure & Henri de Graffigny. *The Extraordinary Adventures of a Russian Scientist Across the Solar System* (2 vols.)
Gustave Le Rouge. *The Vampires of Mars; The Dominion of the World* (w/Gustave Guitton) (4 vols.)
Jules Lermina. *Mysteryville; Panic in Paris; To-Ho and the Gold Destroyers; The Secret of Zippelius*
Jean-Marc & Randy Lofficier. *Edgar Allan Poe on Mars; The Katrina Protocol; Pacifica; Robonocchio; Tales of the Shadowmen 1-9*
Xavier Mauméjean. *The League of Heroes*
Joseph Méry. *The Tower of Destiny*
Hippolyte Mettais. *The Year 5865*
Louise Michel. *The Human Microbes; The New World*

José Moselli. *Illa's End*
John-Antoine Nau. *Enemy Force*
Marie Nizet. *Captain Vampire*
C. Nodier, A. Beraud & Toussaint-Merle. *Frankenstein*
Henri de Parville. *An Inhabitant of the Planet Mars*
Gaston de Pawlowski. *Journey to the Land of the 4th Dimension*
Georges Pellerin. *The World in 2000 Years*
Ernest Pérochon. *The Frenetic People*
Pierre Pelot. *The Child Who Walked on the Sky*
J. Polidori, C. Nodier, E. Scribe. *Lord Ruthven the Vampire*
P.-A. Ponson du Terrail. *The Vampire and the Devil's Son*
Henri de Régnier. *A Surfeit of Mirrors*
Maurice Renard. *The Blue Peril; Doctor Lerne; The Doctored Man; A Man Among the Microbes; The Master of Light*
Jean Richepin. *The Wing; The Crazy Corner*
Albert Robida. *The Adventures of Saturnin Farandoul; The Clock of the Centuries; Chalet in the Sky*
J.-H. Rosny Aîné. *Helgvor of the Blue River; The Givreuse Enigma; The Mysterious Force; The Navigators of Space; Vamireh; The World of the Variants; The Young Vampire*
Marcel Rouff. *Journey to the Inverted World*
Han Ryner. *The Superhumans*
Brian Stableford. *The New Faust at the Tragicomique; The Empire of the Necromancers (The Shadow of Frankenstein; Frankenstein and the Vampire Countess; Frankenstein in London); Sherlock Holmes & The Vampires of Eternity; The Stones of Camelot; The Wayward Muse.* (anthologist) *The Germans on Venus; News from the Moon; The Supreme Progress; The World Above the World; Nemoville; Investigations of the Future*
Jacques Spitz. *The Eye of Purgatory*
Kurt Steiner. *Ortog*
Eugène Thébault. *Radio-Terror*
C.-F. Tiphaigne de La Roche. *Amilec*

Théo Varlet. *The Golden Rock. The Xenobiotic Invasion; Timeslip Troopers* (w/André Blandin); *The Martian Epic* (w/Octave Joncquel)
Paul Vibert. *The Mysterious Fluid*
Villiers de l'Isle-Adam. *The Scaffold; The Vampire Soul*
Philippe Ward. *Artahe*
Philippe Ward & Sylvie Miller. *The Song of Montségur*

MYSTERIES & THRILLERS

M. Allain & P. Souvestre. *The Daughter of Fantômas*
A. Anicet-Bourgeois, Lucien Dabril. *Rocambole*
A. Bernède. *Belphegor*; *Judex* (w/Louis Feuillade)
A. Bisson & G. Livet. *Nick Carter vs. Fantômas*
V. Darlay & H. de Gorsse. *Arsène Lupin vs. Sherlock Holmes: The Stage Play*
Séamas Duffy. *Sherlock Holmes in Paris*
Paul Féval. *Gentlemen of the Night; John Devil; The Black Coats ('Salem Street; The Invisible Weapon; The Parisian Jungle; The Companions of the Treasure; Heart of Steel; The Cadet Gang; The Sword-Swallower)*
Emile Gaboriau. *Monsieur Lecoq*
Goron & Emile Gautier. *Spawn of the Penitentiary*
Steve Leadley. *Sherlock Holmes: The Circle of Blood*
Maurice Leblanc. *Arsène Lupin vs. Countess Cagliostro; Arsène Lupin vs. Sherlock Holmes (The Blonde Phantom; The Hollow Needle); The Many Faces of Arsène Lupin*
Gaston Leroux. *Chéri-Bibi; The Phantom of the Opera; Rouletabille & the Mystery of the Yellow Room; Rouletabille at Krupp's*
Richard Marsh. *The Complete Adventures of Judith Lee*
William Patrick Maynard. *The Terror of Fu Manchu; The Destiny of Fu Manchu*
Frank J. Morlock. *Sherlock Holmes: The Grand Horizontals; Sherlock Holmes vs Jack the Ripper*
Antonin Reschal. *The Adventures of Miss Boston*
P. de Wattyne & Y. Walter. *Sherlock Holmes vs. Fantômas*

David White. *Fantômas in America*

SCREENPLAYS

Mike Baron. *The Iron Triangle*
Emma Bull & Will Shetterly. *Nightspeeder; War for the Oaks*
Gerry Conway & Roy Thomas. *Doc Dynamo*
Steve Englehart. *Majorca*
James Hudnall. *The Devastator*
Jean-Marc & Randy Lofficier. *Royal Flush*
J.-M. & R. Lofficier & Marc Agapit. *Despair*
J.-M. & R. Lofficier & Joël Houssin. *City*
Andrew Paquette. *Peripheral Vision*
Robert L. Robinson, Jr. *Judex*
R. Thomas, J. Hendler & L. Sprague de Camp. *Rivers of Time*

NON-FICTION

Stephen R. Bissette. *Blur 1-5. Green Mountain Cinema 1; Teen Angels*
Win Scott Eckert. *Crossovers* (2 vols.)
Jean-Marc & Randy Lofficier. *Shadowmen* (2 vols.)
Randy Lofficier. *Over Here*

ART BOOKS

Jean-Pierre Normand. *Science Fiction Illustrations*
Raven Okeefe. *Raven's L'il Critters; Rave's Faves*
Randy Lofficier & Raven Okeefe. *If Your Possum Go Daylight...*
Daniele Serra. *Illusions*